SHOT FOR SHOT

The crack of a gunshot halted him. It came from so where ahead. Even Gracie looked up. Two more shots followed.

Curiosity overrode his drunken lethargy and the pair, man and horse, roused themselves out of their stupor and loped up the last of the rise. They found themselves fifty yards from an unexpected sight: two men circling one. The man in the center, a wide-shouldered brute wearing a sheepskin coat, sat tall astride a big buckskin. He held in one hand what looked to be a substantial gun, maybe a Colt Navy, but appeared to have trouble bringing it to bear on the two men, who took care to keep their own horses dancing in a circle around the big man. He tried to do the same, tugging feebly at his reins.

What was wrong with the man? Tucker wondered. Was he drunk? He acted as much. And then Tucker got his answer. The man jigged his horse again, and the big horse tossed its head and stepped hard. Then Tucker saw the red pucker, blackened at the edges. The man had been shot in the back.

Ralph Compton

TUCKER'S RECKONING

A Ralph Compton Novel

by Matthew P. Mayo

A SIGNET BOOK

SIGNET
Published by the Penguin Group
Penguin Group (USA) LLC, 375 Hudson Street,
New York, New York 10014

USA | Canada | UK | Ireland | Australia | New Zealand | India | South Africa | China
penguin.com
A Penguin Random House Company

First published by Signet, an imprint of New American Library,
a division of Penguin Group (USA) LLC

First Signet Printing, December 2013

 REGISTERED TRADEMARK—MARCA REGISTRADA

ISBN 978-0-451-46548-1

Printed in the United States of America
10 9 8 7 6 5 4 3 2 1

THE IMMORTAL COWBOY

This is respectfully dedicated to the "American Cowboy." His was the saga sparked by the turmoil that followed the Civil War, and the passing of more than a century has by no means diminished the flame.

True, the old days and the old ways are but treasured memories, and the old trails have grown dim with the ravages of time, but the spirit of the cowboy lives on.

In my travels—to Texas, Oklahoma, Kansas, Nebraska, Colorado, Wyoming, New Mexico, and Arizona—I always find something that reminds me of the Old West. While I am walking these plains and mountains for the first time, there is this feeling that a part of me is eternal, that I have known these old trails before. I believe it is the undying spirit of the frontier calling me, through the mind's eye, to step back into time. What is the appeal of the Old West of the American frontier?

It has been epitomized by some as the dark and bloody period in American history. Its heroes—Crockett, Bowie, Hickok, Earp—have been reviled and criticized. Yet the Old West lives on, larger than life.

It has become a symbol of freedom, when there was always another mountain to climb and another river to cross; when a dispute between two men was settled not with expensive lawyers, but with fists, knives, or guns. Barbaric? Maybe. But some things never change. When the cowboy rode into the pages of American history, he left behind a legacy that lives within the hearts of us all.

—*Ralph Compton*

Chapter 1

Despite the creeping cold of the autumn afternoon in high country, and the feeling in his gut as if an irate lion cub were trying to claw its way out, Samuel Tucker reckoned that starving to death might not be an altogether unpleasant sensation. Of course, the warm light-headedness he was feeling might also have something to do with the last of the rotgut gargle he'd been nursing since he woke up.

He regarded the nearly empty bottle in his hand and shrugged. "No matter. Finally get to see you again, Rita, and little Sammy. My sweet girls . . ."

Even the horse on which he rode, Gracie, no longer perked her ears when he spoke. At one time a fine mount, she was now more bone than horse. The sorrel mare plodded along the lush valley floor, headed northward along the east bank of a river that, if Tucker had cared any longer about such things, he would know as Oregon's Rogue River. All he knew was that he'd wandered far north. And he didn't care.

His clothes had all but fallen off him, his fawn-colored, tall-crowned hat, a fine gift from Rita, had disappeared one night in an alley beside a gambling parlor in New Mexico. The top half of his once-red long-handles, now pinked with age and begrimed with Lord knows what, and more hole than cloth, served as a shirt of sorts. Ragged rough-weave trousers bearing rents that far south had invited welcoming breezes now ushered in the frigid chill of a coming winter in high country. And on his feet, the split, puckered remnants of boots. These were the clothes Tucker had been wearing the day his Rita and little Samantha had . . .

At one time, though, Samuel Tucker had cut a fine figure around Tascosa, Texas. With his small but solid ranch, and with a wife and baby daughter, he'd been the envy of many. But that was in the past, before the sickness. . . . *Mercy,* thought Tucker, *two years and I can't think of it without my throat tightening.*

"At least I don't have to worry about being robbed," he said aloud. His laugh came out as a forced, thin sound that shamed him for a flicker of a moment. Then once again he no longer cared.

The land arched up before him in a gentle rise away from the river. Here and there, trees close by the river for the past half mile had been logged off some years before, leaving a stump field along the banks. Ragged branches long since cleaved from the vanished timber bristled upward among still-green undergrowth seeming to creep toward him. He traveled along the river, and the gradually thickening forest soon gave way to an upsloping greensward just beginning to tinge brown at the tip.

He was about to pitch the now-empty bottle in the rushing brown flowage off to his left when the crack of a gunshot halted him. It came from somewhere ahead. Even Gracie looked up. Two more shots followed.

Curiosity overrode his drunken lethargy and the pair, man and horse, roused themselves out of their stupor and loped up the last of the rise. They found themselves fifty yards from an unexpected sight: two men circling one. The man in the center, a wide-shouldered brute wearing a sheepskin coat, sat tall astride a big buckskin. He held in one hand what looked to be a substantial gun, maybe a Colt Navy, but appeared to have trouble bringing it to bear on the two men, who took care to keep their own horses dancing in a circle around the big man. He tried to do the same, tugging feebly at his reins.

What was wrong with the man? Tucker wondered. Was he drunk? He acted as much. And then Tucker got his answer. The man jigged his horse again, and the big horse tossed its head and stepped hard. Then Tucker saw the red pucker, blackened at the edges. The man had been shot in the back.

One of the other men shouted, then shot the big man's hand. It convulsed and the pistol dropped. The shooter's companion, thin and sporting a dragoon mustache and a flat-crowned black hat with what looked like silver conchos ringing the band, laughed, looking skyward. As he brought his head back down, his laughter clipped short. He leveled his pistol on the big man in the sheepskin coat.

One shot to the gut and the victim hunched as if he were upheaving the last of a long night's binge. He wavered in the saddle. The man looked so fragile to Tucker. It did not seem possible that this was happening right there before him.

The first shooter howled this time. Then he rode up close, reached out with his pistol barrel like a poking finger, and pushed the man's shoulder. That was all it took. The big man dropped like a sack of stones to the grass. The buckskin bolted and the black-hatted man leveled his pistol at it, but the other shouted something, wagged his pistol in a calming motion, and they let the beast run. It thundered off, tail raised and galloping, toward where Tucker had intended to ride. How far was the man's home place? Was he even from around here?

With a bloodied hand planted in the grass, the big man forced himself up on one knee. He gripped his gut, his sheepskin coat open, puckered about his gripping hand. From beneath the clawed fingers oozed thick blood that drizzled to the grass. Where did the man get his strength? Didn't he know that he was as good as dead, but just didn't yet realize it?

The man had lost his hat in his fall, and a breeze from the north tumbled it a few strides away. His head was topped with a thick thatch of white hair trimmed close on the sides, but the face beneath was a weathered mask, harder than leather, as if carved from wood. And it was the big man's face that froze Tucker. The man had been back-shot, gut-shot, and more, but his expression bore unvarnished rage. Bloody spittle stringed from his bottom lip, his eyes squinted up at his attackers, both a-horseback a few feet away, staring down at him.

Tucker was too far to hear their words, but he heard the jabs and harsh cut of their voices. These were angry men, all three. But a gut feeling told Tucker that the man on the ground had been wronged somehow.

Surely I should do something, say something, thought Tucker. Then he realized that if he did, he too would die. Gracie was a feeble rack of skin and bone, as was he. His only possession, clutched in his hand, was a green glass whiskey bottle. Empty. He didn't dare move. Felt sure that if they saw him, he'd be a dead man in short order.

Isn't that what you want? he asked himself. *Isn't that what you've been doing for more than two years now? Tapering off your days until there is so little left of you that you'll eventually dry up, become a husk rattling in a winter breeze?*

And yet, as he watched this big man struggle to live, to fight these attackers, darting in and yipping at him, like wild dogs prodding a downed deer, Tucker knew he had to help this man. But how?

His decision was made for him when the thicker, shorter of the two men leveled his pistol across his other forearm at the big man swaying on his knees. He squinted down the barrel, and touched the trigger. The pistol bucked and the big man jounced again, flopped partly onto his left side, and lay in the grass, hands clutched tight beneath him.

Chapter 2

Tucker watched as the two killers circled the man in opposite directions. He tensed when at the last minute it seemed as if he might be seen. One of the men had a peculiar habit of jerking his head at an odd angle, a nervous condition, no doubt. The smaller man hopped down from his horse, said something to his companion, then rummaged in the big man's coat. He pulled out what looked like a folded white paper. It looked as though the man was smiling. He stuffed the paper into his own coat, then mounted up.

Tucker kept silent and unmoving, and the men soon thundered off in the direction the dead man's horse had traveled. Long minutes passed, and all sign of the riders dissipated into the chilling air, leaving Samuel Tucker shivering atop his horse. He listened for a moment to the soughing of the breeze through the treetops and stared at the back of the big sheepskin coat. Dead for sure, but Tucker didn't dare move.

He thought about the man and his killers. They had been the first sign of humans he'd had in several days—how many he did not know. Finally he tapped Gracie with his heels and she walked forward, eager, he figured, to sample the green grass before them.

A meadow such as this, bound to be a ranch nearby. Maybe they would know who the man was. As he approached the body, Tucker's shivering increased. He knew it was for more than just the cold creeping in between his thready clothes and the goose-bumped skin beneath. When he was some yards from the body, Tucker reined up and slid off the horse, who grunted and dipped her head to the grass and began nosing and cropping with gusto. He let the hackamore reins trail. He had long ago given up worrying if Gracie would wander off—he fancied she was as tired and as uncaring as he.

If that man's coat had been gray, he thought, stepping carefully, shifting his glance up toward the direction ahead where he'd last seen the two riders recede into the landscape, it might well be mistaken for a great rock marring this otherwise cleared meadow. He ventured forward another step, realized he had the bottle clutched tight in his hand, and held on to it. Not much of a weapon, but it would be better than nothing should those shooters decide to double back to admire their handiwork.

He drew closer, tried to stop the thoughts occurring to him—how, despite the blood and the hole in the back, warm that coat would be. If not for the man's wide shoulders and obvious girth, Tucker suspected he was of similar height. Any bulk and muscle he had once had—and it had been enough to fill out and keep solid his thick frame—had in the past couple of years of wandering dissipated till he was a tall, gaunt man, unshaven and sunken-eyed. But try as he might he could not think of anything other than that warm coat now.

He cut wide around the body and looked down at the man. He saw no breath rise from the mouth, saw no movement of the chest. What he did see was a man lying on his left shoulder, large hands gripping a belly glistening with blood. The shirt over it had once been a checkerboard pattern of white and sky blue checks, but now was a knot of bloody hands and sopping red cloth.

Tucker turned his back on the direction he'd been so cautious about looking, and knelt before the hunched form. Seeing that big white-haired head, clean-shaven face, a nose that had been broken a time or two, the jutting brow and wind-burned cheeks—it all reminded him of his father, dead long years ago, and buried by Tucker's own hand back in Texas. He'd laid him to rest beside the woman he'd pined for all of Samuel's life, the mother Samuel never knew, lost to them both from a fevered sickness.

Tucker cut loose any stray thoughts he had for his own safety and decided that since he had watched the man die, the least he could do was figure out who he was, maybe let his kin know, provided there were any. Barring that, he could try for the nearest town. He looked up at Gracie, who had not moved but a step or two as she dined on the toothsome grasses.

He wasn't sure he could hoist the man aboard her. But even if he could, he wasn't so sure the old horse could carry the dead man. Tucker set down the empty bottle and knelt close before the man, his face tightening as he reached for the blood-specked lapels. *First things first,* he told himself. *Have to see if I can find something on him that might identify him.* He looked around again, half hoping he'd see the man's buckskin headed his way. Nothing moved except Gracie's mouth.

Tucker looked back to the man, reached to part the coat, and a puffed and bloodied hand, the palm cored and oozing gore, snatched Tucker's left wrist and held on with a surprising grip.

Tucker yelped and toppled backward. He landed raggedly, his eyes wide as they met the hard stare of the gut-shot dead man.

The big hand, though mangled, held him fast. A sound like a sigh came from him. Then a blood bubble rose from his mouth and popped, and he spoke in a voice as strong as his grip. "Tell Emma . . . heart . . ."

His blue-gray eyes seemed to brighten as if lit from

within. Then his eyelids fluttered and closed. The sighing sound came again, then leaked out with his breath, and the man was finally dead.

The bloody hand remained gripped on to Tucker's own thin wrist. He pried loose the work-thick fingers, lowered the hand to the grass. "I didn't . . . I wasn't thieving from you," he whispered. "I would not do that. I . . ."

What was the use? The man was dead and he had a woman in his life with the name of Emma. *How do I find such a person? Is there a town along here somewhere?* A river town, he thought. That would make sense. And there was bound to be a ranch close by. Maybe it was this man's place.

But no matter what, he couldn't bring himself to feeling again in the man's coat for something to identify him by. It seemed too big a violation now. He'd just have to do his best, knowing there was no way on earth he was going to be able to hoist the man up onto Gracie—neither of them had the strength for such an undertaking.

Tucker stood, his hands on his waist and his breath hissing out of him. *Just have to leave him, take a chance that something might get him.* He looked down at him again. There wasn't even anything he could do to cover him up. He had no blanket of his own, and the man's coat was on him tight. Then he remembered that the big man's hat had pinwheeled away. He looked around and to his surprise located it not far off. He fitted it tight to the man's head and tugged it down low and snug, covering the man's face.

Other than not wanting to lift her head from what she obviously considered a sweet meal, Gracie proved no trouble for him to catch. He was amazed each morning to find he still had her. Something about the sad old brown-eyed horse, her faithfulness to him even through these lean times, warmed and shamed him, for he knew she deserved better. He was on a fast slide downhill and she seemed content to be along for the ride, a last, bittersweet link with his old life.

He led her around the man and she gave the body a suspicious sidelong stare. They hadn't walked but a few yards when his boot stubbed something in the grass. There lay the dead man's pistol, a Colt Navy. Tucker looked back to the dead man. Still dead. He hefted the pistol. He could tuck it into the man's holster, but he didn't warm to the idea of disrupting the body all over again.

Then it occurred to him that he might be able to use it to identify the man. He dropped the reins and turned the pistol over in his hands. Gracie resumed grazing.

The ebony handles shone from long use. He could pick out no other discerning marks, but as he tipped it up, he noted, etched into the butt, deeply gouged letters.

"P.F.," he said.

Gracie kept eating.

"Bound to help." The pistol slid too easily into his waistband. Finally he pulled it free and kept a grip on it, lest it slip down his pant leg.

It took him three tries to remount. He straddled Gracie's bony spine, his eyes half-shut, dizziness and pinprick blackness crowding his vision. Finally he kneed her forward, and she resumed her walk. He didn't have the heart to urge her to move faster. He knew better than anyone how much effort it took to keep on moving forward, from nothing, toward nothing.

His saddle was long gone. Even the blanket he'd managed to hang on to since he'd sold the saddle had also disappeared a month or more back, maybe in that harsh little Mormon-infested town, though he couldn't be sure.

As they walked, the way became recognizable as a trail. Tucker followed it, and his thoughts soon turned over and over the man's last words: "Tell Emma . . . heart . . ."

"I wonder what that means," he said out loud, and sighed. "Guess we better find this Emma and break the sad news, Gracie. Maybe she'll have a charitable side and feed us."

After suitable grieving, of course. It had been his experience that most people got a leg up and over their heartsickness sooner than later.

Only you have never crawled out of yours, have you, Samuel Tucker? You've been weak as water for a long time now, boy. But the good news is that your weak ways are almost at an end. You can't hold out much longer this way. The very center of your sagging self will give way, Tucker, and that, as someone once said, will be that.

He frowned at the thought. The bitterness of self-doubt parched his tongue and left a dry, sandy feeling in his mouth. He kept his eyes closed as Gracie walked right on past another lane that angled sharply to the right.

Chapter 3

Tucker had approached the point where turning around seemed more and more like the thing to do, maybe go back and try to find where the man had come from. The road might have offered a fork earlier that he had failed to notice. "Well, Gracie, looks like we're sunk."

And then Gracie took a few more steps and Tucker saw thin gray clouds angling straight up and down on the near horizon. Another few steps revealed the tops of neat rows of false-fronted buildings making up a business district. The clouds were smoke plumes from chimneys.

"Fancy that, we know where we're headed after all." He licked his lips, unaware that he was doing so, his thoughts fixed on the splendors of hoisting a filled bottle of whiskey. Then he remembered he had no money, and nothing else to sell, and that's when his stomach gurgled and growled like a baby grizz stuffed in a sack. His thoughts shifted from the wonders of whiskey to a full, hot meal of beef roast, with boiled potatoes swimming in butter, thick gravy over it all, maybe some stewed tomatoes and biscuits. Now, that was worth thinking over. But how could that even happen? His hand went to his belly, to rub down the groaning going on in there, and touched the handle of the Colt.

If he turned it in to the law, as he knew he should, he would get nothing for his trouble, but if he were to sell it to the proprietor of a mercantile, or better yet a gunsmith, he might well make a few dollars. He'd tell the lawman about the dead man, naturally, but he could also afford to eat and drink, fill up on whatever the town could offer him. Though in truth, as long as the town had whiskey, the rest of it could wait.

As they stepped their way down off the half-treed hill, Tucker saw the main road leading into town off through the trees to his left where it curved down from the west, crossed the river at a wide, shallow spot, then paralleled the river for a time before snaking into town and becoming a main street. Of what town, Tucker had no idea.

He didn't even know what state he was in. He only knew it was cold, and drawing closer to winter all the time. The far-off peaks were already dusted with snow, and early snows in mountain towns were no joke. Better to end it sooner than later. If he turned south, he'd meet up once again with warmth, but that would only prolong the end.

KLINKHORN, the sign at the end of the main street read. Odd name, but somehow appropriate. The river valley town looked like a few he'd ridden through, half-built on golden dreams spun by miners, but unlike some of those mining camps, this one appeared to be surviving, even thriving.

Wagons lined the wide street. He saw the sway of dresses and the nodding of bonnets as women went about their shopping, and children chased one another. A matronly lady set to spanking a youngster when he failed to wait for a team of draft animals dragging a work wagon. Tucker spied a saloon sign, a hotel, and beyond, at the far end of the street and set off by itself, a livery. It stood well away from the rest of the buildings, he knew, so the flies wouldn't cause a fuss among townsfolk in hot weather.

Here and there behind the main street sat houses, some grander than others, white-painted-lumber affairs with window shutters and filigree on the roof gables. Others were more modest structures, sitting squat and small; most were tidy.

Chapter 4

Their breath, man's and horse's, plumed slow and steady in the cooling air. It would be dark in a few hours, he figured. Maybe sooner this far north. As if in agreement with him, the dim honey glow of a lamp bloomed behind a gauzy curtain in what looked to be a milliner's window.

It didn't take long for the sorry sight of them to draw the unvarnished stares of everyone he passed. He couldn't guess which they were more alarmed at seeing, him or his skinny horse. Despite his usual lack of care that had settled on him like a comfortable old coat, Tucker found himself looking down to avoid eye contact, and offering an apologetic smile when he did catch someone's wary gaze.

Even children stopped. One barefoot lad in short pants, thin and with tousled hair and a daring, rangy look in his eyes, darted into the street just behind Tucker. He shouted, "Scarecrow horse!" and lashed Gracie with a green whip of a branch, once, twice on the rump. The pain sent her into a churning spin, showing more gumption than she had done in weeks.

"Hey, now!" Tucker shouted, half at the boy, half to settle Gracie.

A man grabbed the lad from behind and dragged him backward, enduring the wily youth's kicks and thrashing arms. "Sorry, mister," said the man, forcing a smile. "He's a waif."

As if that is an excuse, thought Tucker as he slid from the horse's back and steadied her over to a hitch rail before G. Taggart's Mercantile and Emporium. Still under the stopped motion of what felt like the entire town's stare, he rubbed Gracie's flank where already the whip marks rose into weals, each a foot long. Again, he felt terrible guilt, swallowed it down. A healthy horse would have had more flesh, could have withstood such a minor lashing. But the episode had taken more wind out of Gracie's already flagging spirit. She stood at the rail, head bowed, sides heaving, her tongue tip extended from her mouth, trembling and flecked with foam.

"Mister, you ought to take some care of that animal. Or put it out of its misery."

Tucker looked up at the sidewalk. Whichever of the several men standing there had said it, he wasn't sure, but it didn't matter. They were right and they all knew it. Even Tucker. He stroked Gracie's forehead, then stepped up onto the sidewalk. Already the cluster of gawkers had dispersed, hurried their steps as if allowing him to get too close might taint them.

He stepped to the windowed entry door of the mercantile and caught sight of himself in the glass. The gaunt creature he saw startled him. He dragged a hand down his face, smoothing his beard, ran it through his hair, squared his shoulders, and set a hand on the pistol's butt. Then he opened the door.

He settled the door in place behind him, a small brass bell above it tinkling his arrival, heavy footsteps somewhere in the back responding. He saw a nearly full barrel of soda crackers by the counter. He stuffed one into his mouth, barely began chewing it, the sweet sensation of solid food flooding his mouth with saliva. He stuffed another, then another in.

"Them are for paying customers."

He looked up to see a broad older man in a wide white apron and sleeve garters, a gleaming dome of a bald head, two narrowed eyes staring at him through wire-rimmed spectacles.

It took Tucker longer than he would have liked to work through enough of the dry cracker dust in his mouth to respond. He tried, coughed crumbs, covered his mouth, then tried again. "Who says I'm not?"

The merchant crossed his arms as if hugging himself. "Not what?"

"A paying customer."

The man nodded, his eyes squinting at the stranger. "Fair enough. Prove it, then."

Tucker stepped to the counter, pulled the pistol free from his waistband. Already the man behind the counter had his pink hands half-raised and had backed up, his head knocking into shelving holding canned goods and small sacks of beans.

Tucker tweezered the Colt with two fingers, tried to smile and make his voice as reassuring as he could. "No, no, you got me all wrong. I am not here to hold you up." He laid the pistol on the counter. "I only want to sell this sidearm." With a finger, he pushed it toward the merchant, who held his hands chest high. Tucker backed up a step, let his hands hang by his sides.

The big man looked at the gun, then at Tucker, then back to the gun, wearing the same mix of scowl and concern. "Well, yes, uh, I do on occasion . . . buy such things." He looked again at Tucker over the tops of his spectacles. "If the piece is in good working order."

"That one appears to be." Tucker tried to sound hopeful.

The big man turned the gun over in his hands a couple of times, went through motions of removing the cylinder, sighting along the barrel, hefting it at arm's length. "Not many folks carry one of these nowadays. They leave them at home in favor of the newer, lighter models." He turned it over, inspecting the handgrips, then paused, looked at Tucker again over his spectacles. "How'd you come by this piece anyway?"

"That would be a long story, sir. Right now I would like to sell it and be on my way. My horse is plumb wore out and I'd like to treat her to a good feed and a rubdown at the livery. Me, I aim to find a hot meal."

"Mm-hmm. And how much were you looking to get for this old gun?"

"I'll be honest, sir. I don't have much idea of what it might be worth. I'll take all I can get, I reckon." Tucker hoped that sounded friendly. He didn't like the way the man kept looking at the handgrips. What if he knew whose gun it was? Tucker's guts tightened and he knew this was a mistake. He should have gone straight to the law with the gun. What had he been thinking, trying to turn this gun into cash?

He was about to snatch the gun from the man's hands when the merchant said, "Very well, I can give you five dollars, but not a penny more. At that I'm not even sure I can recoup the expense. As I said, these pieces are not highly sought anymore."

Tucker sighed inside and nodded. "That's fine, sir. Fine. I'll take it and be glad of it."

The man set the pistol on a back counter and pulled coins from his vest pocket, spreading them on his big palm and sorting them with a finger.

Tucker looked around at the shelves laden with goods, everything from teapots to spools of hemp rope, leather goods, bolts of cloth, foodstuffs on shelves groaning with the weight of canned goods, bottles, and boxes all sporting colorful labels. It had been a long time since he'd been in such a full store. "You wouldn't consider throwing in a bottle of medicinal whiskey to sweeten the deal, would you . . . sir?"

The man paused, gave him that same long stare. "Even if I sold such a thing, the answer would be no. Our deal has been struck, sir. Besides . . . " He looked Tucker up and down. "You would be well advised to take your medicaments in a less habitual manner. But if you cannot, you will find spirits at any one of Klinkhorn's three saloons." He slapped down five coins on the counter and said, "Good day, sir."

Tucker slid the coins into his palm, held them tight there—his pockets all bore holes—and on his way to the door, he grabbed a cracker, stuffed it into his mouth. Just before he opened the door, he smiled at the glaring man, leaned back and grabbed a handful of crackers, then left.

Gracie stood waiting for him, looking somewhat recovered from her earlier excitement. He walked around her quickly and saw no more marks. He led her down the street to the livery, sharing the crackers with her as they walked. She appeared to like the taste, her soft lips taking them in faster than he could chew his own. "I'm sorry, old girl. The boy just didn't recognize what a fine lady you are. But tonight, at least, you'll be in tall cotton. Who knows what tomorrow will bring? In fact, Gracie, don't even think about tomorrow."

Dark was coming in quick. Lights blossomed from inside several businesses as they passed. Tucker caught a snatch of fiddle music and clapping as a stab of mingled laughter spilled out of a saloon as someone entered. The sounds dulled again with the closing of the door. He licked his lips, aware and not caring what the sight of a saloon did to him.

Back up the street, Glendon Taggart flipped over the OPEN sign in his door and shut it behind him. He stepped down into the street and worked up to a stiff-legged run diagonally across the street toward the lit window of the town marshal's office, a Colt Navy in his hand. The few folks on the street gave him a curious stare. None could recall ever having seen Taggart move faster than a casual walk inside his store, much less run anywhere. And with a gun in his hand, to boot. Their gaze followed the big man's huffing progress all the way to Marshal Hart's office.

Chapter 5

He chose the Ringing Belle because something about the front windows reminded him of home, of his former life long ago back in Texas. Maybe it was the red-painted posts, or the blue curlicues on the hand-lettered sign. That it brought to mind old times, good times before everything in his life went sour, that was enough. He stepped through the door, greeted by the bright glow of too many oil lamps. No matter how much spiffing a saloon did before it opened for the evening, there never was any way of covering up the forever scent of old tobacco smoke, spilled beer, and the high-heaven sweat stink of unwashed, hardworking men. And every bit of it familiar and welcoming to Samuel Tucker.

The place was nearly empty. In a back corner, an old man sat facing the room. He wore a nest of wild gray hair, the sunken cheeks and lips of the toothless on his stubbled face, a set of fringed buckskins that looked older than Methuselah's goat, and on the table before him a slouch hat with an assortment of eagle feathers bristling from one side of the band. He looked as though he missed nothing, taking in the entire scene before him. A nearly full bottle of dark amber liquid sat before him. A squat clear glass half-filled waited by his knuckles.

The back half of the floor was set up with baize games tables, but no one sat at them. The only other person in the place was the bartender, who had the look of a mixed-breed man, but with curious features that made him look half Chinese, half Indian.

"What would you like?" The bartender stood erect behind the bar, no emotion on his face as he stared at Tucker.

He had to ask twice, because Tucker had seen the beef-and-cheese sandwiches stacked on a platter on the bar top. And beside them, a jar of pickled eggs.

Tucker finally shifted his eyes from the food, nodded to the bartender. "I'll take a whiskey. Leave the bottle." The bartender didn't move, just stared with that same dark-eyed look of concern. Ah yes. Tucker smiled and nodded, opened his hand to reveal his coins.

"I can pay. Don't worry."

The bartender placed a gleaming glass and a full bottle before Tucker, who reached for them both. He could taste the stuff already.

"You should eat first," said the bartender, sliding the sandwiches toward him. "Eat." He nodded at the food.

"Thank you. I . . ." Tucker snatched up a sandwich. Overwhelmed for the moment with so much good fortune, he didn't know which to reach for first, and ended up trying for both, made a soggy mess of it, and sucked whiskey from the grainy bread, licked drops of it from his beard. He looked up to see the barkeep smiling. The look did wonders for the stony man's appearance.

"You'd do best to make up your mind before you start a thing."

Tucker paused at that. *Truer words* . . . he thought, then took a big bite of soggy beef-and-cheese sandwich and smiled. He was well into his second, chewing and sipping, the whiskey of decent flavor, not that anything resembling such blood fuel wouldn't be, and softening the meat with the whiskey—his teeth had taken to wobbling at the root lately—when the saloon door opened. The heat of the place, the fine high feeling of food in his gut and whiskey heating his face made Tucker look over toward the door as if he owned the place, and any noise was a distraction to be tolerated, but barely.

A big man wearing a star filled the doorway. Tucker looked back down to his drink. Then his eyes widened and he said through a mouth half-filled with chewed food, "Sheriff?"

"Town marshal," said the man in a big, deep voice.

"Marshal, then." Tucker nodded, chewing vigorously. "Good. I was going to go find you after I finished here."

The man's expression didn't change as he walked closer, arms folded over a broad chest. "What a coincidence."

"Yes, isn't it? You showing up here and all." Tucker began to get that tight feeling at the back of his neck, creeping up his scalp. Should have gone to the law first thing when he rode into town.

"No, it's a coincidence because you say you were looking for me, and I have been looking for you. Didn't take me too long to find you. Soaks usually end up in a saloon before anywhere else."

Slide that one off with a laugh, Tucker, he told himself. He kept chewing, sipped again, then smiled at the man's approach.

The man walked closer, leaned one elbow on the bar, his red-and-black-check wool mackinaw peeled back with a meaty fist resting on the man's solid waist. His knuckles grazed the dark, polished-wood grips of a revolver, snug in a gleaming black holster that creaked with the slightest movement from the big man.

"Why were you looking for me, Marshal?"

A meaty finger prodded a fawn wool hat back, revealing a tall hairless forehead, bushy gray eyebrows beneath. "Uh-uh," he said, shaking the big head slowly, the eyes not moving from Tucker's. The middle of the lawman's face bore a thick, gray-daubed mustache, trimmed above the lip but

long at the ends, that gave his face a stern look that he had
fixed squarely on Tucker.

"Pardon?"

"You tell me why it is you were on the scout for me. Once
you've had your food and drink, that is." The smile that followed was cold, and tightened the rest of the skin on Tucker's
head, like a sudden whisper in a dark room on a cold night.

"My horse, she's poorly."

"I know."

"So I brought her to the livery. On my way to your office,
I . . . I haven't eaten in days, a week. I don't recall. I thought
I'd fill my belly, warm up." He lifted the shot glass, his hand
trembling.

"And did you?"

"Did I what?"

"Warm up."

"I am considerably warmer than I have been in a long
time, yes, sir."

"Good. Now, what was it you were coming to see me
about?"

"Well, sir." Tucker looked at the bartender busying himself at the far end of the bar, clinking noises rising from the
glassware he was probably washing. "Marshal, it might be
best if we discussed what I have to tell you in private, maybe
back at your office."

This seemed to be something the big man hadn't expected
hearing. The lawman's great hairy eyebrows rose, then settled back lower, into a hard state. "I have about had enough
of you, soak." Then the big man reached behind himself, underneath his coat.

Tucker faced him, backed away, his hands raised. "I'm not
looking for any trouble, Marshal. I told you I was—"

"Shut up." Then the marshal pulled free a large ebony-
handled pistol, a Colt Navy, and set it on the bar top between
them, butt facing Tucker. "That look familiar?"

Tucker stared at it a moment, then nodded, the warmth of the whiskey leaving him. He wasn't sure how the big man covered the space between them so quickly, but the next thing Tucker knew, a big hand had grabbed him by the back of the head, those thick fingers locked tight in his stringy hair, then bounced his chin on the bar and pushed his head flat against the polished surface. Pulsing starlight filled his eyes, and chimes rang in his head.

They stood close now, and Tucker saw the man's gut, solid, but straining at the blue cloth of the shirt, smelled the marshal's heavy reek of bay rum, coffee, and cigars. Tucker windmilled his arms, swatting at the man, but it was no use. He was too weak and the man was a tree pinning him in place.

The marshal bent his head down low, the mustache moving like a gray snake. "This look familiar to you? Hmm?" He didn't wait for a response. "See them initials? P.F.? Know what they stand for?" The man spoke in a grunt through gritted teeth, spittle flecked at Tucker's face. "They're the initials of my best friend, fella by the name of Payton Farraday."

He held Tucker, pinned in place, for a few more moments, then released him, flinging him back against the bar. "And you can bet your ass we're going to my office. Some folks call it the jail."

The marshal stuffed the big pistol back into his waistband, grabbed Tucker by the neck, and drove him toward the door. Tucker, already dizzy from the whiskey and his chin throbbing from meeting the bar, lurched a couple of steps, then sprawled face-first on the floor.

He flipped over and scrambled backward to the wall beside the door. "There's been a mistake, Marshal. I—"

The big man advanced on him. "No mistake. A dirt-poor stranger comes into town selling my dead friend's pistol?"

"What . . . how did you know he's dead?"

"You don't think I'd not investigate such a thing as that gun turning up without its proper owner holding it?"

Tucker got his feet under him and slid up against the wall until he stood, eye-height, facing the lawman. "But . . . just seeing the gun doesn't mean he's dead. How did you know he was dead? I left him there, but that was miles back. . . ."

"Two men happened to be heading through there on their way back to town. Didn't have a third horse to bring him in on, figured to send a wagon back for him." He shook his head. "That ain't the way, just ain't the way."

Tucker felt the cold creep of soberness wrap itself around his guts, leach its way into every inch of him. "Those men . . . what do they look like, Marshal?"

The big man smiled, shook his head. "You going to stand there and tell me I'm wrong, I suppose? Not going to make it easy on me, huh? No, I guess you wouldn't at that."

"Make what easy, Marshal? I saw two men kill him, shot him in the back, then in the gut. . . ."

"Oh, two men, huh? You mean, like the ones who work for this town? Is that what you are telling us? You really want to air this out here? Fine with me. Then all the folks here at the Ringing Belle can say they saw me drag off the murderer of one of the decentest men who ever drew a breath in the Rogue Valley."

"Murderer?" It leaked out as barely a whisper, as if he'd been punched. Tucker shook his head hard and fast. "No, no way, Marshal. I may be a lot of things, but I never murdered anyone." He had to think, had to fix this thing somehow, but damn it, his head was fuzzy. None of this made any sense. "No, look, Marshal, I never killed him. It's just like I said. I saw him—"

The marshal drew his sidearm and leveled it at Tucker's head. "I daresay there ain't a person in this town who'd try to stop me or hold a grudge for what I am about to do. Ain't nobody of consequence in here anyhow. My word against theirs." He cocked the hammer back fully, his big face red and shaking with rage.

Now that he was one quick stroke of the big angry man's fingertip from what he'd been chasing for two years, Samuel Tucker found he did not want death. Not at that moment anyway, and not for being blamed for something he didn't do. He wanted it on his own terms.

"Marshal, this is not right." It was the bartender, his muscular hands planted on the bar, no gun in sight, but he stared hard at the lawman.

"Like I said, ain't a soul of any worth in here anyhow. Certainly not a worthless, no-account breed of a breed." He glanced back toward the grizzled old character in the back. The man looked at his bottle, at his glass, his hands, but never once met the lawman's gaze.

The barman persisted. "You have no proof yet that this man killed Mr. Farraday."

"Just who in the hell made you circuit judge?"

"I ask you the same thing, Marshal."

"You are one uppity breed—you know that? But you are a mind-sticker. Sort of fella I won't forget." The marshal winked at the bartender, then sighed and eased the hammer back down. He lowered the pistol and smiled. "Okay, then. We'll play it your way. Turn around and head on out of here. But if you move yourself in any direction but the jail, you best have made peace with whatever god it is that soaks worship, because you will die in your tracks, boy. So help me, on Payton's grave, you will die."

As he walked out the door and down the three steps to the street, Tucker noted how dark the sky had become—and how many people were gathered in the street. At the big man's nod, Tucker headed for the well-lit office diagonally across the street from the Ringing Belle.

"Nice and slow, soak. We are about to have us a nice chat."

Tucker risked a glance back behind him, and saw the bartender standing on the raised sidewalk, staring at them. The crowd parted and most everyone stared, brows knitted in confusion, some looking at Tucker as if he were a pile of steaming dung.

"Nothing to see here, folks. Got us a killer, is all. A cold-blooded, foul murderer." The marshal prodded Tucker in the lower back with his boot, sent him to his knees on the step up to the front door of the jail. "Get up and open that door, soak. We got us some discussing to get to."

They entered and the marshal jerked his chin toward a wooden chair before a desk stacked high with papers, boxes of cartridges, a hat, and other assorted items.

"Take a seat, soak."

"My name is Samuel Tucker."

The marshal shouted out the door, "Everything's under control, folks. Just go on about your business. I'll see to it that justice is served. It's what I'm paid for, after all."

He shut the door, holstered his pistol, and slammed the inside shutters on both barred front windows flanking the door, dropping a steel bar in place across each. That finished, he stood before the seated Tucker, arms folded, and smiling hard down at him. "I don't give a fiddler's fart just what your name is. You are the buzzard who murdered my friend."

"Now, wait a minute, Marshal—"

The marshal lunged at Tucker, drove his fist hard at his head, and knocked him backward in the chair. "I am afraid you won't last till the trial, soak."

On the floor, Tucker's head rang louder than ever, tones like those of an Indian flute whistled in his head, and the edges of his vision blackened. He tried to rise, but the marshal set a boot on his chest.

"You going to kill me now—is that it, Marshal?"

"Something like that. But slow, so you learn some sort of lesson before you up and die on me."

Before Tucker could respond, the big man had dragged him upright, and pinning him by the throat against the wall, laid into him with punch after punch to the breadbasket, his gut, his head. Tucker felt something pop in his chest, figured it was at least a rib or two, and try as he might he couldn't make his arms do anything more than get themselves bruised in the process. *So this is it,* he thought. *In my prime I could have been the match of any man in this town, and probably this man too. But now two years of booze and little else have reduced me to taking a beating and unable to fight back.*

Then a thought came to him. "Don't you . . . don't you want to know what he said? Before he died? Your friend, Payton Farraday . . . He spoke before he died."

As if he'd said magical words, the pummeling ceased. Tucker saw the marshal in twos and threes, the shapes of him blurring, coming together, then separating again, like cards in a deck sliding apart, shuffling. It seemed funny somehow.

Then the big man's face was right in front of his own, their noses touching. "What did he say, soak?" Again, the man spoke through gritted teeth, his big face trembling with rage. He wasn't even breathing hard from the beating he'd been doling out.

"I . . . " Tucker swallowed back blood, ran his tongue around his mouth. The teeth were all there, but looser than ever. Now, that was funny. He almost laughed, and then the lawman shook him like a doll.

"Speak or I'll rip your head from your body."

"Uh-uh, not until you stop this. Put me in a cell, but stop this." He ran his tongue over his split bottom lip, tasted blood. "I deserve a trial and you know it. I can prove I didn't do it."

The man bellowed like a bull grizzly, then slammed Tucker's head into the timber wall again and let him drop in a heap. Tucker heard him walk away, rummage in the desk, then come back with what sounded like keys. Tucker tried to see, but his eyes were beginning to swell. The marshal grabbed him by the back of his shirt. The ragged old garment rode up, bunching under Tucker's arms as the lawman dragged him down a hallway, unlocked a door, swung it open, then dragged him another dozen feet into a darker space and dropped him. The marshal unlocked a cell door, squawked it wide.

Tucker felt himself being lifted. Once again the man's face was close to his. Through the blood and sweat, Tucker could smell the man's anger, like the scent a cornered cougar gives off, raw and rank. But there was something else too. Was it fear he smelled? Raw animal fear?

"You going to talk, soak?"

Tucker managed to shake his head once back and forth before another fist, hard like a river rock, drove into his temple. And the last word on his mind was fear. But not his own.

Chapter 6

"Arliss? Did my uncle tell you when he expected to be back from town?" Emma Farraday gripped the middle rail of the stall and stretched her back. It had been another long day at the Farraday spread. If they had many more weeks like this one, they'd head into the winter in the worst shape they'd ever been in. And as much as she hated to admit it, that was no place they wanted to be—up against a whole lot of snow and a range half-full of stock, mixed at that, and with no hands, save for her and Arliss and Uncle Payton.

"I bet he's visiting with Louisa," said Emma, a smile cracking the dust and grit that had settled on her face throughout the long workday. She straightened up and tugged a glove off one hand. Her red-blond hair, the rich hue of a honeyed sunset, had loosened from the leather thong that held it tied in back. She rubbed her scalp and shook loose her long hair.

"How come he didn't talk with me before he went off anyway? You'd think he was fixing to do something that—" The thought stilled her. He wouldn't. He couldn't . . . "Arliss?" Emma continued. "Tell me Uncle Payton didn't go to town to talk with that foul Bentley Grissom." She turned, looked toward the tack room. "Arliss? Are you in there?"

An old man came out, face sunken from a lack of teeth, his chin bristling with salted whiskers. "I heard ya the first time."

"Then why didn't you answer me?"

He looked at her, eyes wide. "Well, pardon me for a month of Sundays, but a man gets peppered with questions like grape-shot, you think he has time to cogitate on 'em? I got but one thinker." He tapped a long finger to his temple. "And it ain't used to such attacks. Now start at the beginning and we'll work our way through whatever it is you are hounding me about."

Emma tugged off her other glove and tried to hide her smirk.

"You laugh all you want to, but I'm telling you like I told your pappy and I tell your uncle, there ain't no good can come of a man overtaxing his thinker. Mark my words." He resumed tapping the side of his head as if it were a pleasant habit. "You think it does Payton any good? Naw, hell no. He says he wakes up in the morning feelin' like he ain't moving fast enough. Can you imagine?" The old man's nose wrinkled as if he'd stepped in a gut pile.

"As a matter of fact, Arliss, I can. That's how I feel all the time. But I can't do it if he's going to go off and borrow money against the land. Being in debt is no way to live."

"Now you sound like your pappy. He was a good man, but when it come to such matters, even if they asked my thoughts, I just stayed out of it."

"So you don't know if he went to talk with Grissom."

"I didn't say that." The old man turned away, then kept turning and ended up facing her again. "And I didn't say I did know neither." He wagged a finger at her as if scolding her.

Emma smiled. "Arliss, I have no idea what that means, but I'll let it drop, at least until Uncle gets back. I just hope he hasn't done anything to jeopardize the place."

"You ought to know better than that. Why, he loves this spread more than you and me combined. 'Bout the only one who liked it more was your pap."

"I wish you wouldn't keep bringing him up, Arliss."

The old man rasped a hand over his stubbled face. "Naw,

you don't. It's good, you know. Got to keep him alive in us. He's the reason we're all here anyway. Besides, I miss him too. I knowed him a long time, you know. Met 'em all on the trail headin' out here. We parted, and I went off, set to digging in the rocks for more rocks. Why, if there ever was a worse way for a man to spend his days, I ain't done it. I—"

"Arliss."

"What? I was fixin' to tell just how I come to be here and you go and run my train of conversation into the ditch—"

"Arliss!" Emma held up a hand, held her other over her eyes theatrically. "I know how you ended up here. I happen to have heard it a time or two. From you and Daddy and Uncle Payton. And you again. Now . . . " She headed for the barn door. "I for one am hungry enough to eat a small bear. I'm not going to wait on Uncle. You want beans and biscuits or biscuits and beans?"

Arliss held his scowl, his old chin jutting forward like a ship's prow. Then his cheeks rose and his entire face grinned. He pushed his old holey hat back on his head. "With all them choices, I reckon I could eat some of each and a little more of the other. When do we eat?"

"As soon as I make the biscuits and heat the beans." As she said it, she saw Arliss's face lose its broad smile. His brows pulled tight and he looked past her into the twilight behind the barn door. "What's wrong?" she said, and turned.

Her uncle's buckskin gelding stood in the midst of the yard, head down and reins trailing, looking left and right as if confused.

"Jasper, what are you doing here?" Emma scooped up the reins and looked around the yard. "Uncle Payton! Uncle Payton?"

Arliss came up beside the horse. "Oh no."

"What is it?"

He looked at Emma, his mouth set in a grim line, as he held up two fingers, the tips swiped with blood.

"Arliss, what's that?" But she knew.

"It ain't good, girl. The work wagon's rigged. Put that horse in a stall. I'll get Julep hitched. And grab a couple of lanterns. We're losing daylight."

He headed to the barn, then shouted back over his shoulder, "And bring his rifle. I'll get shells and my shotgun."

"What do you think happened, Arliss?" Emma fought to push down a cold snake of fear.

"I don't know, girl, but we can jaw about it later."

The old man led Julep the mule, pulling the short work wagon, back out the rear door of the barn and around to the front. The mule stood, despite the jostling of the small wagon behind her. She was used to quieter commotion where Arliss was concerned, but she took it in stride. He slid the iron bar, post maul, and rolls of wire onto the ground beside the barn. "Emma! We got to go!"

She came out of the barn on her strawberry roan, Cinda, the wire bails of two lanterns gripped in one hand. She leaned down and handed them to Arliss. "Let's go."

"What are you doing?"

"We can cover more ground this way, Arliss. Now let's go!" She booted the roan into a gallop.

Arliss climbed up onto the wagon seat and snapped the lines on Julep's back, the lanterns rattling in the box beneath his feet. He didn't know what they would find, but he knew it was bound to be bad. A man didn't just bleed for no reason. The reason must have been a big one to unseat a man like Payton Farraday. *This family has been through too much,* he thought. *Lord, don't let it be anything like that.* But somehow Arliss knew the night would not end well.

Chapter 7

Emma reached the north meadow and slowed, searching the tall grasses trailside. Payton must have been headed home, since Jasper would have turned up at the ranch sooner had something happened earlier, on their way to town. She hoped she'd find him leaning against a rock, nursing a knock to the head. But that wouldn't explain blood on his saddle.

Every few minutes she'd glance back over her shoulder to make sure Arliss was coming. Try as she might, she couldn't stop her mind from replaying how she'd found her father, shot dead while seeding that same field. It was to be the first of many such pastures and hay fields, he'd told her. Then they would be able to feed their horses top feed. It was a hardy seed he'd ordered special. He'd been mocked at local rancher meetings, but when the grass grew in, year after year, fuller and more lush with each passing season, others had come around, asking how they might order themselves some of the same seed. But it had turned out to be the only such field he would establish.

She remembered that September day two years before. *My,* she thought, *two years ago this week*. She'd ridden out to bring him lunch. Arliss and Uncle Payton had been on the south end of the spread rounding up strays, getting a head count. Her father had been scything great swaths of tall, rich grass. But as she'd ridden up, she saw nothing of him and wondered if he was taking a nap just into the trees at the south end of the field. She'd skirted the edge, not wanting to trample any uncut grass, and glanced in toward the field. Then she saw the section he'd been working, great wide, even cuts, the grass laid low in long rows. And there in the midst of it lay her father on his back. She dismounted and led her horse through the field toward him. While she was well away from him, she smiled, lifted down the tin lunch pail, slung the canteen over her shoulder, and crept forward. He didn't move. She'd catch him napping, a rare treat since he never did anything like that. Called it lazy work.

But as she drew closer, she saw flies clustering over him in a circling swarm, rising and falling, saw some on his face. Soon she saw his sweaty shirt, but it was dark with more than sweat. It had been blood, multiple gunshots in his chest and belly, one in his arm, as if he'd been defending himself.

"Emma!"

Arliss's voice snapped her from her reverie. She glanced back from the edge of the field where the lane from their place met the lane to town.

"Emma! He's here!"

She saw Arliss turn Julep hard right into the field. Beyond them she saw a big rock. Then she realized it was her uncle Payton's coat. She spun Cinda hard and booted her into a run.

By the time she got to them, Arliss was on his knees, hunched over the big man. He'd laid him out flat on his back, the great coat spread wide, her uncle's chest and belly rank and black with wet blood. There was a smell, the pungency of death, clouding her senses.

On the other side of her big uncle's body, Arliss alternately smacked the big man's face and bent low to hug him, then rose again to adjust the man's arms, cursing and smoothing Payton's hair, pushing it back beyond the sun line from his hatband. Arliss babbled that Payton must wake up, had to wake up, damn it.

She knew she should try to track whoever had shot him, but this new, sudden grief and confusion overwhelmed her. Dark descended and Cinda and Julep grazed in the fine, succulent green grasses of her father's prized field. Emma knelt beside Arliss, as close to her as an uncle, and leaned over her dead uncle, unbidden tears trailing down her dirt-smudged face, her uncle's coat sleeves gripped tight in her callused, work-hard hands. She knew that the nightmare was happening all over again, and maybe this time it would never end.

How long they sat like that, she didn't know. With her eyes closed, Emma no longer heard Arliss trying to revive her uncle. Instead, he had subsided into quiet sobs, a low, pitiful sound that gripped her guts tight in its bony hand. She felt grief that she recognized as the same vile ache from two years before. Emma kept her eyes closed and pulled in a long, deep breath. She let it out slowly, forcing it through clenched teeth, then opened her eyes.

Julep raised her head as Emma retrieved a lantern from the wagon. She dragged a match on the strap steel seat brace and lit the lantern.

"We should get Uncle Payton home. Take care of him right."

Arliss nodded. "I'll lay him out on the table, wash him, dress him in his finest."

"We both will."

Arliss looked at her with alarm, shook his head. "Oh no, no, girly. That wouldn't do at all."

"But he was my uncle."

"Yes, and next to your pappy, he was my best friend. But he was a man, and a modest one at that. He'd have been embarrassed to high heaven if you saw him . . . well, you know."

Emma looked down at her uncle and sighed. "I suppose you're right. Let's get him into the wagon."

Arliss guided Julep and the wagon closer to Payton Farraday's body, then made sure the bed of the wagon was free of any last bits of junk from the day's work. He shoved far forward under the seat a knot of rope, a tin of bent and broken nails, and a too-thin fence post. "I didn't think to bring a blanket. It's a hard old wagon."

"I don't think he's going to care, Arliss." As soon as she said it, Emma didn't know whether to laugh or cry, so she did a little of both. It had sounded so much like something her uncle would have said.

It seemed to help the old man too. He shook his head and said, "I swear, girl, with that tongue of yours, if you ain't a Farraday. . . . Now." Arliss cleared his throat. "You lift him by the boots. I'll get him under the shoulders. You set his boots in the bed. Then you can help me slide him in there."

It took them a couple of minutes of grunting, but they got Payton loaded, got the tailgate chained in place.

"I don't expect I'll need the lantern," said Arliss. "Old Julep knows her way home."

They moved along, Emma walking her horse beside the wagon, looking at her uncle's body, his big hat pulled down over his face just as when they'd found him. Soon they reached the spot where the lane toward the ranch T'd off the main trail to Klinkhorn. Emma reined up and Arliss drew Julep to a stop. "Whoa, now. Whoa. What's wrong, Emma?"

"I'm going on to town, Arliss."

"What? No, no, no, that won't do at all."

"You can't keep telling me that, Arliss. I have to see the marshal. One of us has to."

"Then I'll go," he said, making to climb down from the wagon.

"How? How are you going to do that, Arliss? You can't ride horseback anymore, and besides, who's going to tend to Uncle Payton?"

He sat back in the wagon seat. "We'll go in the morning, Emma. Now is not the time. I can't let you risk your neck.

Lord knows who's out there in the dark." He leaned forward. "Your pap and uncle would never forgive me if something happened to you."

"I'm not a little girl, Arliss. And it's something I need to do. Something I am going to do, no matter what you say." She looked down at her uncle once more in the wagon, then said, "I have to go. I'll see you at home later."

As she wheeled the horse around and headed toward town, Arliss shouted after her, "Who's going to help me get your uncle in the house?"

But she didn't even turn in the saddle. Despite the cold silver light of a nearly full moon, he lost sight of her. Soon even the drumming of her horse's hooves was swallowed by the dark. Arliss pictured her, riding in the night, crying, angry, confused, a true orphan now and barely twenty-two years old, but a young girl in so many ways. Her father and uncle had worried so much about her not growing up into a lady, but they were wrong. She was very much a lady, but a ranch lady. *A lady of her own devising, and a stronger woman you'd not find,* thought Arliss.

And then he froze in the seat as he remembered that she had her uncle's rifle with her. He didn't think she'd remembered to take along a holster gun, but he'd told her to grab her uncle's rifle. Even as he remembered seeing it in the sheath on Cinda's saddle on their way out to look for Payton, Arliss felt in vain beneath his boots for the thing, hoping against hope that she'd stuck it in the wagon before she left. No such luck. His hand fell on nothing but the rattling lanterns.

"Oh, Payton, Payton. That girl is too much of a firebrand. I hope she doesn't do something foolish, but as a Farraday, I just know she will. You went and got yourself all shot up, just like your brother. Now how will we manage? Ranch was on shaky ground before, but now? I hope you made that deposit before you got jumped. I reckon I'll be the next one going to town, see what I can see at the bank. I don't reckon they'll make time for an old wreck of a miner with bum knees and no kin relation to the girl. But I smell a rat. And it goes by the name of Grissom."

Chapter 8

The night was cool and a breeze kicked up as Emma rode toward Klinkhorn. She had a good idea who had killed her uncle, the same man she knew had had her father killed. But it had been so difficult then, and her uncle had told her not to worry about it, that he would take care of it, that he would find out who had done it and make them pay. And she had believed he would. But as time wore on, as the weeks became months, and the months became a year, then two, she realized that either he knew who had done it but was powerless to prove it, or it had truly been as their friend Marshal Hart had said, a vicious murder by somebody drifting through. But that had never made sense to her—who'd drift way up here? And why kill a man working in a field? Did they really think they'd find his pockets stuffed with money?

And now Uncle Payton was dead, also by gunshots, and in the same place, almost in the same spot in the field. And that was all too coincidental to her.

She didn't know what she hoped to do in town, but she had to do something. Had to tell the marshal. He was bound to round up a posse. Unless she could convince him that it had been Grissom.

She made the eight miles faster than she had expected, clouds sliding away to reveal a moon offering cold comfort from above. All about her the familiar landscape lay cloaked in a steely glow. She topped the rise, the other side of which led straight down into town, and paused there, puzzled by the light from the long main street and the outlying grid of lanes leading to the expanding homes. She had often wondered how anyone could live so close to others, and had long vowed to herself to never find out. But on this grim night, Emma's first thought on seeing the town was that it looked as if it were on fire, so many lights glowed.

Cinda nickered and Emma responded with a neck pat. She'd long ago taken up the family habit of talking to her horse. She urged the roan into a trot down the slope to the main road snaking into town. "I know, girl. Looks like torches down there. I don't know what's going on."

And as she drew closer, she realized she was right; they were torches carried by more people on the street in the dark of this September night than she'd ever seen milling in town, even during the Fourth of July celebrations. Men, women, even the kids were out.

"Emma Farraday, is that you, dear?" From her right, from between two buildings and carrying a swinging lantern, emerged Louisa Penny, a woman several years older than Emma but who had become a good friend, and someone she'd been able to talk with as she had reluctantly grown into a young woman.

"Oh, Louisa." Emma found herself swinging down out of the saddle and hugging her friend. For long minutes they stood, holding each other, Emma crying long, near-silent sobs, her friend gripping her tight, patting her back and not needing to say a thing.

Angry shouts from far down the street pulled them apart, and Emma dried her red eyes with the hankie Louisa handed her.

"You probably don't even know why I'm here, why I'm crying."

"I had hoped the marshal wasn't correct, but now, seeing you . . . It's Payton, isn't it?"

Emma nodded, her throat hard, her mouth set tight. "But how did you . . . Is that what all this is about?" Emma pointed at the growing cluster of townsfolk down the street, in front of the marshal's office.

"Oh, Emma," said the older woman, holding the girl's wrists. "Nearly every woman in town thought the world of Payton Farraday. But you knew that. You also knew Payton nearly as well as anyone, and you know what he could be like. Slow to anger, slow to smile, but always thoughtful. Slow to . . ."

She turned away, wiped at her eyes. "Now you'll think I'm silly. Just this afternoon . . . he . . . he kissed me, Emma. Like a schoolboy, so kind and gentle. I haven't felt so happy in a long time, Emma. He said he was going home to give you the good news. About the loan. He was so happy."

"What loan?" Emma looked hard at her friend, her eyes sharp and hard. "What loan, Louisa?"

"Why, the loan he took out last spring to help pay . . . Don't tell me he never told you? Don't worry, though, now, because it's all paid off. You'll at least have that small comfort in knowing you're not beholden to that nasty Bentley Grissom."

Emma nodded, more confused than she'd ever felt in her life. What else could possibly happen to make this day the worst she was sure she would ever have?

"Why are they down there, Louisa?"

"Then you don't know. Of course, how could you? The marshal said he was shorthanded. His deputy, Peter Orton, is out on the drive to Ogallala, I think it was. So Marshal Hart probably hasn't had time to ride out to see you. He would want to tell you himself."

"I already know Payton's dead, Louisa. Honestly, sometimes you remind me of Arliss. . . ."

"The marshal caught the man who did it."

"What?"

"Yes, some drifter, a drunk, apparently. The marshal obviously wants a fair trial, but half the town is howling for blood. They want to hang the man tonight from the peak of the livery barn."

"A drifter? Then it wasn't Grissom?"

"Grissom? No, he's a whole lot of things, but I don't think he has it in him to kill a man."

"No," said Emma, looking across the street at the two men leaning against the hitch rail. "But he'd sure as hell hire it done."

For once, Louisa had nothing to say. Then the two men, seeing eye contact had been made, crossed the street, cutting them off.

"Good evening to you, ladies." The runty dark man, Raoul Vollo, swaggered forward around the front of them, while the taller man, whom Emma knew only as Rummler, cut a tight circle behind. Cinda danced as the man ran a hand along her side.

"Get out of the way," said Emma, snarling the words low and menacing. But the smaller man stepped in close, just in front of her. He was her height and his dark, rheumy eyes stared into hers. When he spoke, his voice slipped out like soft cloth rasping over stone, snagging along the way. "I don't think that is any way to talk to a man as important as me. Do you, Rummler?"

The stink of sweat and whiskey and spent tobacco clung to him, wafted off Vollo's rank buckskins, and when he opened his mouth, the pungent tang of spoiled food clouded at her. Emma saw dark teeth that in a few short years would become blackened nubs, then be pulled out altogether.

"Now, what I want to know, *chica*, is when you are going to sell that ranch of yours? After all, you are a woman, and from what I can see, a fine one in all the right places. But what's a woman like you going to do out there with nothing but a few skinny head of beeves and horses? And with that crazy old man wobbling around the place, and two dead men too!" He wheezed out a rasping laugh that forced Emma's teeth tight together.

Rummler had made his way around the nervous roan and now stood behind Louisa. "Why so nervous, darlin'?" When he spoke, the woman tensed, startled, but he grabbed her roughly around the waist.

"No!" she screamed, pulling free and swinging the lantern in a high arc. Rummler had little time to defend himself before the lantern slammed down on his shoulder, spraying glass and flame over his flannel shirt and vest, along his neck and up the side of his head.

"Oh! You witch!" Rummler whipped in a circle, his long arms flailing as if he were engaged in a drunken dance. Since the lantern was made of tin, little fuel oil spilled on him.

"Help me, Vollo!" he screamed.

Vollo let go of Cinda's halter and beat what few weak flames there were with his hat.

Emma grabbed Louisa's hand and tugged Cinda's reins, and the three of them ran down the street toward the crowd, Louisa holding the wreckage of her lantern.

"Curse that nasty man!" hissed Louisa, holding her battered lamp aloft. "That was my best lantern."

They heard Rummler's shouts alternating between curses and murderous oaths directed at them. Only when the women neared the crowd did they look back.

Vollo had Rummler bent over the watering trough on the other side of the street, and scooped water out of it with Rummler's hat. The taller man's jigging had slowed, but he danced side to side as each cold splash dumped over him.

As soon as they drew close to the crowd, the townsfolks' shouts died down as, one by one, they turned their attention to Emma. Concern and sadness marked each face, and Emma found she could not look any of them in the eye, for fear she might break down. She knew her uncle had been fond of the town, and as one of the earliest citizens of the region, he'd felt a justified pride in the place, pleased and proud of what part he had done in helping it grow. The school, the town hall, the saloons, the bank, two churches, all of it. *And here they all are,* she thought. *Looking at me with pity because I lost my father and my uncle, and Lord knows how many of them knew my uncle had taken out a loan to keep the spread floating.* How long could she keep it afloat herself, now that it was just she and Arliss? She pushed the thought out of her mind and tied Cinda's reins to the rail out in front of the jail.

It was Ross Dakin who spoke first. He was one of Arliss's drinking friends. The two old codgers got together once every few weeks to play cards for matchsticks and insult each other. "We're so sorry, Emma," he said, lowering his eyes and shaking his head. He folded his work-hardened hands atop the handle of his three-tine hay fork. "We're fixing to string up that killer. Marshal can't hold him in there forever. Too many of us and only one of him. We'll get him out here. We'll make it right—you wait and see."

This seemed to once again spark the fire of anger in the crowd. It began as nods of heads and mumbles, and soon became shouts of affirmation and anger that spread among the crowd like a prairie fire through dry grass.

Several men held aloft loops of new and used hemp rope, lariats, rifles, and fists. She wanted to thank them somehow, wanted to show them she appreciated their anger, that she felt it too, but something about this crowd, the raw rage on their faces, almost seemed like a game to them. After all, did they really know her uncle? What right did they have to feel this much anger?

Emma stroked Cinda's nose. The loud crowd made the horse sidestep, trying to keep them all in sight, but they were too close and on both sides of her. Emma untied the horse and led her down to the next rail at the fringes of the crowd.

Louisa stepped up beside Emma, stroking Cinda's neck. "I'll watch her until you come out. Don't worry."

"Thanks, Louisa." Emma looked back up the street toward where they had come, but didn't see Vollo or Rummler.

"They went into the Lucky Shot," said Louisa, nodding toward the saloon near where the men had been. "They won't be out tonight. Not under their own steam anyway," she said, her mouth the only thing smiling.

"Just the same, are you going to be okay tonight?"

The older woman nodded. "More than likely. Those two are gutless. Besides, I have a shotgun I keep by the bed."

"Good. But I'm going to tell the marshal anyway. Those vermin should be locked up. No one's safe since Grissom brought them here."

Chapter 9

"Marshal Hart, I have taken the liberty of informing the crowd outside that Payton Farraday has been the unfortunate victim of a savage murder, and that the man responsible has been apprehended by you. I told them that he is an itinerant killer who then had the gall to show up here pawning the dead man's gun." The fat man inclined his head toward the door and smirked. "As you can hear, they are suitably incensed. I daresay they are keen on hanging the man. Whatever shall we do?"

"'We,' Grissom? You got a mouse in your pocket?" The marshal rattled the dented enamel coffeepot, found it empty, and slammed it back on the stove.

"What has got you all bunched and puckered?" Grissom leaned back as if he were stretching his back because of some fat man's ache, his enormous belly arching outward, his pudgy pink hands balled behind his back. He wore most of his smirk.

The marshal sighed and flopped down into his chair behind the desk, rubbing his cut knuckles with a cupped hand. "The last thing I need is a vigilante crowd out there. Whether you know it or not, whether you like it or not, I am the law around here and you are the mayor of this half-a-horse town, and that's all there is to it. And besides, don't you think announcing a thing like that was a little premature?"

"What do you mean?"

"I mean." He closed his eyes for a moment, then lowered his voice and resumed speaking, quieter and in a more clipped tone. "I mean, Grissom, that we only have a pistol in our possession. The word of those two fools who work for you could land you in my jail. You want that?"

"But they assured me—"

"Yeah, and I don't doubt that they did the job, but no one's supposed to know that until someone discovers the body, right?"

Grissom smiled. "A trifling detail, Marshal. It will all burst open wide very soon."

"You better hope so, Grissom. Elsewise, you'll be spending a lot more time here in the jailhouse."

Grissom moved with a speed that astonished the big lawman. He bent low over the desk, his oily pink face inches from the marshal's. "You think that's what I am, eh? An idiot? I thought we had come to an agreement of sorts. Now I see that I was incorrect."

They stared like that, the words quivering between them like a sunken arrow. Finally, in a low voice, the lawman said, "I am tensed up because your boys failed."

"No, on the contrary," said Grissom, standing upright. "They succeeded well, I should think. When they rode into town smiling, I knew my troubles were nearly over. And my plans could have been even closer to fruition had the drunk you arrested happened to have died of gunshot wounds sustained while resisting capture."

He wore no smirk, just stood there sweating, his broad forehead and his wide, whisker-free pink face staring at the marshal. The seated man could not meet his stare.

"I presume he is not dead. Otherwise you would be parading him outside by now. You have enough of the peacock in you, Hart, for that."

"I'll tell you why, 'cause it ain't right. It ain't lawful. Not while there's cause to believe he's innocent. At least in the eyes of the town."

"Oh, this is rich, Marshal. Rich, especially coming from you. But tell me, why must the pangs of justice twinge within you now, of all times?"

Again, the lawman could not meet the mayor's gaze.

"Oh, don't tell me you think he might be useful to you. Perhaps in usurping me somehow, hmm? That is what you want, after all, isn't it?"

A log shifted inside the potbellied stove, clunked against the firebox.

"Cold in here, Marshal. I was you, I'd warm things up a bit. Put another log on the fire, so to speak."

The big lawman stood up, his chair squawking on the wood floor. "That a threat, Grissom?"

But neither man got a chance to say more, because the door flung inward. Escorted by a wave of sudden shouts and angry oaths, Emma Farraday strode in wearing an old patched sheepskin barn coat and no hat on her head.

The marshal came around the desk and closed the door, touched her arm lightly, and escorted her into the midst of the room. "Emma, I was going to ride out to see you, soon as I was able. . . . You've heard, then."

"Where is he? Where is the devil? They said you had him here."

"He's here, but I had to subdue him, Emma. He's passed out in a cell back there." He nodded toward the big wooden door with the inset bar window at the back of the room. "He's a drunk, looking for whiskey money, I suspect, nothing more."

"I'd like to know how you found out, Marshal. We only just found Uncle Payton ourselves."

"I am afraid that is my fault, dear girl," said Grissom, trying to look despondent. "I spoke too soon, perhaps. You see, a man came into town—"

"Grissom, who's the marshal here?" Hart glared at the fat businessman.

"Somebody better tell me what is going on." Emma looked at each of them in turn. "My uncle has been killed and I want to know why—and I want to know how you found out so soon. I barely rode into town before everybody on the street was telling me how sorry they were." The woman's top lip curled as if she were about to growl like a dog.

She turned her gaze fully on the fat man. "And then those two bums who work for him, Vollo and Rummler, actually smiled when they told me how sorry they were to hear about it." Her gaze never left Grissom's face. "They also tried to manhandle Louisa Penny."

"What? Is she okay?" The marshal's nostrils flexed wide, his brow creased.

"Yes, she's fine. I can't say the same for Rummler. She smacked him with her lantern, singed him up a bit."

Grissom pooched out his lower lip. "I am sorry to hear all this, Miss Farraday. As men in my employ, they will naturally be reprimanded in the harshest terms."

"Great. Fat lot that will do. But I am curious, Grissom, about what they said to me."

"Oh, what was that, my dear?"

"Well, when they weren't attacking us, they smiled, walked around my horse, and asked me when I figured I was aiming to sell up, move out. Being a woman and all, one of them said. Me being a woman, I guess he figured there's no way I can run a ranch half as competently as a man."

"My dear," said Grissom, his head canted to the side, a resigned look of pity in his eyes.

"Don't call me that. Ever. In fact, don't even talk to me."

"Fine, fine. But I will say this last thing." He caught her hard-eyed stare. "To the room, naturally. They are an uncouth pair, Vollo and Rummler, I'll grant you. But their hearts were in the right place. After all, running a ranch alone is no way to live. In fact, it's a sure way to bankruptcy."

"I am not alone. I have Arliss Tibbs. Next to my uncle and father, he's one of the most capable men I know of."

Grissom snorted, covered his smirking mouth with a hand. "Begging your pardon, Miss Farraday, but Tibbs is hardly a paragon of manhood. He's a broken-down old man whose best days surpassed him long before you were even born."

"We are through talking."

"I shall keep that in mind."

"Grissom, get out of here." The marshal grabbed the fat man by the scruff of his suit coat and walked him to the door. The marshal lowered his voice, whispered to the fat man, "You are a low caliber of a man, Grissom, standing here and trading licks with a girl whose uncle was just murdered."

"Unhand me, damn you. Or else. And you know what I'm referring to."

"Shut up!" the marshal barked, and propelled the fat mayor out the door. The activity roused the crowd's ire, and a fresh wave of shouts and oaths filled the lantern-lit street.

Before Emma could ask him what that exchange meant, he said, "Would you like Luke Slater to attend to Payton's . . . needs, Emma?"

The girl, her eyes rimmed red, turned her gaze on him. "What? No. Payton was my uncle and Arliss's friend. We'll tend him at home. Just like we did for Daddy. Then I'll bury him up back, beside Daddy. They were nearly inseparable as brothers when they were both alive, so I figure now it'll be the same."

"Yes, I'd guess your father would want it that way. They both would."

"Are you going to tell me just what is going on? Who did you arrest for killing my uncle, and how did you know he was dead?"

The marshal scratched above his ear. "Like Grissom was going to say, Glendon Taggart come to me a few hours ago, all hot and lathered. Seems a mangy old drunken drifter on a near-dead horse rode in this afternoon, had nothing but an old pistol. He sold it to Glendon for five dollars, then went and got drunk with the money. But Taggart noticed 'P.F.' on the butt of the handgrips, your uncle's initials. Seems he recognized it as your uncle's gun. So he brung it to me for a look-see. And he was right. It was Payton's Colt Navy—had it since the war. I'd recognize it anywhere." He picked up the gun from the desktop, handed it to Emma.

Emma hefted the pistol. "Yes, this is definitely Uncle Payton's. He loved this old thing. Polished it all the time."

Marshal Hart smiled. "Yeah, I told him I don't know how many times that he ought to get himself a decent new rig." He patted his own hip gun and smiled. "True to Farraday form, he did the exact opposite of what I suggested. But the gun suited him."

"Didn't do him much good, though, did it?"

"No, no, I reckon it didn't at that."

Emma let the lawman lift the gun from her hands and put it back on the desk. "Marshal, how did you—"

"How did I know Payton was dead? I didn't. Hoped somehow this man had just taken it from him, but then the man confessed when I went to the Ringing Belle to question him about the pistol. He was already half in the bag and working on getting himself all the way in. I reckon that's why he was so belligerent."

"Then he killed my uncle for money?"

"That'd be my guess. But who knows what goes on in the mind of a drunkard?"

They were quiet for a few moments, and then the marshal said, "If you want anything, Emma. I don't have much, never have, being a lawman and all, but I'm sure I could arrange credit for you at the bank, something like that to get you by."

She looked at him, alert again, as if he had suggested she strip down for him right then and there. "I will not take credit. My daddy never did, Uncle Payton never did, and I sure won't. Especially not from a bank owned by that fat sorry excuse of a man Grissom."

"Now, Emma. Before you go spoutin' off about Grissom—and I'm not saying I like him any more than anybody else around here—you might want to reconsider what you thought you knew about your uncle's dealings with the man."

"What do you mean?"

Hart sighed. "Well, way I heard it, your uncle had borrowed a good bit of money last spring to keep your place floating."

It sickened Emma to hear it, but it confirmed what Louisa had told her, and even what Arliss had hinted at. But it was just too early after his death to go learning confusing things about her uncle. "My uncle Payton never would borrow from a bank, and especially not from a bank owned by Bentley Grissom. You must have heard wrong, Marshal."

He stared at her a long moment, then said, "Yeah, I guess I must have at that. Besides, I only mentioned you going to the bank because I know it's been rough and all, lately."

"The only thing I want from you, Marshal Hart, is to see him. The murderer."

"Emma, like I said, he's not conscious. Between the knock I had to give him on the head and the booze he'd been into at the Ringin' Belle, well, he's in no shape for visitors."

"I want to see him now." Her jaw muscles were set, her face tight with barely controlled rage.

"All right, all right." He grabbed the key ring from his desk.

Emma glanced at the desk as they walked by, then stopped before it. "I will take Uncle Payton's pistol with me when I leave."

"I can't let you do that, Emma. It's evidence, for the time being."

Her narrowed eyes and flexing cheek muscles told him what she'd say before she spoke. "I'll be taking it with me, Marshal."

He sighed again, not for the last time that night. "All right, Emma. But you bring it home, put it under lock and key. A pistol like that ain't nothing a girl should concern herself with."

She reached for it and he grabbed her wrist. "I don't think you'll be bringing it back there, Emma." He nodded at the door to the cells. "You can have it when you're ready to head home."

"Fine. Open the door, Marshal. I have an uncle to get ready for burying, but I need to see his killer first."

He opened the door and lifted down a lantern from a hook. "Come on. He's in the last cell, back there on the right."

She walked ahead of him down the hallway, stopped at the last cell, and squinted into the dark. "Hold the lamp closer, Marshal Hart. I want to see him."

From the cell, they heard a groan, then in the shadows saw the man's head rise off the wooden platform. "Heart?" he said, his voice shaking and weak, as if it belonged to a man far older. "Heart? That's what the dead man said. Heart." Then his head flopped backward and clunked on the plank.

"Hey! Hey, you in the cell," shouted Emma. "Don't you fall asleep! What else do you remember?" No sound came from within the cell. "Hey! Marshal, wake him up. He had to be talking about Uncle Payton."

"I can't, Emma. He's better off to square up with his Maker, 'cause he'll be swingin' soon as the judge comes on through."

"Throw water on him, something. I want to hear what he was about to say." She looked around, as if expecting to see a waiting bucket of water by her feet.

"Emma, listen to me." The marshal tried to turn her around, steer her back up the hallway.

She jerked her arm from his grip, squared off in front of him. "If you won't do anything, then let them in!" She waved an arm toward the front of the building. "They'll know what to do with the worthless killer." She forced back hot tears and gritted her teeth.

"You know I can't do that, Emma. They'd string him up and then what would we have? A murdering mob."

"To hell with the law, Marshal. He's guilty of murdering my uncle Payton!"

"I know, Emma, but what would happen next time? It gets easier and easier and pretty soon you have a town no one wants to live in, a town where everyone fears their neighbors. And Klinkhorn doesn't need to be that way. Let the law do its job."

She stared at him, not saying a thing, anger radiating from her taut features. "I'll be back tomorrow," she said, then left him standing there in the dark in front of the cells.

He heard the front door open, the sounds of the crowd flood in. He heard Emma's voice shouting at them from the front steps, heard footsteps, lots of boots on wood, coming up onto the sidewalk. He reached for his pistol, let his fingertips just dust the curve of the polished handgrips. Would any of them have the courage to try it? To try to take him? It would be so easy to just let them. So easy. But no, he had to know, had to know what the drunk had heard, had to know what the drunk knew.

The boot steps did not draw closer, and then the voices became a dull rumble again as the door slammed shut. He let his gun hand drop, raised the lantern, and gave the prisoner one last look. The man lay still, one leg bent, an arm draped across his stomach. He could be sleeping, was certainly too weak to fight back. *You shouldn't have stopped yourself, Granville Hart. Should have finished the job. After all, that's what you pride yourself on, isn't it? Always seeing a thing through.*

"Heart, he said heart. . . ."

The marshal listened for more, but the prisoner was silent, so he left, trying to figure out just what tomorrow would bring. And the day after that. One way or another, he would see this thing through to the end.

Chapter 10

"Vollo! Rummler! Get your asses in here . . . now!" Bentley Grissom bellowed from behind his closed office door at the back of the Lucky Shot Saloon. He squeezed his cigar so hard between his thick fingers that it split, snapped in two. Before he noticed, the glowing end had singed a smoking black dent in his leather desk blotter. He stuffed a wad of his handkerchief in his whiskey glass and dabbed the smoking spot.

"Vollo! Where in the blazes are you two?"

This time, his shouts produced results. The door cracked open a hand width, then a little wider. Raoul Vollo's long nose and tangle of dark hair poked into the room, his eyes scanning for Grissom. "Ah, boss. Everything okay? We heard you shouting. We were worried about you."

"How touching," said Grissom, a fake dripping smile on his face. Then it slumped as quickly as it had appeared. "Get in here, both of you."

"Now, boss? We was just celebratin'—"

"I am not going to say it again, you foul piece of trash."

"Now, boss, that ain't no way—" But Rummler shoved Vollo into the room and came in too, slamming the door behind him. He realized it had been too loud, and winced as if he were picking his way through a crowded theater. "Sorry, boss. Been having a few drinks."

"So I see." Grissom looked at Rummler. "What happened to you?" He jerked his chin toward what Rummler assumed were the burned patches on his shirt, the welter of blisters on his neck and cheek.

"Aw, it was this crazy woman. . . ."

"It's always a crazy woman with you, isn't it?" Grissom shook his head.

"You don't approve of the way I conduct my affairs, boss?"

Grissom stared at the two glassy-eyed men sitting before his desk. "I don't give a rat's ass what you fools do with your time, so long as it doesn't affect me or my plans. When it does, you'll know it. Like now, for instance." He sat back down in his horsehair-stuffed leather chair. It squeaked and something sounded as though it were cracking. His eyes shot to their faces, squinting, daring them to smile. They did not. They were learning.

He steepled his fingers under his chin. "I have just returned from a meeting with Marshal Hart. I am sure by now you have heard the news that he has a man in custody who says he witnessed the slaying of Payton Farraday." He palmed the desktop and leaned forward. "What do you say to that?"

Vollo looked at Rummler, then cleared his throat. "Does that mean that he seen us, boss?"

Grissom closed his eyes and sighed. "Yes, that is precisely what that means. Fortunately for you two hoodlums, he has also admitted to the killing. At least that is what the good marshal has told me, which I doubt is the whole truth, but it is good enough for me."

Neither man spoke, so he said, "Considering how you've conducted yourselves thus far, I'd say you have both drifted through life relatively unscathed. How much longer such dumb luck will carry you, I have no idea. But I'd prefer to not test its limits while you are in my employ."

"We didn't see no one out there," said Rummler.

"But you, it seems, were seen. Fortunately for you and me, the man who did the seeing is a drunken wreck whose veracity is undermined by the fact of his very existence, it seems. Plus, my own personal lawman will see to it that should he somehow see you two—and I do not want him catching sight of either of you, do you hear?—it will appear as if he is conveniently conjuring a fabrication to save his own neck from a good stretching. Now, enough with the confused looks on your doltish faces. Just what is it you were celebrating, boys?"

Vollo smirked, exchanged a knowing look with Rummler. "Like you don't know?"

But Grissom stared them down.

"Okay, sure," said Rummler. "It's what you just were jawin' about. You know, because we finally got one over on that uppity Farraday. Really, though, we coulda done the deed a long time before now. You just had to say the word. It wasn't no big deal. He's just a man, after all."

Vollo laughed. "Yeah, a man with a whole lot of holes in his hide!"

"Not that you would understand anything having to do with finance or business, but for what it's worth, and since you did manage to crawl through another day on earth without getting yourselves killed, I will tell you that the paper you brought to me from Farraday's pocket was the last piece of the puzzle I have been patiently waiting on for a couple of years now."

"But, boss, all that money he brought to the bank? We could have got it off him before he ever made it to the bank." Rummler rubbed his temples, shaking his head slightly, as if he were trying mightily to gain an understanding of something that seemed too foolish to waste time thinking about.

Grissom sighed. "You idiots. If we had taken the money before he made the deposit, I wouldn't now have the money and the receipt proving he made the deposit." Grissom beamed at the two squinting men.

Vollo turned to Rummler. "If he don't have the money and a little ol' slip of paper is all he wanted, then why are we celebrating?"

"Tell me you aren't as dumb as you sound. Give me some sort of indication that you are toying with me. Please." Grissom regarded his two employees, but received no response. He sighed. "Who owns the bank, gentlemen?"

Vollo shot a hand like a pistol toward the still-standing Grissom. "That'd be you, boss. Sure as daylight follows night, you 'bout got this town sewed up tighter'n a bull's backside."

Despite the fact that these buffoons were paid to pander to him, to fulfill his whims, to strong-arm when needed, to protect when needed, to remain out of sight when required, Bentley Grissom had to admit he liked hearing them laud his efforts. And those efforts had been mighty.

It had indeed been a long couple of years, but they had not been fruitless, and if it all went to hell tomorrow, he at least had lived beyond the means he had assumed he would have while here in the wilderness mining burg turned hub of commerce and promise. It was that very sort of thinking that endeared him to the local populace, and it was what had gotten him elected as the town's first mayor. And now that he had a taste of such a life, he wanted more. Perhaps the senate, the governor of a state, who knew what the future held?

Grissom selected a new cigar from the box on his desk. He sniffed its length, smiled, and bit off the end, then caught both men watching him. Rummler licked his lips as if the cigar were a snack.

"Oh, pardon me," said Grissom. "Are you fond of cigars too?"

"Yes, sir, it is a point in fact that I am partial to a bit of fine tobacco now and again."

"I see. Would you like one?"

Rummler licked his lips again and nodded.

"Too bad. You'll get nothing from me." He sneered at them, an openmouthed frown of disgust. "You are lucky I've not shot each of you before now. Imagine, celebrating when one of the town's founders has been brutally attacked and slain by a vicious little drunken drifter. You should show more respect."

Confusion was writ large on the faces of the two ratty men. As the meaning behind Grissom's words dawned on them, smirks blossomed on their faces.

Grissom leaned closer. "I'm not kidding. Now go before I change my mind and shoot you. If you must drink, do it in your rooms and not in my saloon. I'm sick of the look of both of you."

Vollo half rose from his chair. "Hey, now, Mr. Grissom, you ain't got no call—"

Quick as lightning, the fat man let fly with his half-filled whiskey glass. It sailed straight and true right into the center of Vollo's face. The heavy glass snapped the nose sideways and his eyes bulged. Grissom saw it as if it were happening slowed down somehow. Even as he flipped backward in the chair, Vollo screamed and covered his blood-gushing nose with his hands. He lay sprawled on the carpet, mewling.

"I said get out. Both of you. I will talk with you in the morning."

Rummler stood in the midst of this exchange and backed toward the door, his hand resting on his gun's polished ebony handle. "You got no call, Mr. Grissom. No call to act this way. Besides, we ain't been paid yet."

"You'll get paid in the morning. Well paid, as promised. But for now, drag that moaning, bleeding mess out of here. And see that he doesn't soil my carpet."

He turned his back on them and waited until he heard the door click. Not for the last time did he wonder if he shouldn't have long ago hired men who were both good and detrimental to the health of anyone he decided needed removal from impeding his plans.

He also sorely desired to not have to pay those two buffoons in the morning, even though they did indeed do as he'd asked. But now that the most important final piece of the puzzle was in place, he could not—would not—risk having them foul anything up. They weren't the sharpest knives in the rack, but if they spent any amount of time thinking about their predicament—once they sobered up, that is—they might well figure out their true worth to him going forward, and they would be right in calculating it, as he had done, at a very low number.

But their risk to him, should they decide to blather about anything they might or might not have done while in his employ, might well further damage his already-shaky standing in the community of Klinkhorn. It was a standing that, much as it pained him to admit, had sunk considerably lower than it had been since he'd arrived three years before. Still, it might not do to dispense with the buffoons just yet. Better yet, if he could get someone else to deal with them, or perhaps rig it somehow so that they managed to deal with each other, that way he might avoid the entire headache and mess. There was one man who was so beholden to him that he would do anything to keep his secret well hidden.

Grissom's office, in a rear corner of the Lucky Shot Emporium and Dance Hall, formed the hub of most of the town's business. He'd come to town three years before, filled with grand ideas and little else. He'd even weighed less then. One thing led to others; opportunities presented themselves. Yes, those were heady days, learning about the region, far from prying eyes and ears and loose mouths that might have recognized what he had been up to all along.

Chapter 11

Back in the saloon, Vollo held a cloth soaked in tepid dishwater to his newly battered face. It felt soothing. "What got into the boss? He ain't never been that way before."

Rummler nodded. "He sure does have himself a temper."

"Who doesn't? He's also got more money than God. Oh, my nose hurts."

"With some folks, money ain't enough unless they're lordin' it over others. I seen it time and again. And I expect that busted nose of yours will throb for some time, Rollo." Then he turned a smile on his partner. "I do know one thing that just might help ease the pain of that face of yours."

"A drink! Damn it, Rummler, you are right as rain, as usual." Vollo slammed down a slug of whiskey and rapped his knuckles on the bar top. His glass was filled right away. "What?"

"That prissy young Farraday girl is just about all on her lonesome now. All she has is that gimpy old man Arliss Tibbs. Boss seems keen on, as he says, 'dispensing' with the entire clan. Worse we could do would be to deny that pretty young thing a romp or two with a couple of fine men such as ourselves, before she's dispensed with, that is. And that old biddy friend of hers could stand a bit of handling too."

"You mean the one who lit you on fire? I'm beginning to think you like the older ladies, eh?" Vollo laughed, the whiskey doing a decent job of keeping the pain in his face toned down to a dull throbbing. "But no joke, Rummler, that's the best idea you had all day," said Vollo.

"I hear tell the Farraday girl is about as pure as a mountain snowdrift in January."

Vollo licked his puckered lips again. The thought of such a task pulsed his blood and set his twitchy left eye to jouncing.

"Then get your hat, Vollo, because it's time to take a moonlit ride."

"Tonight?"

"Hell yes, she's probably going to go home tonight, all alone on that dark road, nobody to guide her. And she'll be sad and confused, feelin' like she's been left alone in the world. Why, Vollo, it surely just about makes me heartsick."

Vollo slid off the stool and stood weaving, his broken nose and purpling eyes a hideous mask. "Let's go find that thing and comfort her, then."

Chapter 12

By the time Emma stepped out of the jailhouse, she wanted only to be home, back with poor Arliss, to help him with her uncle. She had miles to go to get home, and she knew Arliss would be sick with worry. *Should have taken the marshal up on his offer of an escort back home.*

As she crested the little ridge above town, she looked back and saw lights, fewer than before, winking through the trees.

"Don't be silly, girl," she said, swinging Cinda back around and onto the road home. She felt mixed up about everything she'd learned in town. She should have felt relieved to know that Marshal Hart had jailed the man who'd killed her uncle. But the coincidence of it happening in her father's meadow didn't sit well with her.

"Aw, hey, now, why don't you go ahead and be silly, girl?" The voice snaked out of the dark ahead. It was that foul Rummler. Which meant Vollo was somewhere close by. Those two were as tight as coughing and sneezing.

Emma felt a wash of anger, at once familiar and tiring. "What do you want, you vermin?" Emma held Cinda, the reins taut, kept her legs tight and boots tensed in the stirrups. She crept her hand toward her uncle's rifle in its boot under her left leg, slowly shifted the reins, made to loop them over the saddle horn.

Behind her she heard the slow approach of a second horse.

She must have ridden right by Vollo in the dark—the thought chilled her.

"Now, what have you gone all quiet for, missy? Could be you're about to shuck that rifle of yours? I wouldn't do that, I was you, as Vollo there has got himself into an aching madness that can't be helped but one way. And if he don't get his way soon, why, he's just going to have to shoot something."

She had to buy herself a little time. She didn't think they could see her any better than she could see them, which, at present, wasn't any more than a dim shape, since the clouds had decided once again to hide the moon glow. For once, she hoped they stayed that way.

"Well, now," said Emma in what she hoped was a husky voice, though she had no idea if that's what would appeal to men. Though she figured anything at all might appeal to such dregs as these. They were what her uncle had called "bottom feeders." With that reminder of her uncle and of the day's harsh events, she shook her head no, bent low, and shucked the rifle from the boot, praying it was loaded. She assumed it was, because her uncle would never have carried an unloaded weapon.

"Useless as a toothless dog," he'd say, laughing.

The dark night managed to keep her hidden, and she hoped that the men were drunk enough to become confused by her maneuvering.

"She's pullin' the rifle, Rummler!" Vollo's voice croaked from behind her.

Even in the dark, he sounded odd, as if he was drunk and having trouble breathing. From ahead, she heard the tall man peel back his pistol's hammer.

"Don't do it, little sister!" Rummler barked, his horse jigging and stamping.

From the sound of its hoofbeats, Emma could tell he didn't know where to turn, where to shoot. Fast as she could, Emma jerked Cinda's reins left, then booted her hard. A throaty nicker boiled up from the horse's throat and she lunged forward, fighting the tug of the reins.

Any hopes Emma had of bolting free of the two drunks slipped away when a zipping sound like a bee seared the air just behind her head, followed tight by the sound of Rummler's pistol cracking the dead black of night. Emma felt a tickle at the back of her neck, and wondered if she'd been shot. Time for worry later, she thought, if there was to be a later. *I'm moving now and that's all that matters.*

The sound had spooked Cinda, and the horse reared, then was knocked off-kilter by something large and heavy that pinned Emma's leg between it and Cinda's belly. Her horse landed hard, grunted, and thrashed with her head at the other horse, but Emma knew their route had been cut off. Taking to the side of the trail would be a dicey proposition—the spruce were too thick along the road, and the night was too dark for such a gamble. A second later she felt a rough hand snatch at her, heard one of the men, might have been Rummler, too close and grabbing at her.

She swung the rifle across the front of her and connected with something that snapped, followed by a howl of pain. Something broke. Maybe the man's fingers—too low to be his face.

But the victory was short and not sweet in the least. For the big heavy thing rammed her again. It was one of them, riding his horse into her on purpose. As it hit her a third time, it pinned her leg again and hot pain flowered in her knee. It felt as if something pulled apart, tore inside. She put it out of her mind and concentrated on staying in the saddle. If she fell off now, in the dark amid the legs of three thrashing, confused horses, she wouldn't stand a chance.

Cinda's front hooves rose, slammed down, then rose again, before lurching with a fresh blow from the other horse, and staggering. Emma pitched her right boot out of the stirrup, the leg throbbing from the pummeling. Her left boot stayed in the stirrup and Cinda lunged forward, dragging Emma with her. The roan bucked, slamming Emma up and down against the saddle, in counterpoint, jarring every bone in Emma's body, and forcing her teeth together hard.

As she slammed forward and back, her gut lurched against the saddle horn and something clunked against it—Uncle Payton's Colt Navy! She'd forgotten that she'd jammed it in the waistband of her denims when she left the marshal's office. And it also occurred to her that it had been emptied of bullets anyway. But it might make a decent club, should it come to that. She jammed it down, hoping the commotion wouldn't dislodge it.

It was all Emma could do to keep her grip on the side of the saddle, the awkward curve of the cantle affording no easy grip. Then, from close behind, closer than she expected, Vollo's voice rasped out a barking laugh. It sounded wet and raw.

"You monster!" she shouted, and drove the rifle backward, hoping to repeat the damaging blow she'd dealt Rummler a few seconds before. But at that moment, dull light bloomed over the welter of thrashing horses. Ragged banks of clouds, like thick smoke, dragged and broke across the face of the moon. Emma caught sight of the far-off orb as she felt her right boot slide back into the stirrup. She rammed each foot forward hard, securing her seat on Cinda and swinging the rifle left, then right.

One swing felt as though she'd caught Vollo. She glanced left quickly and saw that his hands gripped his already bloody face, sporting swollen lumps of flesh, and streams of fresh blood dribbling through his fingers. The stricken man offered a flat grunt and his horse dropped back.

As if to help Emma, the clouds slipped closed over the moon again, like curtains on a stage play, and Emma booted Cinda into a hard gallop out of there. They might well follow, but at least she could put distance between them.

She heard Vollo's ragged yelps of pain, heard Rummler

screaming, "You'll regret tangling with us, damn your hide!" He cranked off another round, a wild shot.

Emma heard it whiz close by. She swung back around, reins held loose in her left hand, and levered a shot, squeezed the trigger, and let it go. The brief flash of flame gave her away, as she knew it would, but she dropped low and hoped Rummler was too scared to try another shot. She was wrong. Something whistled and whizzed close by her head. She felt Cinda give a slight lurch, then resume her pounding run down the road they'd traveled for years. She hoped Cinda hadn't been hit, but she kept on running hard. She trusted that the horse knew her way.

She sent another shot in rapid response and was rewarded with a diminishing strangled cry of pain. It sounded as if she'd gotten him. And she hoped it was a mortal shot. The thought, which she found cold comfort in, didn't bother her in the least. At this moment all she wanted was to get home, sit before the fire, and not think about anything that had happened that day. Her back felt chilled and wet. Too cold for dew, but the night's cold crept into everything.

It wasn't until she neared the long turnoff to the Farraday spread that she straightened and reined up, guessing she'd done enough damage, at least for the night, to the two boozed-up fools hoping for something they would never get from her—not while she drew a breath.

As she neared the ranch house, light glowing from within the kitchen's two windows, she saw Arliss hefting a lantern, crossing the room, and coming out onto the long roofed porch. Emma found herself releasing a long-held breath, almost as if she hadn't breathed the entire trip back home.

She rode Cinda through the open door of the barn into the dark within, light from Arliss's lantern slowly approaching, illuminating the hay-strewn, hard-packed earthen floor, then the walls, then Emma and her horse. She looked up, offered a tired smile to Arliss. They said nothing to each other for a few moments while she loosened the cinch. She grabbed the saddle horn and found it split, the leather ripped as if peeled apart by a big hand, the wood underneath splintered and savaged. And there was something else there too, lodged in the wood. It was a bullet from Rummler. Must have been that last one he'd fired, when she'd lain low, hoping he'd not be able to mark where her flash had come from. She'd come that close to catching it in the back.

Then Arliss held up his lantern, touched her shoulder. "Girl? What's happened to you?"

"Why?" she said, turning her head toward him.

"Your back's bloodied, coming clean through to your chore jacket."

Then it occurred to her. That first shot from Rummler. Could have been Vollo; didn't really matter. She remembered thinking she'd felt a tickle at the back of her neck. She reached up, touched high on her neck, just where her long hair was gathered. The bullet had buzzed like a bee between her loose ponytail and her neck. So close to getting shot . . . twice. Those boys would bear a close watch. She felt colder than ever.

"Who done this to you, girl? Emma? You tell me what's gone on in town." Arliss's voice shook when he spoke, and she recognized it as that rare but unstoppable anger rising in Arliss Tibbs, something that even her father and Payton did their best not to rouse.

She turned and faced him, this old man, gimpy leg, nearly toothless, hard of hearing and cantankerous, and the nearest, dearest person she had left in her life. Emma hugged him, suddenly so tired and weary. He hugged her, patted her shoulder, made funny soothing sounds.

"I'll help you with that saddle, get Cinda here a stall, some feed and water. She looks plumb tuckered. Nearly as rough as you." He spoke as he worked, bucked the saddle onto the rail while Emma led the horse to a stall, rubbed her down with sacking, gave her feed and water from buckets Arliss had already drawn from the well for her.

"Come on inside now, girl. We'll get you cleaned up, fed. You can tell me all about it. From the looks of things, you got a heap of tellin' to do too. Then we rest up. Big day tomorrow."

"Uncle Payton?" she said.

He nodded. "Him and me, we been busy."

Chapter 13

The sound of clanging metal cleaved straight into Samuel Tucker's skull with all the finesse of a dull ax and pulled him into a grudging sitting position.

"Good news, soak! You made it through the night without getting lynched. You about ready to rise and join the land of the living—at least for another couple of days?"

Tucker heard the voice as if it was echoing through water before it finally dawned on him that it was the marshal. He tried to open his mouth, tried to rub his head, tried a whole lot of things, but none of them seemed to want to happen at the same time. His head pounded like a fusillade of cannon fire.

"You . . . you were in a hurry last night . . ." Tucker stopped talking. It hurt too much. He lightly touched his forehead with his fingertips. Lumps, and on the back of his head too. And what felt like dried food back there in his hair. *No, Tucker,* he told himself. *That would be blood.* His ribs ached, and his chin felt as though it had swelled to the size of a can of peaches.

"What was that, soak?"

Tucker risked opening an eye, and found out that one eye was all he could muster. But he saw the big lawman smiling at him through the bars. Daylight fingered in through a small barred window at the end of the hallway. It looked to be set in a door, maybe to the outside. He slowly shifted his gaze back to the marshal. "I said you don't have the guts to come on in here and call me that."

Next thing he heard was the jangle of keys. *Oh, I just can't keep my mouth shut. And now he's going to beat me more.* Tucker tried to tighten his gut, turn his face to the side so the fist might not clock him square on the sniffer.

"Relax, soak. I brought you some breakfast."

With his open eye, Tucker saw the man set down a wooden tray with a bowl of what looked like gruel, a ragged end of bread, a cup of steaming coffee, a short wooden spoon, and a cloth napkin. The marshal left the cell and returned in seconds with an enamel basin half-filled with hot water, steam rising from its surface. "You are a wreck, boy. I suggest you clean yourself."

The marshal left the cell again, locked it behind him.

"Hey, Marshal."

The man turned around.

"Don't think I didn't notice that you called me 'soak' when you came in here. Despite my very warning against it."

The marshal actually smiled. "Wasn't sure you'd notice."

Tucker slid closer to the tray, stopped to rest beside it. "I'll let it slide this time."

The lawman left, shaking his head and smiling.

Tucker sat in the empty cell, looking at the bars across from him forming the wall of the next cell. From what he could tell with his one good eye, there were two cells back here, one window, and a door that sounded and looked as if it led to the outside, maybe to an alley out back.

"Great," Tucker said aloud. "So you know where you're at, Samuel Tucker. Now what?" First things first, he had to get this food inside him, clean up as best he could, then try to convince the marshal that he didn't do it. At least spend time thinking about all the reasons why he couldn't have killed that man so that when the traveling judge came, he'd have some sort of defense worked out.

He set to on the food and coffee with vigor and soon left the bowl gleaming clean, the tray free of any bread crumbs, and the coffee cup drained. It tasted as though he could use more, but he'd have to wait to press his luck with the marshal. From what he recalled of the night before, that big man had been a hard case to deal with, and quick to rile. Last night, last night . . . Had there been a girl? Here in the jail? As his mind scratched at the scrim of fogged memory, it slowly revealed bits and pieces of the previous night, none of which made sense.

He knew, from previous mornings when he'd been hungover from a big night in the bottle, that time often revealed enough moments to allow him to function again for another day, relatively assured that he'd not committed any major crimes. And he knew for certain this time was no different. As he mulled this over, the marshal returned and stood before the cell.

"I can identify the men who shot that Farraday fella. In fact, I am sure of it."

"So can I, boy." Hart leaned closer to the bars. "'Cause he's sitting right in front of me. And that would be you, boy."

Tucker closed his eyes, resisting the urge to scream. "Marshal, pretend for a moment that I am innocent. Wouldn't you want to see that an innocent man jailed in your prison doesn't pay for someone else's crime?"

A broad smile sprawled out on the marshal's face. "I couldn't care less, and you shouldn't either. 'Cause you won't be in my jail. You'll be swinging from that old tree up by the pioneer cemetery."

Tucker sighed and kept on with his argument. "Because if I am innocent, but paying for the crime, that means the two men who did it are walking around free. Odds are they're from your community too."

That seemed to interest the marshal. "What makes you say that?"

"Touched a nerve, did I?" said Tucker. He tried to smile, but it hurt too much. "Stands to reason, Marshal. It wasn't but a few hours to dark when it happened, so those killers would have headed to the nearest town to hole up, spend the money they stole."

"They stole money, you say?"

"I know they took something from the man's pocket once he was down. Looked like a folded paper. What it was, I don't rightly know."

"And how do you want me to go about finding them?"

Tucker resisted the urge to ask, Wasn't that the job of a marshal, to find people? Instead he said, "Well, I could tell you what they look like, and then you could have them rounded up somehow, bring them on in. I could tell you if they are the men or not."

"Mm-hmm. And it never would occur to you, a man who is in jail and who is, by all accounts, a worthless drifting soak, to lie about such a thing to save your own murderous hide, eh?"

Tucker gripped the bars, rattled them feebly. "Look, damn it, Marshal—"

"Don't you curse in my presence, mister."

"Curse? I said 'damn it.' I bet you say worse all the time."

The big lawman leaned close to the bars. "That's twice. I hear it a third time, and you will wish you had been eaten alive by grizzlies as a child."

"Will you at least let me tell you what they looked like? Maybe you'll see them around town, and then if they kill someone else, you'll be able to tell yourself that you could have done something about it but chose not to. That should provide some comfort."

The marshal's face tightened and his jaw muscle worked as if he were trying hard to not do something he really wanted to. "Don't you dare lecture me, you cowardly little tramp."

The two men stared at each other, equal height but one a

too-thin rag of a man, the other a wide-shouldered law dog with a big mustache and thick eyebrows peppered with silver. He sported thick shoulders and a round gut gone soft and beginning to spill over his gun belt. There was also a quarter century between their ages.

"But if it will make you feel like you aren't being railroaded, then by all means, describe these coldhearted killers who gunned down one of my best friends—a man I have known since the war, a man who I came to this territory with, along with his brother, when you were wetting yourself and eating bugs off a dirt floor back wherever it is you come from. Texas is my guess."

Tucker liked that he had touched a nerve. He had no intention of letting go of any thread that might at least allow him to wedge a boot in the door before they stretched his neck.

"There were two of them, Marshal. One wore a brown hat and was taller than the other. Or at least he appeared so on horseback." Tucker stopped for a moment. The lawman stared at him with half-hooded eyes like those of a lizard in the sun, seeing everything that went on around him.

"The other one was shorter, sported a dark dragoon mustache, wore a black hat with what looked like silver conchos. Oh, and they looked to be shooting Colt's sidearms. Their mounts were—"

The marshal turned away. "I am done listening to your sad conjurings. Save the rest for the judge."

Tucker watched the man's broad back retreat up the short hall. He reached the door and paused, his back facing Tucker.

"What is it you are afraid of hearing from me, Marshal?" Tucker's voice, full and sonorous, the only thing not thin about him, echoed in the otherwise empty cells.

The lawman cranked the skeleton key in the mechanism and just before he pulled the ring handle, he said, "You keep this up and there will be very little of you left to hang . . .

provided the judge can make it here in time." His voice was cold.

From the other side, he settled the door, locked it, and soon Tucker heard the front door of the law office open and close. There was nothing working in his favor, everything working in the marshal's. And that's all it would take to convince anyone who might need convincing that his neck should snap like a carrot.

Chapter 14

Grissom looked at the two men in his employ and shook his head. "My word, I didn't think that after last night you two sorry cases could look any worse. But I was wrong."

Rummler held one side of his forehead as if it were cracked porcelain and he was waiting for the glue to dry. "It wasn't our fault. Chasing down a . . . horse thief. Right, Vollo?"

"More likely a filly. And if it's the one I suspect it is, you watch your step there. That filly bites and I haven't given you any orders in that direction—you hear me?"

The men nodded and Grissom watched as Vollo worked the brim of his grimy hat. The fat man knew what was coming, but he liked to see the lead-up to it, just the same.

"We are finding this town expensive, as you know. There is food, and horses need shoes . . . These things are . . ." He shook his head, looking for the word.

"Expensive?"

"Yes, Mr. Grissom. That is the word. So I am glad you see what I mean, eh?"

"I don't quite understand what you are trying to tell me, Raoul. Would you like to start a business? As a farrier, perhaps?"

Vollo looked as if he'd been slapped. "Oh no. I don't even know what that is, but I don't think I would like that. What I need is—"

"Oh, shut up, Vollo." Rummler winced as he raised his own voice. "What we need is our money, Mr. Grissom. You know, for what we done yesterday. That paper and all."

"Aaah, now I see. I thought for a moment there that all my businesses in this town would soon be challenged by two savvy new merchants. But I see now that I was mistaken. I breathe a sigh of relief, sirs, at this satisfying turn of events."

"I swear, Mr. Grissom, you ought to go into politics. You got all the fancy patter down flat. I have heard a few of them statesmen palaver here and there in meetinghouses and saloons and on the street and such. I always make a point to listen, though I have no idea what it is they go on and on about. You got the gift, sir, and no mistake."

Grissom smiled broadly, tilted his head, and nodded. It was true he could wax eloquent at times, he knew as much, but even from someone such as Rummler, it was a pleasure to hear.

As he counted cash into two stacks before them on his desktop, it occurred to him that perhaps Rummler was a deeper pool than he had earlier surmised. The man, he felt sure, had been stroking his feathers to get their money out of him as painlessly as possible.

He pushed the money toward them. *If I don't have them killed before they spend it,* he thought, *I will surely recoup the investment in my saloon.*

As they pocketed their payments, grinning and wincing with each movement, Vollo indulged in a moan. "I am so sore today. I need a drink."

Rummler nodded slowly.

"Your sore head or elbow or backside is of no concern to me. What I am concerned with is that drunk in the marshal's cage. I want him dead." He watched the two men smile through their wounded faces and lopsided gauze wrappings. "Just not yet."

"Not yet? Why forever not, Mr. Grissom?" Rummler

squinted at him as though he were having a hard time making out just where Grissom stood.

"Because Marshal Hart is no fool. If he senses a reason why he needs to keep that boy alive, though it is a reason he won't share with me, then I want to go along with it—for a little while. But my patience only wears so thin."

"Well," said Rummler, "just tell us when your patience reaches its end, and we'll snap it for you."

"Bold talk for a quivering, wounded wreck. But we'll see. For now, I'd like you two to do what you are good at."

"That would be drinking, boss," said Vollo, offering Rummler a wink that looked as though it cost him physically just to execute it.

"The thing to which I refer is leaning against the porch post and making sure that nothing happens at the marshal's office without me knowing about it. Understand?"

The two men nodded, and Grissom could see on their faces that this simple task sat well with them.

Then Vollo asked the inevitable question. "What sort of things?"

Grissom sighed. "Anything, you fool. Anything at all. If the marshal leaves, I want to know. If he stays, I want to know. If a blowfly lands on the roof, I want to know. Am I clear?"

Again, the two stared at him as if he'd just asked them to run naked through the street. He shook his head, then motioned them to leave as if he were waving away a bad smell—partly true in their case. The door had nearly closed when he shouted after them, "And no drinking on the job."

He smiled as he heard their low moans.

Chapter 15

It was dark early the next morning when Emma woke. She was cold, her muscles were sore, and as the previous day's events came to her, she rolled onto her side in the little bedroom she'd slept in her entire life. She usually hated to stay in bed, preferred to get the day moving, but today there seemed little point. She was alone in the house now. Arliss kept to himself in his quarters in the lean-to built onto the side of the barn. She knew she should get up, but the effort seemed too much for her.

Then the faint, strong tang of coffee on the boil reached her. Arliss had come in, tended the stove, and put on coffee to boil. That old man was too good to her. Especially considering she had fallen asleep the night before to the far-off rhythmic sound of his hammer blows and rasping saw as he worked to build her uncle a proper coffin. He was a skilled carpenter, and she knew it gave him grim pleasure to be able to do this last thing for his friend, but she hoped Arliss hadn't overdone it. He was no spring chicken, as he liked to remind anyone in earshot.

She stretched, flexed her back and arms, and lightly touched the kerchief around her throat. It held in place the bandage Arliss had insisted she keep on the back of her neck where the bullet had grazed her. The nick was tender, but not enough to slow her down.

She dressed in her dirty clothes from the evening before and topped them with a wool sweater and fresh wool socks for her feet. She laid out on her bed a buckskin riding skirt and cotton blouse, suitable attire for a funeral. But first, she would have to dig her uncle's grave up beside her mother and father. It would be a long chore but one that needed doing. And one that she felt she needed to do—her own last effort for her uncle. Arliss would argue with her, but she would not let him down in that hole. He had done more than enough.

As she entered the small cabin's main room, Emma avoided looking at the blanket-draped form of her uncle laid out on the table. She had told Louisa that they intended to bury her uncle today, after the noon hour, so Emma was sure men would come later to help place him in the coffin, then carry him up back to the plot where her mother and father were buried.

The morning was a chill one, with a cold rain just beginning to fall. Emma tugged on an old slicker hanging on a peg by the back door and headed to the two-holer behind the house. She caught sight of Arliss limping his way back to the house from the barn and waved a hand, but he had his mackinaw canopied over his head and didn't see her.

By the time she got back to the kitchen, he had two cups of hot coffee poured and was warming what was left of last night's biscuits. He looked rough, dark eyed, and older than he usually did. Tired or heartsick? More likely both.

Finally he spoke, his voice a croaking sound he hoped was more early-morning frog in the throat than a sign of coming sickness. "I've built a right pretty box for him to rest in. I expect he'd like something a bit grander, but it's what we got."

Emma tried to smile, said nothing. Arliss knew full well that her uncle Payton didn't have a fancy bone in his body. A plain box, especially one built by Arliss, suited him perfectly. Right down to the ground, he would say. And in it too, she thought, wincing at the apt thought.

She finished her coffee, set the cup in the dry sink, and tugged on her coat. "I expect I'll get started on the grave. This rain will soften the soil, but it could hinder if I wait too long."

As she suspected, Arliss bolted down his coffee and biscuit. "I should do that, Emma. It ain't no work for a—"

Her look stopped him from saying "girl," as it always did.

"I'd like to help," he said in a quiet voice.

"Of course."

The rain made the initial digging easier, having loosened the hard-packed earth, but then it continued, cold drops pelting down, running off their hat brims. By that time they were nearly five feet down, and the bottom of the hole was a muddy soup. Arliss had long before crawled out and worked the edges to keep the rain from slumping the dug soil back into the hole. They finished just before the first wagon from town arrived.

Over the next hour, buggies and single horses and buckboards filled with townsfolk all arrived, their raised arms tenting tarpaulins over their heads, the oiled cloth shedding most of the wet. They angled their rigs off to the sides of the long, narrow lane to the homestead. The men stood in groups in the barn, dressed in their best bib and tucker. Women and children brought baskets of food to the house, kept a near silence on their chatter, out of respect. Mostly, though, people could not understand what had happened—over and over the words "stranger" and "makes no sense" and eventually "Grissom" came out.

Soon Emma could no longer bear being in the house. Cleaned up and dressed in her clean clothes, her long hair loosened, mostly to hide the bandage at the nape of her neck—she definitely did not feel like talking about her adventure of the night before—she went to the barn, nodding politely at the looks of sad concern directed her way from all the men. Arliss was busy in the back corner, talking to some of the men in a harsh tone, and didn't see her as she approached. He sounded angry, as if he were scolding the men.

"Arliss, I think it's time."

He looked at her, nodded rabbit-quick, and silently walked to the coffin he'd made, other men assembling around it. Then they all trailed Emma to the house.

The men brought the box, the fitted cover, and a hammer and nails to the house. Arliss had laid out Payton on his own quilt, one made for him long years before by an ancient relative. It was a beautiful piece of handwork and some of the ladies clucked quietly, about such stitchery going to bury a man, never to be seen or appreciated again, but they caught reproachful glares and quieted themselves.

They all filed past, said their piece, and then Arliss and Emma did so. She managed to keep from breaking down before all those people, people she'd known her entire life. Some of them she liked, some not as much. But all of them had genuinely liked her uncle, dozens of them, so many that Emma was convinced, looking around the place, that most of the town's residents were there.

The one whose absence surprised her was Marshal Hart. She asked Arliss about it, but before he could answer, Louisa overheard. She'd been told he would miss the funeral because he was afraid that in his absence, given the anger of the townsfolk the night before, some stragglers might take it into their heads to lynch the man.

Cold rain chilled them all to the bone as they stood clustered about the grave four and five people deep. The man who ran the town newspaper, Wilfred Tinker, a friend and poker pal of Payton's, read a passage from Shakespeare, who Emma was surprised to learn had been a favorite author of her uncle's. Emma vowed to read more, as her uncle and father had forever nagged her about. Then six men overhanded the ropes until the casket settled with a gentle splash in the last six inches to the bottom of the hole, water rising on it.

They would make a marker later, as her father had done for her mother, and they had done for her father. They'd had the advantage then of Payton's immense strength to help sledge out the large, flat rock that Arliss chiseled her father's name into.

After the service, as they all trailed back down off the little hill toward the house and barn, someone said, "Month from now, this rain'll come down as snow." There were a few murmurs of agreement, and then they all went back to talking quietly in the barn until the women called them all in for a stand-up meal. Seeing them all there made Emma both grateful and tired. She appreciated their support, but wished they would all go home.

There was little said that night. She and Arliss sat by the fireplace, too bone tired and too numbed from all that had happened to do much more than shake their heads and watch the flames dissipate into glowing coals. Then they too dwindled.

In the dark room, Arliss's voice surprised her. "You had your uncle here last night. I expect I'll stay tonight. Lord knows what them two craven devils will do."

Emma knew he meant Vollo and Rummler. She was too tired to argue, but she was curious about something. "When I went out to the barn earlier, it sounded to me as if you were chewing out those men from town. Was I just hearing things?"

He sat for a long moment, and she'd begun to think he'd dozed off when he said, "I was givin' them all what for, yessir. Trying to get them to do something for me—for your uncle. And to a man they said they would do anything for me, for your uncle. But not what I was askin'."

She almost hated to ask, but she had to know. "What did you ask them, Arliss?"

"I count a good many of them folks who come here today as my friends. Or at least I did. But not a one of them will raise a finger against Grissom." He looked at her for the first time in long minutes. "I asked them boys to help me take care of Grissom's boys, Vollo and Rummler. And do you know, they hemmed and hawed and whined about their bank loans and children's safety and their houses and businesses? My word, you'd think Grissom owns everything under the sun."

"Doesn't he?"

"No, girl!" He smacked a gnarled old hand against the worn armrest of the rocker, the runners working as if part of a machine. "That's where you're wrong. Man like Grissom can grab everything he can see and it will never be enough for him. But it won't be everything. No, no, 'cause what a person's got that can't be bought is in here."

He tapped his temple again, as Emma had seen him do a thousand times before when he was trying to prove a point. "And here," he said, thumping a fist against his own chest so hard she thought he might pop something. "I'm talking spirit and fight and that thing deep inside that tells us if what we're doing is right or wrong. You see what I mean?"

She nodded.

He looked back at the dying glow of the fire. "But them folks who live in town, they got nothing but fear in their hearts and heads. And that ain't no way to live. I was hoping to stir them up. But the fear's got 'em too hard, too deep. Even when they know something's wrong, they're too afraid to do anything about it." His voice grew quiet and she barely heard him when he said, "Have to do it myself."

She wanted to tell him not to do anything foolish, but with Arliss, she knew telling him not to do something was just like begging him to do it. And besides, there was a part of her—and she didn't mind admitting it to herself—that wanted to see Vollo and Rummler squirm, then die.

She shook her head. "Daddy's bed is all made up, you know."

"I know, I know." His rocking chair worked faster. "I

might settle down there later. Right now I'll set a spell. But you look about ready to slide off that chair and hit your head. Best you get to bed, girl."

She rose and hugged him before he could get up. Then she covered him with a wool blanket, and kissed his bald forehead. "Good night, Arliss. Thank you for . . . everything."

"You're near as kin as I got." His voice was low and watery. "I'm thankful for you, girl."

Emma squeezed his shoulder, then went to bed.

Chapter 16

Hundreds of miles to the south, along a rail line in Nevada, thick chains rattled as a ramp lowered from the middle of a stock car. The angle was steep, but two great black horses picked their way down with ease, each led by a man wearing a black hat and black duster. The horses carried identical flat black saddles, saddlebags, and sheaths for long guns.

A third horse, an Appaloosa, followed, led by a man of thirty-five years, dark blond hair worn fashionably long, as was his matching waxed-and-curled-at-the-end mustache, daggered chin hair, and bushed sideburns; a thick cigar jutted from beneath the mustache. His horse carried a richly carved dark brown leather rig, a single rifle boot, and a war bag lashed securely behind the cantle. This third man was spotlessly dapper, his knee-height boots shone with a high polish, and he wore a cream-colored jacket trimmed in leather, starched white shirt, string tie, all topped with a fawn hat. He bore the look of a man who makes his money by pointing and nodding.

When all three men were assembled trackside, the third man wagged a brown-leather-gloved hand at the ramp, and the stock car's attendant, who cranked hard from inside the car on a ratcheting handle, raised the ramp. The three men did not wait for the train to gather steam and resume its journey.

With the dapper man in the lead, they walked down the slope close by the tracks, then headed northwest, the lead man setting a brisk pace. Minutes later they were lost from sight by the train, but heard it rolling forward, gaining speed, and chugging west. Regular gouts of thick black smoke thrust high above the pines.

Once they reached a wide, long meadow, the two men in black flanked the dapper man in brown. The one on the left said, "Where we headed, my lord?"

The man in the middle made no comment for a few moments, the horses chuffing and the day growing darker before them. "We are headed to a little town called . . ." He retrieved a folded paper from his breast pocket. "Klinkhorn, I believe it is called, though why on earth anyone would wish to name a town as such is inconceivable. We are to meet a man named Bentley Grissom. We have corresponded for several months and he has made me a most interesting business proposition." He folded the paper again and tucked it away. "From the looks of the skies, gentlemen, we are headed toward inclement weather."

"Begging your pardon, Lord Tarleton," said the other man. "But is there really anything of value out here?"

The dapper man laughed. "Tell me, what do you see all around you?"

"Hill country, dark clouds, trees . . ."

"And what is it we have been doing since leaving Denver weeks ago?"

"Buying property."

"Yes, and more to the point . . . ?"

The man in black slowly smiled.

"Yes, you see now. And you?"

The other man in black had been waiting for Lord Tarleton to call on him. "Yes, sir. It's the trees, sir."

"Well done, man. I am, as the Americans say, a tycoon of various things, and soon will become a lumber baron. Logical when one thinks that an empire such as mine needs a constant supply of raw material. And this untouched wilderness is filled with old-growth species."

Lord Tarleton pulled in a deep lungful of air, exhaled, then puffed thoughtfully on his cigar. "The first time I read about the magnificent West of America, with her untouched wilderness, so unlike Britannia, I knew I had to see it for myself. It barely seems possible that I've been here less than five years and already my holdings are equal to those of my dear old papa back across the wide Atlantic."

The two riders in black had dropped back a few paces and now exchanged glances. Lord Tarleton's money was good, better than most situations men handy with guns might find for themselves, but by gosh, the man could brag. Every chance he got. But they could live with it. After all, they'd signed on, and when he was drinking, the lord could be fun— and generous with his cigars and whiskey.

"Do you know, gentlemen, why I chose to take you on this sojourn? To get out and away from the bustle and strife of Denver?"

One man cleared his throat. "I assumed it was just in case you ran into folks who needed persuading—some that didn't want to sell up."

"Precisely! I make this journey, pockets jingling with hard cash, and yet it astounds me, time and again, to learn that some people have less than no interest in becoming rich. They choose instead to whine and cry and carry on as if I were robbing them of something they might one day pass on to their offspring. But the land is useless if you can't afford to feed the growling bellies of those tots. Am I right, gentlemen?"

"Yes, my lord," they both muttered.

"Ah, what better time to trek deep into the hinterlands on horseback than in the fall of the year, when the much-loved foliage and russet hues bedazzle the hills?"

An hour later, the clouds had parted and they crested a rise that revealed a long view of seemingly endless miles of vast, rolling forest, a mighty river coursing through the very heart of it like a silver thread in a woman's gown, sparkling as sunlight shafted through the dissipating cloud cover far ahead. The three horsemen paused, taking in the wilderness before them.

Lord Tarleton eyed the course of the river, envisioning lumber camps, sawmills, fleets of schooners at the shore waiting to carry his lumber all over the world. There were enough trees here to build a ladder to the moon—and have lumber left over for a fine mansion—maybe on this very spot, overlooking a kingdom befitting an English lord. The thought, Tarleton told himself, bore merit.

Chapter 17

Emma had startled him, peeking around the office door. Marshal Hart saw her and stood, his chair clunking the wall behind him. "Emma, come in, come in. Would you like a cup of coffee?"

"Sure, thanks."

She sat in one of the side chairs. The pretty girl he'd seen so many times smiling in town with Arliss or her uncle Payton now looked thinner, eyes dark for want of sleep. He handed her a stoneware mug of hot coffee, then sat on the edge of the desk. "I didn't know you'd be coming into town so soon . . . after the funeral. I am sorry I didn't make it out there."

"That's okay. Most of the town showed up."

"Oh." If that was meant to make him feel bad, it worked. "I'll be out by and by to pay my respects. I was afraid to leave the prisoner here. Felt sure they'd lynch him, should I leave him for more than five minutes. People are riled up in Klinkhorn. Your uncle was a well-liked man."

"I know. Thank you, Marshal."

"You didn't come here to listen to my excuses, Emma. What can I help you with?"

"I came to talk with you about Vollo and Rummler."

"Oh, what about them?"

"When I left here two nights ago, I rode home, but they bushwhacked me."

"What?"

"Well, they tried to. It was dark. They shot and I shot back."

"They hurt you?"

"Nothing to speak of. They nearly had me at one point, but I managed to get away." She half smiled. "And I think I might have winged one, maybe managed to break the other one's nose. That Vollo, I think."

He'd have to talk with Grissom again. The last person he wanted to see today.

"Marshal, can't we do something about them? They're blights. Nobody here likes them." She stood, paced the room. "For that matter, nobody likes Grissom."

He sighed. "Emma, we can't just run people off for no good reason."

"No good reason? They tried to . . . Well, I don't want to think what they had in mind. Oh, I guess Arliss was right."

"What'd he say?"

"That everyone in Klinkhorn was afraid of Grissom, in his debt somehow."

"I'd guess he's more right than wrong. I'll see to it, Emma. Believe me, those two won't know what hit them. Now, it's funny you should show up, Emma. That skinny soak in there wants to see you, been asking for pretty near two days now."

She stepped forward, jaw thrust out. "I'll see the buzzard again."

As Marshal Hart turned the keys in the thick wooden door that led to the cells, Emma Farraday once again smelled the reek of years of unwashed men confined in too small a space with little fresh air and even less natural light. It was midday outside, but in there it was as dark as the inside of the Devil's belly, as her father used to say.

"You'll want to keep back from the cell door, Emma," Marshal Hart whispered low.

"Why?" The voice croaked from the dark before them.

"Shut up, prisoner. You will keep your peace until spoken to, and then only respond when you have permission. You understand me?"

There was no answer.

"I said, 'Do you hear me?'"

A sigh sounded low and long, and then a less croaking voice said, "Yes, I understand just how it is."

Hart's boot slammed the bars down low by the floor. "Shut it, you."

"Can't have it both ways, Marshal," said Emma, smiling.

He regarded her for a moment, unsure how to take that remark. He'd known Emma her entire life, and didn't think there was anything devious about the girl.

From the office up front, they heard a man's voice calling to the marshal, repeating his name, as if trying to find him.

"What?" shouted Hart.

"Oh, there you are," said the man, and they saw the outline of someone in the doorway. "Marshal, there's a ruckus at the Ringin' Belle. Some sort of fight between a whore and a man says she tried to rob him."

"I'm busy, Clem. Can't you all take care of it?"

"Well, that's just it, Marshal. Everybody's kind of figurin' you've spent plenty of time nursemaiding that killer in there and not enough time tending to your duties around town."

"Oh, they do, do they?" But Hart knew there wasn't much he could say to that argument. "Aw, hell," he grumbled. They were right, of course. He turned to Emma. "Since I know how you feel about him, I guess you won't try to bust him out. I'll leave you two to talk . . . if that doesn't bother you, Emma."

"No, that's fine. I'm curious to know what this murderer might have to tell me that seems so urgent to him."

The marshal headed back up the hallway. "I'll be back directly. You're not going to shoot him, are you?"

"Marshal," said Emma, "do I look like the type of person who'd do that?"

"There ain't a type, Emma, if you'll pardon me saying so. But if there was, you might just fill the bill." He shook his head and closed the door behind him, but did not lock it. They heard him talking with the man who had brought the message, the sliding of desk drawers, his big boots sounding as they crossed the wooden floor, and then the door clunked shut behind him.

A few long moments passed when no one spoke. Emma stood before the cell, though well back from his reach.

"Ma'am?" Tucker finally said, staying in the dark of the cell.

"What? What is it you want from me? What more can I possibly give you?"

"Ma'am. I know you think I'm guilty. That I'm the one who killed your uncle, but it's not true."

She snorted, looked away.

"I'm not lying, I promise you."

"Uh-huh. That's why you showed up in Klinkhorn with my uncle's pistol, then sold it and got drunk with the money."

"No, that's not . . . Well, it's sort of true, but I tell you, I was starvin'."

"For drink, yeah."

"No, I wanted to do the right thing, but . . ."

"But what? You're a murdering drifter. Why should I believe you?"

Tucker nodded in the dark of the cell. "Because the marshal said they're going to hang me soon, and I can prove I'm innocent."

Emma wanted to reach through the bars and strangle him. Instead, through gritted teeth she said, "Prove it."

He moved closer to the front of the cell, and the scant light from the barred window fell on his face. And when Emma saw him, she gasped.

"That bad, is it?" Tucker tried to smile, but it hurt too much. He guessed what she saw. Earlier in the day, when the morning light had lit the cell block strongest, he'd been able to see his wavery reflection in the washbasin water. His left eye was a puffed, bruised mess; he was unable to see out of it, though he guessed there might be a bit of light coming in through it now. His forehead bore similar welts, and most of his head felt like a bumpy log too, though his hair probably covered those lumps.

His lips had split and were slowly crusting over. He didn't think his nose had broken, amazingly enough, but it was puffy. And his chin throbbed every time he moved his mouth. He had also chipped a couple of teeth. The rest of him ached all over, mostly his gut where the big lawman's ham-sized fists had driven in time after time.

He was sure a couple of ribs were cracked. It hurt to draw deep breaths. And his own hands were scabbed about the knuckles and the small finger on his right hand was a purpled, swollen thing that looked like a raw sausage gone rancid.

Emma regained her hard demeanor. "Nothing you don't deserve—and more—for what you did to my uncle."

"I can see how you'd think that, but I'm telling you I didn't do it. How else could I describe the two men who shot him? I saw it all."

"Why didn't you help him?"

"I am ashamed to say I did not—it's true. But I had no weapon, no money, nothing at all except my horse, Gracie." At the recollection of her, his throat tightened, as it had each time he'd thought of her since he ended up in jail. "I wonder if you could look in on Gracie. Whatever happens to me, she doesn't deserve to be mistreated. She's a good old girl. I miss her so."

"Where is she?"

Emma's voice was hard and tight, but he figured that her asking was some sort of positive sign.

"I took her to the livery when I . . . when I got the money from the gun. She needed a feed, a rubdown." When the girl didn't answer, he continued. "I'd be obliged if you'd see that she's being cared for. She's hard to miss, pretty thin, but a stately old girl." He smiled, thinking of her spirited ways. "Maybe you could find a home for her, a pasture where she can spend her final years in peace. Lord knows she deserves more than I ever gave her."

"Fine. I'll see to her. What about these two men you say killed my uncle?"

"They were each a-horseback, one on a bay, the other on a roan, decent horse, that one, but the other, not so much. Been abused, worked too hard. Sounds familiar. The man on that horse was runty, not very tall. He wore a black hat, looked like he needed a shave, and his tunic was probably white at one time. He also wore his guns cross-draw fashion, and I can't be sure, but it sounded almost as if he was foreign, probably Mexican. The other man was taller, also grimy and in need of a shave. He wore a somewhat white shirt, black vest, and a brown hat."

The girl studied him, and he couldn't be sure, but it seemed almost as if her features had softened a bit. Was there something of recognition there?

"That all?" she said.

"No, but they . . . This won't be pleasant to hear, I'm afraid."

"I've been through worse, believe me."

"Okay. They had shot him in the back before I saw them. I was on the southern edge of this pretty green meadow, saw that all three were riding toward me, though by the time I climbed up out along that ridge just this side of that river, they had shot him in the back. He had the big pistol out and was trying to make it work, but it was almost like he couldn't figure out how to do it. Then they circled him, laughing and whooping it up. Shot him again a few more times, in the hand, in the belly. He fell off the horse, but kept trying to get to his knees. By the time I really saw him, he'd already been shot at least a couple of times. They would have killed me too. Sure as shootin'."

"What happened next?"

"His horse ran off, and then he fell over and lay on his side. They were laughing the entire time. Finally the short gunman climbed down out of the saddle. They were laughing, and he rummaged in the man's coat pockets, then pulled out what looked like a piece of paper. White, I think. He unfolded it, read from it, then shouted to his friend, 'We got it!' or something like that, and climbed back up on his horse. Then they rode off toward what I later found out was this town.

"I went to see if the man was truly dead, but he was. Or it looked like he was. Then I will admit to giving thought to seeing if he had any money." He looked down at his feet as he said this. "I've never stolen from anyone."

She snorted as if she'd heard a lie.

"It's true. Even with the pistol, I intended to use it as a way of identifying him in town."

"Why did you leave him there?" Her voice cracked as she asked.

"Look at me, ma'am. I can barely carry myself through the day, let alone heft a big man like him. And besides, his horse was gone and Gracie isn't in any better shape than I am. I had to leave him there. I did manage to find his hat, though, and I snugged it down over his face. I was afraid of leaving him exposed out there like that. Seemed the only thing I could do."

"But you sold his pistol in town."

"I know I did. But I hadn't meant to. I had every intention

of going to the marshal's office right off. Explaining things to him, but then I smelled some home cooking and along about that time some kid whipped Gracie on her flank with a green branch. I felt so low, had to do something for her. So I cashed in the gun at the store."

For a moment neither of them spoke, and then Emma said, "That's quite a story."

"Yeah, well, it's the only one I have. But there's something else."

"What?"

"Your uncle. He spoke to me."

"What?" She looked to him, desperate and angry and hopeful and sad all at once.

"It's true. I swear it."

"I thought you said he was dead."

"No, I said I thought he was. But as I was checking his belly and chest for wounds, he grabbed my wrist in his big hand. Like to scared the daylights out of me. He looked straight into my eyes and he said, 'Tell Emma . . . heart . . .' And that was it.

"At the time I didn't know who Emma was or what he meant by 'heart,' but now I wonder if maybe he wasn't talking about Marshal Hart."

"But why?" She said it as if to herself, so Tucker didn't say anything. Then she looked at him, and he saw tears welling up in her eyes. And for the first time, he saw how pretty she was. And how sad.

"I wish I had never come this far north, ma'am. I . . ."

"Me too," she said, and turned and stalked out of the cell block. Tucker didn't bother shouting to her. There was more he wanted to tell her—things that could help prove he didn't do it, things he might never have known, like why hadn't he rummaged in the man's pockets? Why not take the entire gun belt? Why not take bullets? Those things would make sense, but not taking them made no real sense.

And why wouldn't he take the man's horse if he'd been the one to kill him? It had certainly been a more reliable mount than poor old Gracie. Why stop there? Why not take his fine clothes, his boots? Why, for that matter, would he ride just a few miles back toward where the man must have come from and wave the dead man's gun around? And then he stopped short.

Why, indeed? He'd done just that and now he was painted guilty, despite the obvious fact that no one in their right mind would have done that. But these people didn't care. Even the thin string of hope he'd held on to, the notion that maybe the marshal had had something to do with it, that he'd suspected some sliver of guilt in the man, even that had dried and crumbled when the dead man's niece walked out of the cells, away from him. He'd bet he'd never see her again, unless it was one last time from the scaffold, as she watched him drop and twitch out his last.

The utter hopelessness of his situation washed over Tucker like a dunk in a cold stream. He stood in the dark cell, pressing his cheeks against the cold bars as much for comfort as for support. He closed his eyes and felt his last flicker of hope fade, then pinch out, like a blown match. He was surprised he had even that much hope left, considering how far he'd fallen in the past couple of years.

He heard a slight rustling sound and opened his eyes. She'd returned and stood once again before him. Instead of arms folded as if to defend herself, her hands were thrust into her coat pockets, jaw stuck out, and she regarded him as if she'd come to some sort of decision.

He met her stare. "Haven't you ever made a mistake, a bad mistake?"

"Not yet." She eyed him, considering the weight of something big. "But I have a feeling I'm about to."

She turned and walked away once again. As Tucker watched her leave, he couldn't be sure, but he thought he felt a twinge of something he hadn't felt in a long time. Maybe it was hope. Maybe it was the relief of knowing there was someone who might have heard what he was saying. He closed his eyes again and felt the coolness of the bars on his face.

Chapter 18

"You what?" Marshal Hart stood by the little stove, a short length of split birch in his hand, the door to the stove open and puffing smoke into the little room.

"Open your damper, Marshal." Emma nodded at the smoking stove.

"Oh, right." He spun the wire handle in the pipe, poked the coals with the end of the wood, then stuffed it in and clunked the door shut. "Emma, I don't understand you. A couple of days ago you felt like the rest of the folks in this town. Wanted to string him up. This one seems cut-and-dried to me."

"I know that, Marshal, but he told me things that made me doubt that."

"Such as?"

"Among other things, he said two men did it, and the descriptions he gave me sounded an awful lot like Vollo and Rummler."

"You wouldn't just be saying that because you're so fond of them, would you?"

"No, I might not like those jackasses, but I wouldn't do that." Emma shook her head. "Tempted, but no."

"What is it exactly you're asking of me, Emma?"

"I guess I'm asking you to call it off. Let me oversee him, at least until we can prove him guilty or innocent. Or until there's a trial."

Marshal Hart grinned and shook his head. "That simple, huh? You have it all worked out?"

Emma shrugged, nodded. "Look, Marshal, if there's anyone who has the right to doubt him, it's me, right?"

He considered this a moment, then said, "Maybe."

"So if I'm not totally convinced he's guilty, then that should say something."

"I suppose, but it's a pretty shaky argument there, Emma."

"I know. But what if he really is innocent? What if Vollo and Rummler really did do it? Knowing what I know of them, it wouldn't surprise me at all. No man should hang for something he didn't do. I can help prove him innocent, if he's telling the truth."

"What do you expect me to tell the rest of the town, Emma? They all want his hide."

"Don't tell them anything. You're the only one with a key to the cells, the only one who goes in there anyway, right?"

"This is harebrained, Emma. You know that, don't you? Why not just leave him here, then go prove him innocent and we'll let him go?"

"Because I don't trust the townsfolk."

"What if someone got wind of the fact that he wasn't really here anymore?"

She shrugged. "Tell them he escaped? Look, Marshal, if you won't do it for me, what about for my daddy and Uncle Payton?"

He felt his face redden, narrowed his eyes. "Emma, that is not a card you want to play lightly."

Emma nodded. "I know, Marshal Hart. But something about all this stinks to high heaven. And a man's life might be at stake. Otherwise, do you think I really would have done that? We've already lost good men for no reason in this town, two of them who were close to me. Why risk another person's life? I have a feeling that Vollo and Rummler are involved in this somehow and I want a chance to prove it."

"I'll grant you that they are rats of the lowest order. But that doesn't mean they killed Payton and the prisoner didn't."

"Doesn't mean they didn't either."

Marshal Hart regarded her a long moment, smoothing his mustache with a thumb and forefinger. He chewed the bristly ends, thinking that this just might be a solution to a real problem. This could work out well—or it could put him in deeper with Grissom. He darned sure knew the residents of Klinkhorn would not be impressed. If that man wasn't under his roof, it would be awful easy for someone to kill the skinny soak, and then all manner of problems might disappear. At the least it would save him the trouble of housing him until the judge happened by. Because he certainly hadn't yet sent for the judge.

"I am headed to lunch," he said. "But as a rule, I always leave my keys in my top desk drawer. Always seemed safe enough. Pity about the cells back there. Bad as most of them prisoners are, they really should have more than the one window set in that door." Hart looked at Emma. "You know the door I mean, that one that leads to that blind spot in the alley out back?"

He stepped to the door, looked out. "Fixin' to rain again." He looked at Emma. "Might want to cover your load for the trip back to your place."

"Marshal? Aren't you worried about my safety? With him possibly being a killer and all?"

"You? Nah. There might, just might, be a grain of truth in what you're saying. Besides, something about him just don't seem the type."

"I thought you said there was no type."

He headed through the door, chuckling. "Just like a Farraday to trip me up at every turn."

Chapter 19

"Keep your mouth quiet and your head down. And drape that blanket from the cell over your head. We can't let anybody see you, or you're done for—and I expect I wouldn't be too popular in town either." Emma looked past the mule toward the front of the alleyway. "Hurry up! You want to get caught before you're even started?"

Tucker shuffled out of the jail's back door, a gray wool blanket with holes draped over his head and shoulders. It managed to cover him all but for his boots. He reminded Emma of an old woman or a monk, enough so that she had a hard time keeping from laughing.

As he struggled up onto the wagon's bed, he said, "You always this bossy?"

"Only with people who might be killers. Now get up in the front and I'll drape this canvas over you."

He lay down, angling his thin form around boxes filled with canned goods, a keg of flour, and sacks of cornmeal and dried beans. "This is what you eat? No fruits or vegetables?"

"We have beef, venison."

"That's not a vegetable or a fruit, ma'am."

"Stop calling me 'ma'am,' damn it. My name's Emma. But you can call me 'boss.' And besides, if eating fruits and vegetables lands you in the shape you're in, I'd as soon stick with my beans and biscuits, thanks very much."

She rummaged for the tarp. "If you're so all-fired excited about fruit and vegetables, you can scout up some and cook them for us. Now shut up or you won't have to worry about fruit ever again."

She threw the tarp over him, dropped a coil of new rope on top to keep it from slipping off him, and climbed up into the seat. Then he sat up again.

"What now?" she said, keeping an eye on the alleyway.

"What about Gracie?"

"Who?"

"My horse. You said you'd—"

Emma sighed. "She's fine, I'm sure. The livery's the best in town."

"It's the only one in town, I'll bet."

"Well, yeah. Now lie down, damn it, or I'll drag you back in there. I swear it."

"I'm not going anywhere without Gracie."

Emma closed her eyes. "Okay, okay. We'll go get her. But you're paying for whatever she eats. Now lie down! Make a move and we're both in a world of hurt. You understand?"

They rolled out of the lane behind the long row of buildings, at the end of the street just across from the livery. Emma stopped the mule, set the brake, and hopped down. She leaned over the side of the wagon, fidgeting with the canvas, and talking low. "Keep still—you hear me? I'll be back with your horse in a couple of minutes."

"I might owe a little cash on the bill."

Emma sighed. "Of course you would." She lifted the coil of rope and slammed it down hard where she guessed his head was.

"Ow!"

"Oops," she said, lips unmoving, but she was smiling.

She leaned her head into the cool, dark interior of the stable. "Halloo, anybody here?"

Off to the right, in an empty stall used for storage and

filled with a clutter of dust-caked saddle blankets, heaps of old rope, and puckered tack, Horace Marquand emerged from a pile of straw, bits of chaff clinging to him. "Hey there, Emma. How you doing today?"

"Hey, Horace. I'm okay, thanks. Got a request for you. I'm here to lay claim to that old horse belonging to that worthless buzzard in the jail."

From behind her, she heard a muffled oath. She coughed, made a show of clearing her throat.

"You need a drink? Help yourself to the pump yonder. Ladle's clean."

"Thanks. Just dusty down here."

"Yeah, that's a stable for you. What you want with that horse, girl?"

"Marshal said it was payment of a sort for what that lousy, no-good, murdering coward took from us."

"Aw, heck, that ain't no fair trade. She ain't but a rack of bones. Best chopped up, used for coyote bait."

"I know, but it's all we're getting out of this mess."

He nodded, scratched his stubbly chin.

Here it comes, thought Emma.

"I have had that horse for a couple of days now. . . ."

"What's he owe you, Horace?"

"Well, now, Emma. It don't hardly seem right you paying off the debt of the man who . . . well, you know."

"Yeah, I know. What's he owe you?"

Marquand scratched his chin again. "I could let that horse go for a couple dollars."

"Two dollars, Horace? I best see what it is you've done for this horse to justify two dollars. You yourself just got through telling me it wasn't worth a bean."

"Aw, Emma, I'm just trying to make an honest living here. Times are hard, as you well know."

"What's that supposed to mean?" She narrowed her gaze at him.

"Nothing, but money's not going near as far as we all would like nowadays."

"Tell you what. I'll pay you a dollar now." She handed him one. "And another if when you lead that horse out here she looks worthy of a second dollar. Seeing as how I happen to know that bum in the jail already paid you when he brought the horse here, I'd say that's the best offer you'll get all day."

Horace disappeared back into the barn, muttering and rubbing his chaff-specked hair. He emerged a minute later with a horse that had seen better days. In fact, Emma wasn't sure she'd ever seen such a rough-looking beast. And yet there was something there in the sorrel's eyes, an alertness. Time would tell. The horse was no dewy colt, but Emma watched the horse walk toward her, stood off to the side to see her gait, and recognized a decent frame, good height. This was a real horse, underneath the patchy coat and jutting hipbones, all angles and points.

"We'll get you fattened up, eh, girl?" She let the horse sniff her hand, traced the horse's jawline back, and rubbed her neck. The horse lowered her head and nodded slowly, liking the attention.

"Your horse, then, Emma." The man held out the old, knotted reins.

"She come with a halter? Anything?"

"Just that sad excuse for a hackamore."

"I'll have to think about that second dollar, Horace. She isn't in nearly as good a shape as I was led to believe she might be, especially after two days under your roof."

"You are a Farraday, make no mistake." He shook his head and retreated to the interior of the dark barn.

Emma tied the old horse to the rear of the wagon and made the long, slow turn around the livery, then headed on up Main Street, knowing full well that every person in town had stopped and was watching her lead the horse of the man they all knew to be her uncle's killer. What was going through their minds, she could only guess. As she passed the Lucky Shot, Vollo and Rummler walked out onto the porch and leaned against posts. They each gave her a hard stare.

Instead of doing what she wanted to, which was to whip the mule into a run and drag her loaded wagon bouncing on out of there, she halted right in front of them and sat for a moment.

She cut her eyes toward them, but kept her head rigid, as though she were staring straight ahead. This bothered them, she could tell. It took a few seconds before their bluster and bravado bubbled to the surface.

"Well, lookee here, Vollo. Got ourselves a honey with a wagon full of goods."

From the wagon, she heard a muffled curse, saw the canvas shift slightly.

"Don't you dare," she said, low and even, barely above a whisper. If he popped up out of the wagon now, they were both sunk.

"You talking to me, girly?" Rummler stepped down off the porch. "What you got in there, girly? Anything good to eat? I'm a mite peckish." He reached toward the side of the wagon to lift the canvas.

With speed born of anger, Emma snatched up her uncle's rifle from where it leaned by her feet. She levered a round, then laid the barrel across her right forearm. It happened to be aimed at the tall man.

In a loud, clear voice that carried up and down the silent street, Emma said, "Well, whatever happened to that head of yours, Rummler? Tangle with a bobcat? Or maybe you got yourself grazed by a bullet from a rifle not unlike this one while you and your nasty little friend, Vollo, were trying to rape a girl on her way home the other night?"

The man's gray face reddened. "I . . . I don't know what you mean." He waved at her as if dismissing the rants of a crazy woman.

"Speaking of worthless buzzards," she continued in a near shout. "How's that nose of yours, Vollo? Looks as if something like a rifle stock—why, not unlike this one here—might just have slammed into it, maybe while you were half-drunk and grabbing at a girl on her way home the other night."

From behind Vollo, a large shape emerged, cut a wide shadow on the worn porch boards in the afternoon sun.

Bentley Grissom hooked a finger around a thick cigar and plucked it from his puckered pink lips, blew a plume of smoke, and said, "Bold talk for a girl who'll soon not have a pot to piss in, nor a window to toss it out of."

That caught Emma up short. In all the commotion, she'd not given much thought to the loan Hart and Louisa had both mentioned. Grissom's fat, confident tone and smug smile stopped her cold. She felt her own confidence shrink like a parched plant in hot sun.

She couldn't let him talk to her that way in front of everyone. How easy it would be to shoot him now, just pump a handful of shots into the big sack of fat, and take Vollo and Rummler too while she was at it. She was sure no one in town would mind. The fat man owned them all six ways from Sunday and had a lock on their Sabbath too, she'd bet.

She was about to reply when Marshal Hart stepped up behind Grissom and looked her square in the eye. He shook his head, warning her to shut her mouth.

She couldn't help herself. "You go to hell, Grissom." His name tasted like poison on her tongue. She spat in the street and snapped the lines on the mule's back. The last thing she saw was Vollo and Rummler smiling their foul, dumb grins. Above them, Grissom's heavy-lidded eyes regarded her from deep in his face, and his grinning mouth and fat, wet lips continued to suckle on the black cigar.

Behind him, the marshal shook his head, as if he were sorry for her. She clucked the mule faster, the rifle cradled in her arms.

"Oh Lord," she said, sighing when they'd left the last straggling shanties of Klinkhorn behind. "Just like Daddy and Uncle Payton and Arliss have told me. I will never learn to keep a civil tongue in my mouth."

"I believe they are right. You are a lost cause . . . boss."

"Shut—" She stopped herself and sighed again.

Neither of them spoke for long minutes. Then he said, "I need some air. It's stifling under here."

"No, you might be seen. Be thankful that you're warm. It's getting cold out here."

"I might be warm, but this wagon's rattling me to death."

"Good. Save me the trouble. . . ."

What was happening to her life? Two days ago she had been convinced all was well. The ranch seemed to finally be something that might become profitable, the memory of her father's death was healing, Arliss was as cantankerous as ever, and Uncle Payton had begun to pay calls on Louisa Penny.

Now, within a couple of days, she'd lost her uncle and she found out that he had taken out a loan on the place. And though it sounded as if he'd paid it off, she had no proof— and worse, if what the prisoner said was true, Vollo and Rummler had taken the loan receipt from her uncle, on behalf of Grissom.

Though they had been keeping a slow pace, Emma eyed their back trail frequently, checking on old Gracie at the same time. The old horse kept right up with them. When they were a few miles from home, but well onto Farraday land, Emma saw the canvas rise at the end of the bed, close to where the horse was tied. The prisoner had somehow wiggled himself around enough that his head now resided where his boots had been. He popped up and reached for Gracie.

"Hey! Lie down back there. You want to get us shot?"

He flopped back down. "I haven't had a chance to say hello to Gracie."

"I don't care. You keep this up and you'll not have a chance to do much but die. Now lie down." That was the last she saw and heard of him until they wheeled on into the yard.

Arliss strolled out of the barn, but his smile slumped when he saw the horse tied to the back of the wagon. "What in blue blazes is that?"

Before Emma could stop him, Arliss had grabbed the front corner of the tarp and whipped it back. "I hope you brought me a can or two of them peaches. I'm partial to a can of—" He staggered backward, hands held up in a pugilistic stance. "What the hell is this! Emma, get my hay fork. We got us a stowaway!"

Samuel Tucker sat up, blinking at the sunlight, and rubbed his face.

"Now, Arliss. Before you get all worked up, you might as well know the truth. Arliss Tibbs, this here is . . ." She turned to Tucker, her brow wrinkled. "I don't know your name. Not sure I ever heard it, in fact."

"It's Tucker. Samuel Tucker." He stepped forward, held out his hand to Emma. She shook her head, then looked down at her scuffed, dusty boots, keeping her arms folded.

"Emma Farraday," sputtered Arliss. "Why, you could knock me over with a feather, not taking a man's hand extended in greeting? I never."

Arliss thrust out his hand and Emma said, "He's the man who was arrested for . . ."

Tucker let his hand drop, then squared off before Arliss, hands on his narrow hips. He was a tall man, broad of shoulder, even if the shoulders had little meat on them. "As Miss Farraday was about to say, I am the man arrested for the murder of Payton Farraday."

Chapter 20

"You have 'made certain inroads in securing the deeds' to the land to the immediate southwest of this run-down town? What exactly does that mean, Mr. Grissom?"

Bentley Grissom was about to respond when Vollo let out a snort and shook his head. He was sneering at Lord Tarleton's men.

"Vollo, Rummler! Go mark your territory outside, and take those two with you. Buy them drinks, but all of you gun hands get out of here. We're talking business, and it's none of yours."

"I'll thank you kindly, Grissom, to leave the ordering about of my men to me and me alone." Tarleton didn't look up from the map, kept his finger on the blue vein curving through the center of it. "Reginald and Shepler, perhaps you might look into that matter we discussed earlier. I have a few more minutes to spend with our gracious host. Now, about the deeds you may or may not have secured, Mr. Grissom."

The four men left, Vollo and Rummler annoyed that the other two men waited them out before leaving the boss's office.

"Yes, yes, ah." Grissom leaned over the map, his face glistening with oily sweat.

Tarleton backed up, folded his arms. He was not at all impressed with the look of the man. His letters had indicated he was some sort of local power lord with a lock on all the businesses, the comings and goings in this, the only town in the midst of this outrageously timber-rich region. But the truth of it was that this man's impression of himself far outstripped the reality. *What does he see when he looks in the mirror?* thought Tarleton. *If it's the greasy rotund man I see before me, then a wide and deep strain of delusion runs in his family.*

He looked again to where the fat man pointed on the map. Even his fingernails were begrimed.

"Something wrong, Lord Tarleton?"

"What? Oh no. Not at all. I am merely thinking of the future."

"Then you and I are like two peas in a pod, sir. Both of us looking to the next bend in the road. That's how I got to where I am today."

"Indeed." Tarleton looked around Grissom's office at the back of the saloon. It was a pine-paneled room, a low ceiling, and with two overlarge and rather vulgar paintings of saloon girls. His eyes rested on the rather visually demanding twin attributes of one of them.

"You like my beauties, eh?" Grissom rubbed his hands together. "I can see we have even more in common than I thought. I'm not surprised—it's why I invited you to my private office first, to have a drink, make you feel comfortable here in Klinkhorn."

The Englishman stared at Grissom as if he were speaking in a foreign tongue, so he kept talking about the paintings. "I had them commissioned by a roving painter to hang out front in the saloon, but I recognized the true artistry in them and chose to keep them back here in my office instead. They keep me occupied." The fat man indulged in a long wink and nudged Tarleton on the arm.

The Englishman immediately withdrew the limb from such further abuse as though he'd been shot. "Mr. Grissom.

This visit to your charming little town has proved a most interesting diversion. My men and I will be moving on to greener pastures unless you can produce proof sufficient enough to convince me that you have indeed a lock, as you say, on this surrounding acreage. You were correct about one thing: from what I have seen, the forests hereabouts are of sufficient enough quality that they may merit deeper investigation by me and my team of professionals. If that is the case, then I will consider making Klinkhorn my base of operations for several weeks in order to investigate the surrounding region."

Grissom nodded, and his mouth dropped open. Just enough to let the flies in, thought Lord Tarleton.

The Englishman continued. "It is imperative that I travel the length and breadth of the tract in order to gain a solid grasp of its size and level of timber quality so that I might gauge its potential value. That is the first step in assessment."

Grissom licked his lips, didn't quite know what to do with his hands. It sounded to him as if this man was on the hook. Now he just had to land him. He could hardly believe it. He'd read about Lord Tarleton, wealthy land baron and one of the first of the English gentry to rove into the West. And best of all, the man was beyond rich—and paying top dollar for huge tracts of untouched timber! "Whatever I can do, sir, to assure you—"

"You can start by not simpering and patronizing me. We'll get started first thing in the morning reconnoitering the region. The entire region." He turned to face Grissom. "Provided that you can, in the next two minutes, prove to me that you have full dominion over the lands in question." The Englishman's gloved hand smacked hard, knuckles down, on the elaborately detailed map.

Grissom's entire body tightened, his throat constricted, and he felt the air choking off within him. Then it came to him. Yes, why not? It seemed to him that Tarleton believed that since the frontier, as he had called it all afternoon, was a place jumping with outlaws, he would expect no less when it came to legal documents. So all Grissom had to do was show the man the promissory notes, the titles of holding, any bank documents that showed the initial holders were hopelessly indebted to him. And definitely not the receipt of debt paid he'd been forced to sign when that damnable Payton Farraday had surprised him and come in to pay off the loan. The Farradays' lands were far and away the key to this entire deal.

Grissom clutched at the man's sleeve. "Would you allow me just a pinch more time? In addition to this saloon, I own the bank here in town and I have all my important documents locked up secure there, in the vault. I'm sure you understand such precautions, being a man of the . . ."

The lord stared at him, unamused. "Fine, then. Let us proceed to your bank and you can show me what it is you have. I will hold off forming a determination until then."

Several minutes later, Grissom led Tarleton up the street to the bank, then closed it to business and shooed the employees out. He drew the blinds and ushered Lord Tarleton into the vault room, an antechamber of the vault itself. It had been annoying that Tarleton insisted, without consulting Grissom, that his two hired guns be allowed in there with him.

"I'm not comfortable with having . . ." Grissom leaned closer to Tarleton. "With having your men in here . . . near the vault."

The Englishman closed his eyes and sighed as if he were on a stage, projecting to the back rows. "I can assure you, Mr. Grissom, that they are not interested in the scant holdings of your vault." He turned to his men. "Am I incorrect, gentlemen?"

"No, sir," they both said in unison, their hands held crossed before them, as if waiting to pluck their pearl-handled long-barreled Colts from their finely tooled black leather cross-draw holsters and shoot Grissom dead. He swallowed. This was getting embarrassing.

"Fine, fine, fine." Grissom slid back a curtain to reveal, built into the wall, a black-faced steel safe, four feet tall by three feet wide. In blocky gold type, the front read EXCELSIOR, MODEL No. 102393.

Funny, thought Lord Tarleton, how the people who had the least in life often took measures to protect their meager possessions. A town like this had no need for a bank, as far as he could tell. Why didn't these people just keep their meager money with them, their important papers buried under their houses? Wasn't that what the dime novels said they did out here on the wild and woolly frontier?

Grissom glanced over at his assembled guests, smiled weakly, wishing now that he had not sent Vollo and Rummler packing. They were probably going to be useless to him for the rest of the day. Knowing them, they'd taken the curt dismissal as a sign that they needed to brood and suck down his watery booze. The buzzards.

He lowered himself to his knees, hoping he didn't break wind in the process. It was so embarrassing when that happened. He grunted, positioned himself in front of the tumblers, glanced back over his shoulder. "Ahem, if you please, gentlemen. I am a banker, after all. And mayor of Klinkhorn. And a business owner as well. The people of my town respect me in all positions."

"Yes, yes, of course, my good man."

Grissom liked that. The lord had called him a good man. He was, yes, he truly was a good man looking to do the best he could for his community. And if he made a few dollars in the bargain, so much the better. Where was the harm in that? He dialed the last number into place and heard the faint but delicious sound of the tumbler click into place. He spun the star-shaped stainless handle, lifted up on the bar lever, and the safe door glided outward, its hinges barely uttering a complaint.

Grissom looked in and spied the familiar several small stacks of paper currency, and deeper in there were a dozen short stacks of gold coins, one gold ingot, and several small buckskin pouches that contained gold dust. He plucked a pistol-length leather satchel an inch thick from its spot, wedged against the side of the safe. Grissom slipped the small leather folder into an inner jacket pocket, then grunted backward a few inches, his knees popping and his massive haunches looking, he feared, like two pigs fighting under a blanket.

The safe door had nearly closed when he heard a small noise, like a squeak, come from Lord Tarleton. The Englishman had his hand held out, as if he were trying to stop the door from closing.

"Something wrong?" Grissom looked from the Englishman's eyes to the safe. Then he swung the door open again. "There something in here you are curious about, Lord Tarleton?" He was beginning to think there might be a whole new angle to this dandy that he hadn't recognized before.

Tarleton straightened, licked his lips. "The, uh, leather pouches. Are they . . . would they contain genuine gold pokes, I believe they are called?"

Grissom pulled one of the sacks out, hefted it. "Yes, sir, I believe these are Milky Peters's pokes. Or rather they were. He'd been having a rare run of good fortune at his strike— about the only one around here who actually works a claim instead of talking about working it from inside my bar." He looked at the sack in his hand, then winked and tossed it up to Tarleton.

"Oh my," said the Englishman, catching it and not even trying to hide the delight in his eyes. He smiled, not able to take his eyes off this genuine article representing the wildness of frontier life.

"I daresay Milky won't have any worries if you were to

take a peek at that. Feel of it, as the old-timers say. Before you touch it, you should know one thing," Grissom said, holding a warning finger upright in the air.

Tarleton stopped, suddenly afraid he might be about to commit a serious error.

"You will develop a taste—and I'm talking a hard hankering—for real, honest-to-God raw gold that no amount of praying or digging or sluicing will satisfy." He winked and struggled to his feet.

"Is there"—the lord had untied the pouch and was probing the depths with a fingertip—"much in the way of gold in these parts?"

Grissom's smile drooped. He looked at Tarleton's two men and leaned close to the lord. "In a word, yes. And I happen to own much of the land where the best strikes have been found."

"You said earlier that the pokes were the property of this Milky fellow. But from your use of 'were,' I take it that they are now your property?"

"Yes, indeedy, lord, sir. You see." He straightened, grunting. "Milky's off on a little trip back to Deadwood to visit his ailing ancient mother. But he needed money for the journey. I advanced him ample cash to get there, have a good time, bury the old girl in style, and get back here. And in return I only asked that he leave me his meager poke. . . ."

"That does not sound like such a good deal, Mr. Grissom."

"And the deed to his claim, sir." Grissom patted his breast pocket. "Upon his alleged return, he will pay me back the money borrowed. Should he not return, I will keep the poke and the deed."

"And just what are the odds that he will return?"

"Slim to none, sir."

"Aaaah, you are a clever man, Mr. Grissom." Tarleton prodded the contents of the bag, his eyes wide and a smile curving his waxed mustache. "A very clever man indeed."

Chapter 21

It was the first time in a long while that Emma recalled seeing Arliss Tibbs speechless. The old man backed away, lowered the work-worn hand that had been about to shake hands with a killer.

"You said you were the one who killed Payton?" But Arliss's eyes swiveled from the boy to Emma. "I'm confused." But his fists were balled, and as he spoke, he trembled with rage.

"Arliss, please—"

"Somebody best get to talking and fast. I got work to do and I don't like mysteries, much less one that involves a killer of a friend of mine. I heard all about you from my friends in Klinkhorn."

"Arliss." Emma stepped up close to him, her back to Samuel. "You trust me, don't you, Arliss?"

"Yeah, as it happens, I do. But that don't—"

"Then trust me when I tell you that I believe he didn't kill Uncle Payton. Okay? He's here for the time being. We're trying to figure out what to do. But we're down a hand, he was going to rot in that dark cell, and we have a whole lot of work to do before snow flies—and no time to do it in. And in between all that, we're going to try to figure out who did it and why."

Arliss looked at them both again, his lower lip trembling.

Then he turned and walked toward the barn. "Ah, to hell with you both."

"If it makes any difference to you," she shouted at his re-treating back, "I'm at least convinced he's not lying to me."

Arliss kept walking and disappeared into the barn.

"Thanks for trying," said Tucker.

"I meant it, stranger. I don't know exactly what happened, but I do know that the descriptions of the two men you saw convince me that you might be innocent—because they are the lowest of the low, bad men doing bad things on a daily basis. And they're employed by Bentley Grissom, a man people in town call 'the Devil you know.' He's mayor, owns the bank, holds the note on lots of the businesses downtown, and owns a couple of them outright, including the Lucky Shot Saloon, where his office is."

"Busy man," said Tucker, stepping up to the wagon to help carry the groceries.

"Yes, he is. And I forgot to mention he says he's a lawyer. So he can write up all manner of documents to suit himself—and you can bet he does just that. Most everybody in Klink-horn is indebted to him in one way or another."

"And the Farradays?"

She started up the steps to the long, low front porch of the house. "Up until my uncle was killed, I didn't think so. But someone said he'd taken out a loan with Grissom, which didn't seem like something he'd do. But someone else said he'd paid it off just that day he was killed."

Tucker stood, a sack of beans swinging from each hand.

"What?" said Emma.

"Remember, I told you I saw those men taking that paper from his pocket?"

"Yeah," she said, her lips pursed. "Probably the—"

From behind them, Arliss said, "Most likely it was his receipt for paying off the loan. The one I wished he had told you about, Emma. Grissom wouldn't have wanted him to pay it off, else he'd lose control of Farraday lands, so he set Vollo and Rummler onto him to snatch that paper back."

Tucker nodded. "That way there would be no proof that he'd paid it off."

Arliss stepped up to Tucker, looked up at him, and pointed a finger at the tall man's face. "Ain't none of this is proved yet. And even then, you got some sort of explanation to get around on my good side. Might be you won her over, but me, I ain't so easy to convince." He turned away, then spun back, his finger extended closer to the tip of Tucker's nose. "And I sleep with my double-barrel loaded with buckshot!"

Samuel Tucker felt as though he'd had about enough, and faced them both. "I have a pretty good idea of what you think of me, not just for what you think I did—which I did not do, I will add—but also because of the way I look. It's true that I don't have much meat or muscle on my bones, and my horse isn't much better off. I have my own reasons for the life I lead. But I didn't kill Payton Farraday. The only thing I'm guilty of is in being at the wrong place at the wrong time."

"And selling his gun to Taggart at the mercantile," Emma said, staring at him.

Tucker nodded. "That is true. But I explained to you my intentions. I can only say that I was dry-gulched by hunger. Me and my horse."

Emma stared at him for a long moment, then finally said, "Speaking of that bone rack, you should see to her. I'll fix up something for us all to eat. You going to be any use to us, you better get some meat on your bones." Emma blushed almost immediately, then said, "Arliss? Maybe you could show him a stall for the horse, and where he can bunk."

"You're dang tootin' he'll be bunkin' in the barn. 'Cause I'll be in the house." He fixed Tucker with a hard stare. "Even if you ain't a killer—and I ain't saying you ain't!—I know how things are with you drifters." He pointed at Emma. "She's my charge now. I'm responsible here, so I'll be in the house." He turned and pointed that finger up at Tucker's nose again. "And I sleep with a—"

Tucker nodded. "Double-barrel shotgun. I know. You said."

Arliss stalked off toward the barn, shouted over his shoulder, "Loaded with buckshot!"

Tucker watched him for a second, then said, "Is he always this way?"

"No." Emma headed back inside. "Sometimes he's grouchy."

Chapter 22

That night, Tucker woke up to see Arliss standing above his bunk in the barn, a shotgun cradled in his arms.

"Arliss." Tucker sat up. "What . . . can I help you with?"

The old man stood staring at him, then handed him something in the dark. "Take a slug or two. Help you ease out of them booze tremblings. I seen your hands shaking earlier."

Tucker regarded him a moment, then shook his head. "No, I appreciate it, but I have to work through this on my own."

"No, sir. You're in my barn, you go through it my own way. I been there, fella. I know what I'm talking about." He held the bottle out to him again.

Tucker took it slowly, uncorked it, and licked his lips, though he tried not to. He swallowed a stiff jolt, then another, and felt Arliss pulling the bottle from him. He struggled against it a moment, then let go and dragged a shaking hand across his lips.

"I won't give you the bottle. I'm teaching you to fish, like they say in the Good Book, or somewheres. If I give you this here bottle, you'd guzzle it down, wouldn't be able to help yourself, not whilst you got the serpent curled around your gizzard so tight you feel like you might bust wide open. But if I teach you to ease off it and ease back into clear-eyed livin', you might just be of use to yourself—and to us."

The old man shifted his shotgun and took a slug himself.

"We got a powerful need for another set of hands around here. Lots of work. Course, being a bone rack like you and that horse of your'n are, I can't expect you to be of much use to us for a while, but I got tasks that you can do. And there's one thing we can provide is a bit of food and plenty of hard work so you'll sleep hard, wake up feeling better each day, like you knowed something."

"Thank you. You were right—that was just what I needed."

"Good. Now you can do me a favor and don't tell Emma." He glanced toward the wall, beyond which sat the house, and lowered his voice. "She ain't much of one for drinkin', so any yammering you do will be on your own head. Now get some shut-eye. You're a talkin' fool, and I got sleep to tend to."

With that, he turned and stalked out into the night, muttering a blue streak to himself.

"Thanks, Arliss," Tucker said to the empty barn. And for the first time in a long while, he fell asleep without dreams of the past clawing at him.

Chapter 23

For little more than a week, the odd trio at the Farraday spread kept their heads down, worked hard to ready the place for early snows that most often hit in late September and early October. They moved their small herd of beeves to winter pasture, separating the culls, cut firewood, and felled and dragged timber to season for next year's projects. Arliss wanted to build a proper smithy and an open-sided building away from the barn where he could butcher beef and chickens easier. His current slaughtering space was wherever it happened to be convenient.

Tucker fit in well, even if entire days went by without him being addressed by either Emma or Arliss. But he didn't take it personally since he noticed that they rarely spoke with each other, except at mealtimes. It was a quiet place filled with hard work and heavy with grief.

He grew accustomed to the routine, took comfort in it. With each day that slipped by, he felt himself regain strength, felt muscles form again where he hadn't felt muscles on his arms and legs for years. His craving for booze, always tapping on his shoulder and whispering a fluttering call for attention, was not something he indulged in or particularly missed, tired as he was at the close of each day. And each night he slept better than the night before. His bruised face and battered ribs slowly changed from dark purple and blue to lighter greens and yellows.

The days had turned increasingly cold, even at midday. Arliss decided he wanted to butcher a few culls and get them to the folks in town who had requested beef. They'd spent a couple of days doing just that, and since it was work that Tucker had had experience with, he was pleased to be of use to them. He even suspected he impressed Arliss, though with the old man, that was a difficult thing to tell.

They'd stopped for a big noonday meal and Emma and Arliss were watching in amazement at Tucker's capacity for food. He was putting on weight, feeling fitter, and eating more beans, biscuits, and beef than either of them could have taken in in a week. He'd also managed to find wild carrots and onions and, to their surprise, the presence of the vegetables had added considerably to the meals.

Arliss buttered another biscuit for himself, picking at it and trying not to raise his eyebrows as Tucker ladled another scoop of whistle berries onto his plate. They didn't much mind, as he had turned out to be more than a fair hand at the cooking. Even better that he enjoyed it, as cooking had never appealed to either of them.

"So, I wonder how ol' big britches, Marshal Granville Hart, is managing to keep the lid on the town, what with this one gone and all." Arliss wagged his bushy gray eyebrows. "Sure folks must know by now that he's escaped from the calaboose."

Tucker paused, his mouth full. He'd barely given the town much more than a passing thought all week. What had the marshal been doing to keep his disappearance a secret? Surely someone would have noticed he wasn't in there.

"We'll find out soon enough," said Emma.

"How's that?" Arliss asked.

Emma sighed. "Arliss. We have to take the beef and eggs into town—soon as you finish butchering those culls. I don't expect it will warm up anytime soon, but those folks are depending on us bringing beef in."

"Yeah, yeah, I forgot. Okay, me and Tuck here is about ready to start in on the last of the butchering anyway." He looked down at the biscuit he was picking at, then tossed it on Tucker's plate. "You might as well eat that too. You been eyein' it for five minutes. Besides." He smiled. "I'm savin' room for a snort in town, and maybe a beer or three."

Emma lowered her gaze at Arliss, eyes narrowed.

The old man shook his head, looked at Tucker. "Ain't that just like a woman, though? Take away a man's fun afore he's had any!" He slapped the table and rose, his chair stuttering on the wooden floor.

"At least we can talk with Grissom before you meet up with your chums at the bar."

"Yessiree, I aim to give that sloppy sack of guts a thing or two." He held up a fist menacingly.

"I'm serious. Doesn't seem likely that a piece of paper could mean all that much. Must be some other form of proof that we don't owe Grissom money, right?" She looked at Arliss.

The old man only shrugged. "It's a devil of a thing, not knowing where you stand."

She rose from the table and snatched up her plate. "I know where I stand. I was born here, I was raised here, and I will die here. Now or later, it makes no never mind to me. If he's going to try to steal this place from us, paper or no, debt or no, he'll have to do it over my dead body."

Tucker felt plenty of things he wanted to say, but it was too soon to express his opinion here, too raw.

"I wish you wouldn't talk like that, girl," said Arliss. "We'll get to the bottom of it, but I can't take another Farraday leaving me. And if you go, where in the hell would old Arliss get to? Riddle me that, smarty!" He smacked the table a last time and left. Even Emma's apology from across the room didn't stop him.

Chapter 24

"Morning, Glendon." The short, bald man leaned in the door of G. Taggart's store, saw that it was free of customers. "Got a minute?"

Glendon Taggart, he of the "G. Taggart" on the sign out front, stood in his usual spot behind the counter, tallying figures before his wife got on his back again about them.

"Doing the accounts, eh?" Chet grinned, tried to read the tallied figures upside down.

Taggart slammed the accounts book shut. He'd known Chet ever since they'd both arrived in Klinkhorn four or five years back. Chet was the owner of the feed, ranch, and hardware store down the street, but the little bald man could be annoying. "What can I do you for today, Chet? Business slow over at the shop?"

"I tell you what, Taggart. I don't seem to be able to pay Grissom's 'special taxes' that he said us merchants were obligated to pay."

Taggart nodded, even sighed in what he hoped sounded like sympathy. "And I'll tell you what, Chet. I understand, but I am in the same boat. Hell, we all of us listened to him when Mr. Bentley Grissom rolled into town in that wobble-wheeled buggy of his three years back. That alone should have told us something. Then he proceeded to sell us a bill of goods—told us what we wanted to hear and then stayed!" He chucked his spectacles on the counter and folded his arms. Damn Chet anyway for getting him riled. He did this every week. "Klinkhorn has never been the same since," he said as a closing shot.

"I can't disagree, Glendon," said Chet, his head wagging as if he were palsied.

But Taggart knew they were plowing ground already turned a few dozen times a month around kitchen tables and business counters and card games and horse stalls all over town. And no matter how many times they yammered on about it to each other, nothing changed. Grissom had the entire town in a tightening grip about the neck. And they had let it happen so long now that they couldn't afford to go against the grain where Grissom was concerned.

Plus, there were Grissom's promises of big business coming in, of their need to expand their business, the laying in of more and more expensive inventory. And that had necessitated that they partake of Grissom's bank's low lending rates. Why, in the beginning the man had practically given away money. Most business owners in Klinkhorn had felt the same way, and he had been all too eager to lend everyone in town money.

The man's promises so far had proven hollow. But they were all realizing it too late. The man owned controlling interest in most of the town's buildings, a good many tracts of land in the surrounding region, plus the Lucky Shot Saloon and the office of mayor of Klinkhorn, for what that was worth. And if the rumblings around town were true, the biggest feather in his cap would be the controlling interest in the Farraday spread—all seven thousand acres of it.

"Why are you here anyway, Chet?" The merchant placed his big ham hands on the counter. "You know something I should?"

"Might be I do." Chet half smiled, leaned against the customer side of the counter.

"Out with it, or out of my store."

"Why, Glendon," said Chet, wincing as if he were about to be struck. "I thought we were friends."

"We are, damn it. That's why I don't like these games. Out with it."

"It's that foreigner, the English fella."

"What about him? We've seen strangers here before. Used to be a mining camp, you know."

"Yeah, but that fella has something going on with Grissom."

"That's no surprise. We all do."

"Yeah, but ain't none of us renting all the free rooms in town for his men."

"Men? He only came in with those two on the black horses." He thought about it. They had been an unusual sight, armed as they were with double rifle rigs, double cross-draw hip irons, and Lord knew what all else under them dusters and in those elaborate black leather saddlebags.

"That's what I been trying to tell you, if'n you'd let me get a word in sideways. Word leaking out is that the English fella is some sort of royalty and he's bringing in all sort of men who work for him."

"What for?"

Chet shrugged. *Useless,* thought Glendon. *He could at least have come in here with useful information.* "Where did you hear this?"

"Same place we hear anything about Grissom—those two fools who work for him."

"Rummler and Vollo," said Taggart. He thrust his bottom lip outward, chewed it a bit. "When the wife comes in, I might just wander on over to the Lucky Shot for a beer." Taggart winked. "Can't get any less information than you've managed to offer."

"Aw, I don't need this treatment from you, Glendon. I have a wife for that." He headed out, the door's top bell ringing behind him. As soon as it settled into place, he popped his head back in. "You'll let me know if you hear anything, right?"

"Yes, Chet. You'll be the first to hear."

Chet smiled and whistled on down the boardwalk.

"And then everybody will know. If I find out anything, that is."

Chapter 25

As she emerged from the narrow trail behind the house, Emma didn't know who was standing before her, up on the hill where her mother, father, and uncle rested forever. He was a tall man with wide shoulders and a narrow waist, lanky and lean, but well muscled. He held his hat in his hand before him, as if out of respect for the three graves, and not just as someone gawking out of curiosity. Then the figure shifted weight to his other foot and she recognized the older but mended work denims and shirt that had belonged to her uncle, and she realized it was Samuel Tucker. And a sudden knot of anger gripped her in the throat.

"What are you doing up here?"

He turned, eyebrows raised. "Emma—"

"You didn't know them, don't have any reason to be here. You may work for us, but you don't have any right to be up here. This is a private place. Besides, what do you know of death and grief? You're just a drunk and a drifter."

As she said it she felt shame heat her face. But it was already said, too late to pull it back in. Instead she stood, arms folded in front of her.

Tucker stepped away from the foot of the graves. "It's very peaceful here." He glanced at her. "But you're right. I did not know them, Emma. And you're right too that it's a private place. And for intruding, I apologize to you."

He looked at her face until she met his gaze, held it. She noticed that his dark hair and sunburned face had cleared, now shaved and scrubbed, with mostly healed bruises and cuts, and with brown-green eyes free of the yellow tinge and tiny red veins that had made him look worn down to a useless, frazzled end.

"I wasn't always just a drunk and a drifter. Up until two years ago I had a ranch of my own. I bred horses, mostly. It was a fine place. I had five hundred acres of decent land near Tascosa, Texas. And I had . . ." His smile slipped and his voice cracked. He swallowed and spoke again. "I also had a wife and a daughter. Rita and little Sam, short for Samantha. Rita insisted we name her after me." He gritted his teeth, looked up at the branches of the pines standing tall over the quiet knoll.

"What hap—"

Tucker plunked his hat on his head. His cold tone cut her short: "They're dead. Both dead. Taken from me by sickness. So yes, Emma Farraday, I may be just a drunk and a drifter, but I know my share of death and grief."

"I am so sorry, Samuel. I didn't know—"

"That's right—you didn't." He walked by her on the trail. She caught his sleeve.

He stopped, looked down at her. "I have nothing and I want nothing. As soon as my debt to you has been sufficiently paid, I will leave you be."

He tugged free of her grasp and strode away, looking for the first time like someone she'd never met. Someone taller, broader, bigger, and sadder than the man in the cell had ever been. It seemed as if she were seeing Samuel Tucker for the first time—and for the first time since her uncle's murder, she knew with full certainty that Samuel Tucker hadn't killed Payton.

She watched him walk with purpose back down the wind-

ing, treed trail. Then she turned back to the graves and saw
sprigs of late-fall clover had been set at the foot of each. She
stood there thinking about the conversation she'd just had,
then bade her mother, father, and uncle a good night and
made her way back down the trail.

At the barn, Arliss was busy brushing a gleam back into
Gracie's coat. What he'd done with the old horse in just a few
short weeks amazed Emma. But then old Arliss had a way of
surprising everyone around him, often on a daily basis.

"You've worked wonders with that old bone rack, Arliss."

He spun, brush and currycomb held out as if to defend
himself. She laughed. It was rare to be able to sneak up on
him. She'd spent half her youth trying that, but he'd always
make some sly remark when she was a few feet from spring-
ing on him like the wildcat she'd been pretending to be.

"You have to get up early in the day to fool this hombre,"
he'd say. "It's my Apache trainin'. I was adopted by the tribe
as a young man, see, on account of my skill as a mighty
hunter and warrior. So I didn't have to learn anything about
them skills, but sneakin' around, ain't none better than a
Apache. They'll scalp you clean whilst you're having your
morning coffee. You won't know it till you go to brush your
hair and there ain't nothin' to brush!"

She'd always laugh nervously, never quite sure how seriously to take Arliss. But today, so many years later, she felt
bad that she'd gotten the drop on him. He seemed riled about
it too.

As if reading her mind, he said, "Age is gettin' to me, I
reckon. I'm like old Gracie here. Still got some use, but not
on the big tasks. Yessir, I like this old horse. Reminds me of
me."

Emma rested a hand on his shoulder. "Arliss, you're never
going to get old."

"How's that work anyway? Reason I ask is if I could just

bottle me some, we might could make a mother lode of a strike, take care of all our woes."

Emma smiled, took the brush from him, and began working on Gracie's sleek neck. Arliss set to work currying her tail.

"Arliss?"

"Mmm-hmm."

"You think he had anything to do with . . . Uncle Payton being shot?"

"Tuck? Nah."

Emma stopped brushing. Gracie swung her head around, annoyed that her trance had been interrupted. "You said that pretty fast," said Emma.

"I tend to do that when I'm sure of a thing."

Emma resumed brushing. Gracie half closed her pretty lids, snorted in contentment.

"Why do you ask, girl?"

Emma didn't respond right away. A few moments passed, and then Emma said, "I feel the same way you do. I'm sure of it. But when did you know?"

"Pretty soon after you drug his bony carcass home. Course, I didn't let on that I felt that way. Had to put on an act—elsewise we'd spoil him for work and for himself. He needs to learn to build himself back up to be a man again. But I seen first off that he was pitiful and had been on a long toot, but . . ."

He stopped currying and leaned on the horse. Gracie's flank twitched and she looked at them both. "See, girl, there's two types of men in this world. Men who are just good, the type who go ahead and give something all they got and go through their days not even thinking about not hurtin' anybody or anything because it just don't occur to them to hurt something in the first place. You see? Then there's the other type: rascals who are always looking for an easy road, looking to scare up a meal without having to work for it, people be damned. Them are the type we got in them devils we know, ol' Grissom and his boys."

"But not Tucker."

"No, Emma. Not Tucker. I do believe he's one of the good ones. But you didn't hear it from me." He winked at her.

"That goes along with what he told me."

"Oh, what was that?"

"I surprised him up at the graves."

"What was he doing up there?"

"Said it was peaceful. I'm afraid I said some things that I didn't mean."

"Just like a Farraday. I swear, a spikier crew I've never met."

"Yeah, well, he ended up telling me a bit about himself. He's from Texas. Had a spread down there . . ." She looked at Arliss.

"That all?"

She shook her head. "He also had a wife and a baby girl."

"Had?" said Arliss, paused, his leathery hands flat on the horse's hide.

"Yeah. A fever maybe, some sickness got them. I gather he lost it all."

"That would account for his drinkin', then. And it just goes to show what I said before. I'd wager that man couldn't hurt a bug . . . unless it plumb riled him. And then it'd only be for the right reasons. But good men like that"—he wagged the currycomb at her—"once you get them fired up, they can be awful sudden men, and when they're on the boil, you best keep clear."

Emma brushed Gracie for another silent minute, then handed Arliss the brush. "Thanks, Arliss. I have to go . . . do something." She kissed him on the cheek. Just before she left the barn, she leaned back in and said, "Arliss? You're one of the good ones."

He shook his head, blushing, then shouted, "If I'm so all-fired fancy, how come I ain't allowed to have a beer or three? Heh?"

He resumed brushing the grateful old horse. "Gracie, I do believe we are in for an interesting time of it." He chuckled and brushed.

Chapter 26

"Arliss, I believe I'll visit Louisa when we're in town. She promised to help me with finishing off that dress."

Arliss nodded, flung another forkful of dung onto the pile by the door.

Tucker cinched down the last of the cloth-wrapped beef and leaned against the side of the wagon. "You wear dresses?"

"Why would you say that?"

"Well, I've only ever seen you dress like a cowhand."

She felt her face flush with shock, then familiar anger. Why did this man get under her skin so? What right had he to say something like that to her, much less say anything to her? Despite her welling urge to drive her fist into his nose, blacken his brown-green eyes, she held her fists and her tongue. And instead she shrugged into her sheepskin jacket and tugged on her worn leather gloves. "Because that's what I am." She pulled her hat down low and looked at him. "Another thing? I'm also your boss. Get to work or get gone."

Tucker watched her as she led the horse on out the front door of the barn.

Behind him he heard a low wheeze. He turned to see Arliss, bent over, one gnarled hand slapping a knee. He was about to ask if he was okay because the old man looked as if he was choking. Arliss turned his whiskery old face up to look at Tucker and Tucker realized he'd been laughing so hard, tears were running down his face.

"What's so funny, Mr. Tibbs?"

When the red-faced codger could catch a breath, he wheezed out, "Didn't think you had one."

"What?"

"Spine enough to rile her. She's got your number, boy. Got you pegged, sure as I got rheumatics in every blessed bone in my body. Hoo-ee!"

Tucker stared at the empty open door. "I just don't know what to make of her. Can't figure her out."

"And you never will, boy."

Tucker turned back around. "How's that?"

"I say you never will quite know what makes her tick either. 'Cause she's a Farraday! They're all like that. Good news is that you got a whole lifetime ahead of you to work on it."

Tucker grimaced. "What makes you think I'm sticking around where I'm not wanted?"

"Oh, you'll stick." The old man turned, shaking his head as he set back to work pitching dung. "You'll stick. Love'll see to that."

"Love? You're crazy, old man."

"Yeh, no argument there." He touched a finger to the side of his nose. "But I do know a thing or two about Farradays and a thing or three about love. I been down that road myself a time or two and it's a rosy path. But it can be a thorny thing too. Best keep your boots on and be careful where you step."

"You might know Farradays and you might know love— I'll not argue any of that—but you don't know a thing about Samuel Tucker."

"I know enough to know she sees something in you that excites her and scares her. And from what I can tell, it ain't all bad. I do believe I'm beginning to think I was wrong about you." The old man held up a finger in warning. "Beginning, I said. I ain't all convinced yet. 'Specially since you ain't done a lick of work yet today. Now get on it or I just may have to light into you, take a round or two out of you myself, you insolent pup!" He swung the hay fork in a wide arc and cackled as Tucker jumped back and headed for the door, shaking his head and mumbling to himself.

"He'll do," said Arliss, smiling in the dark of the stall. "I reckon he'll do. Heh!"

Chapter 27

Tucker watched Emma and Arliss headed on up the road in the wagon, Julep setting a brisk trot. She'd recovered most of her smiling demeanor, despite what he'd said earlier about how she dressed. He hadn't been wrong, but it seemed he didn't know how to talk when he was around her. With Rita, it had been easy; he'd known her nearly his entire life. But this woman, Emma Farraday, now, there was a spitfire with a streak of wildcat one minute and an easy smile and relaxed chat the next. He didn't know what he felt, but he knew it was foolish to feel anything for her more than gratitude that she'd saved him from a certain hanging.

Tucker walked back into the barn, finished saddling Jasper, the dead man's horse. Oddly enough, it had been the horse they both had insisted he use since he'd gotten there. "Only one that won't sag trying to hold up your big bones," Arliss had said.

Arliss had wanted him to venture out across the river to the far valley to look for a late-calving cow and her calf. The old man said that in years past they'd had a number of cows head in there looking for a private, woody place to bed down and calve on their own. Tucker knew many of them did such things when their time came.

He filled his canteen, checked the rifle in the boot, extra shells in his coat pocket, and welcomed the recent loosening of the tenseness between them all. It had been a long few weeks, not being able to do much of anything other than work, and eat and sleep. Yet oddly it had been enough. Felt as though he didn't need more in his life. At least at the moment. He'd not felt so good, so hopeful in a long time. Odd, that, considering he was a fugitive holed up at the home of the very man he'd been accused of killing.

He felt odd once again that he was wearing the clothes of a dead man, riding a dead man's horse, using that man's gun and saddle, and eating his food at his table.

"Are you your own man anymore, Samuel Tucker?" he asked himself out loud as he rode out across the near meadow, scattering close-pastured stock that thundered away a few dozen yards before halting stiff-legged, staring at him with ears perked. He shook his head. Cows were cows the world over; he guessed they'd do the same thing every day, a hundred days in a row.

The bases of the two closest hills sat dark with trees, the valleys thickly forested with immense firs. Never had he seen so many trees, so much lush green growth. Even this late in the year, it seemed there was grass for the stock to eat.

What would winters be like here? He'd hesitated to ask Arliss and Emma, lest they take his question to mean he was angling for a place to stay. He was aware that his presence in their lives had put them at the raw edge of danger with Marshal Hart. And if what they'd told him was the truth, Grissom was the most powerful man for many miles. And becoming more powerful by the week, it seemed.

He rode for the better part of an hour, the sun nearly overhead. The day was turning warm and he loosened the buttons of his light red-and-black wool mackinaw. That too had belonged to Payton. He was grateful that they were of the same large build, lest he have fewer clothes to wear, especially in the encroaching cold season.

Jasper stood tall, blowing in the cool of the forest. Far

below, near a stream just south of this valley connected with the Rogue River, he saw a skipper mule deer drinking from the stream. *Now, that would be a fine treat,* he thought, already sliding the rifle from its boot. The big buckskin stood as if used to such behavior as Tucker tied the reins tight to a stout low branch.

He raised the rifle, slowly cocked back the hammer all the way, sighted on the thick fur of the deer. Its cold-weather coat had come in nicely. Right there, at the shoulder, a clean kill. His forefinger tightened on the trigger, tighter, tighter— the deer raised its head, alarmed, then shifted its stance, obscuring his shot by a tree halfway between them. He would have to wait for the deer to step a pace to either side. He eased off his finger's pressure on the trigger and resisted the urge to swear.

Upstream, to Tucker's right, he heard twigs snapping, the steady alternating *crunch, snap, crunch, snap* of an incautious man's feet on deadfall branches, then the heavy, rasping breath of a man unused to exertion. All this Tucker heard at the same time as the young buck, and the skipper bolted into a brown blur. No way to get a shot now.

Only then did Tucker swing his gaze around and spot the man. There he was, far below, oblivious of both Tucker, far above him on the valley slope, and of the long-gone deer he'd startled. Tucker eased off the hammer, slid the rifle back in its boot, never taking his eyes off the bumbling stranger.

The man had something balanced over his left shoulder, looked like polished wood of some sort topped with something that glinted now and again as sunlight hit it while the man struggled forward through the thick trees. He wheezed and soon stopped, almost directly below Tucker on the slope. Tucker watched him a moment more, and soon heard men's voices coming from the same direction as had the wheezing man.

They were talking, discussing something of humorous interest to them all, for the talk elicited great side-smile hoots. They too tramped into view and Tucker saw what they were then—a gang of men looking to survey land, judging from the implements they all carried. And by the looks of them, most red-faced and chests working like a smithy's bellows, they were also unaccustomed to working vigorously out-of-doors. They also hadn't come all that far hefting and lugging such gear.

What were they up to? This was Farraday land—that much Tucker knew. With Arliss and Emma in Klinkhorn, Tucker felt an odd sense of duty to investigate, set these men straight if need be. The Farradays owned enough land around these parts that there was little chance these men were off their course somehow or cutting across Farraday land to get to another spread. No, Tucker sensed there was something afoot—or maybe a mistake. He hoped it was the latter. No better time than the present, he told himself and headed downhill, cutting a zigzag pattern through the trees and leading Jasper by the reins. It didn't take the men long to spot him.

Tucker saw that several of them wore sidearms, and their hands instinctively hovered near them. The rest of the men stood, heads cocked and brows pulled tight in concern, no trace of smiles on their faces.

"Ho there," said Tucker, waving an open hand as he approached. None of them said a thing for a few moments, so he kept walking toward them. Finally they must have taken him as posing little threat, for they relaxed.

"Hello there," said the first man he'd seen, who by now had recovered his breath, though his face was red from the exertion of his walk through the woods. "You lost?"

"I was just about to ask you all the same thing." Tucker had stopped just short of the group, keeping himself back enough that if need be he could drag the buckskin between himself and the men, should any trouble start. It might just buy him enough time to shuck that rifle from the boot and draw on them. He had no sidearm and hadn't wished for one until now. Neither Emma nor Arliss carried one and they hadn't offered him the use of one, so he hadn't much thought of it, but he sure wished he had one now.

"How's that, mister?" The burly man looked annoyed with Tucker's statement.

"This here is Farraday property, pretty near as far as you can see in most directions for quite a distance. I don't imagine you're here by accident."

Another man, slimmer, taller, and more dapper than the rest, stepped forward. He wore an elaborate mustache and chin hair. A dandy if Tucker had ever seen one. "You suppose correctly, sir." The rest of the men seemed to melt back from this man. *Must be the boss dog,* thought Tucker.

The man's speech bore an accent. English, if Tucker wasn't incorrect. He'd met a couple of English waddies in the past, some Australians too, and he always confused their accents. "As I say, then, this here is Farraday land."

"Yes, yes, I heard you. We were just about to make a last set of measurements, but I suspect I am a fifth wheel here. My men will do the necessaries. You and I can head back to our camp. I will fill you in on the proceedings, lest you think we are violating the place."

A couple of the men snickered, but a harsh glance from the foreigner shut them up. *Camp,* thought Tucker. What sort of camp would these men have set up? And what could they possibly be measuring?

The man turned to walk back the way they had come, but paused to wait for Tucker. The other men had already moved to a nearby level spot. Some began to set up their gear, what he saw now were wooden tripods with folding legs and brass contraptions atop. Others walked ahead with their own gear. Surveying the land, had to be. Maybe it was some government project? If it was a government job, from what he'd heard there wasn't much a private landowner could do about such intrusion. Railroad? He'd be sure to ask the questions. But for now, he'd keep his mouth shut and gain what information he could.

The Englishman didn't seem to have much interest in conversing with him wherever it was they were headed, which suited Tucker just fine. That way he could keep an eye on him. Every once in a while, Tucker glanced behind him to make sure he wasn't being bookended into a trap of some sort. They climbed up a rise and there below him lay a bustling camp. He saw the same number of men, maybe more than the eight he'd seen back there in the woods, some of them walking in and out of a white canvas tent.

A cook fire sat at the center of the camp. Several trees nearby had been felled, one of them quite large. One man straddled it, measuring and scratching his findings in a notebook. Leaning against a narrow work wagon were more and varied instruments that looked expensive to Tucker, judging from the brass fittings and implements perched atop. Near the tent were a couple of tables, their surfaces cluttered with scrolled papers. Others, unfurled, looked to be maps.

The Englishman had stopped at the top of the rise and spread his hands wide as if to present the scene to his new guest. The expression on his face was one of pride and amusement, as if to say, "Look what I have created." "Our day camp," he said.

"Certainly looks like you have something important going on here," said Tucker.

"Oh, but we do, sir. We do. Of the utmost importance."

"Mmm-hmm, and what would that be, Mr. . . ."

The man held up a finger. "All in good time, sir. First, I hope you will partake of a cup of coffee with me. I'm feeling fatigued from our morning's exertions and would like the bracing effects of a cup of strong coffee, brewed the way American cowboys make it. Or so I have been assured anyway. You appear to be one yourself. Perhaps you will be the judge?"

Tucker regarded him a moment, then said, "Lead the way. I'll not refuse a cup of coffee presented in so skillful a worded manner." *But I will keep a sharp eye on you,* he thought as they walked down into camp.

The other men barely glanced their way, though they did part like tall grass before the Englishman. Tucker kept the reins in his hand, and stopped at the edge of the camp a few paces from the smoking campfire. "So, mind telling me what this is all about?"

The man handed him a tin cup of steaming coffee. Tucker held it by the handle, didn't sip, just watched this boss man.

The Englishman blew across the top of the cup, then sipped and smiled. "Aaah! So good." Then his eyes rested on Tucker's face for the first time since they got to camp. "An explanation is in order. I am Lord Tarleton and, among other things, I am a businessman. One of my primary interests is in logging and lumbering, and this part of the West, not all that far from the coast, all things considered, is ideal for such ventures. I have been traveling this region for many months now, throughout northern California, into Oregon, and so on. The Rogue River, which courses close by here, is a large enough flowage for me to get timber to the coast, where I will render it into lumber and load it aboard fleets of schooners for points all over the world."

Tucker sipped his coffee. "Sounds impressive."

"Indeed, it is, it is. And that is only the beginning. Why, I have—"

"Pardon me for interrupting, but what you have is nothing. As I said before, this here land is part of the Farraday spread. And I happen to know they ain't interested in having it logged off. Even if they were, I've seen your kind, mister, and what you leave behind. I've seen stump fields in my travels, and they ain't pretty."

To Tucker's amazement, the dandy man before him nodded in agreement, a solemn look making him appear as if he'd just come out of church. "I know. I know exactly what you mean. It's brutal, really, the way some people treat the land. I can assure you, this place"—he waved a hand at the landscape around him—"will be dealt with selectively and with respect for its natural beauty."

"That's good to hear, but you are missing one thing, and it's the Farraday spread's stamp of approval. And since they own this land, you ain't likely to get it."

The man smiled, and it felt mighty annoying to Tucker.

"I think that perhaps you had better talk with your cherished Farradays, ask them about a mortgage against their land on which they defaulted. Ask them about the deep debt they have accrued. Better yet, ask my friends Bentley Grissom and Granville Hart. That would be Mayor Grissom and Marshal Hart, of course."

Before he could respond, Tucker heard a voice behind him, familiar somehow.

"So that's where you got to . . . workin' for that little hussy and the old man."

He turned to see two grimy men on horseback. As he stared at them, recognition filtered to him like the forest sunlight. Of course, that's where he'd seen them—they were the men who had killed Payton Farraday. He'd not been this close to them before, but they were the men, no doubt. He'd heard them then, from a distance, and then in town, while under the canvas tarpaulin in the back of the wagon when Emma had brought him out of Klinkhorn.

They walked their horses toward him, their pistols drawn. He'd blown it. They would take him to jail—maybe worse. Rummler and Vollo, those were their names; he'd heard enough about them from Emma and Arliss. He'd hated them before for what they'd done to the Farraday family and seeing them only deepened his hate for them.

"This here man," said the taller, slimmer of the two—Rummler was what Tucker believed was his name—wagged the pistol at him. "Is a coldhearted murderer. He is having you on, Mr. Tarleton, Your Highness."

"That's a lie," said Tucker, reaching toward his rifle.

"I'd not do that, killer man," said Vollo, shaking his head.

"No, it ain't a lie neither." Rummler's gaze never left Tucker's face. "See, Your Highness, there was this killing just before you and your boys rode on into Klinkhorn. Funny thing, it seems this man who is trying to say that you ain't got no right to be on this property is himself the very killer of a man by the name of Payton Farraday."

"Again, that's a lie. These men are the ones who shot him. I witnessed it and was jailed wrongly for it."

All this time, the Englishman stood sipping his coffee, one arm hugged about his chest. Only his eyes moved as they flicked from Tucker to Rummler and Vollo. Finally he said, "This is all very interesting. I propose that you two escort the man to town. If he is innocent, all the better. If not, all the worse—for him anyway. For now, either way justice will prevail."

He turned to face Tucker. "Pity our meeting couldn't be under better circumstances, but it really is for the best."

Rummler sneered at him. "Vollo, get his rifle off'n him and make sure you check him over for any other weapons."

The smaller, smellier of the two wore a dirt-smeared smock that looked to be the same one he'd worn the day Tucker had first seen him. He rode close, leered down at Tucker, who tried to keep the buckskin between him and Vollo. But the horse shied and shook his head, unruly at the last. Vollo skirted the big beast, snatched the rifle from the boot, and held it up like an Apache holding up a prize scalp.

"We'll get him to the marshal's office, get him locked up again," said Rummler. "Half the town wants to hang him. The other half wants to watch."

"Don't listen to them, Tarleton. They have no idea what they're on about." The entire time Tucker spoke, he backed up slowly, aware that there was no way he could yank the horse around fast enough. They'd shoot him where he stood just for trying. And probably get away with it too. Still, he kept talking, kept trying to postpone whatever it was that was about to happen. "I witnessed with my own eyes these two kill the very man they claim I killed."

"Just like a killer to say such fancies, Your Highness. Now let's go, killer man, before I lose my patience."

Tucker looked at Tarleton, who he knew now saw him not only as a potential murderer, but as someone who was opposed to his ideas of logging off this land.

"Vollo, once he gets up into the saddle, you keep an extra-sharp eye on him."

"Of course. It will be my pleasure to shoot him if he gets out of line." He laughed, showing ragged, blackened, stumpy teeth, and his braying sounded wet and raw, as if a sickness had already eaten away most of his throat.

"We'll be seeing you later in town, Your Highness, sir." Rummler and Vollo nudged the buckskin forward.

Tucker sat his horse, pleased at least that they hadn't tied him . . . yet. Perhaps they were afraid to get too close to him. But he knew one thing for certain—they weren't going to bring him to town. He knew they couldn't afford to let him live. From their point of view, he might be able somehow to convince the marshal or other townsfolk that he might be telling the truth—and that was something they didn't want.

For several long minutes after they left, Lord Tarleton stood sipping his coffee, saying nothing. His men slowly went back to their tasks. "Reginald, Shepler." The two gunmen emerged from either side of the clearing. "One of you follow them, let me know what you see. But don't interrupt the proceedings unless you feel you have to. The other of you, back-trail him and see where he came from, find out what you can of this Farraday bunch. I suspect Grissom is not playing a proper game of cards with us. Anything we can learn will be of use when it comes time to dispense with him. Now go, go." He shooed them away. "I expect a full report from each of you back in town tonight."

"Yes, Your Lordship," they said together.

He turned his back on them and heard them ride out of camp. The other men's usual chatter and work noises remained subdued. They knew better than to question anything he might do or not do. They were all too well paid for that. And if by chance they did, then they would not be employed by him any longer. They might also not ever be employed anywhere else. He had allowed the barest of such hints to circulate among them. But they knew that he and his two trusted gun hands were the only ones who really knew for certain what happened to men who questioned him.

Lord Tarleton smiled as he poured himself another cup of coffee. He looked forward to seeing this newest game play out. The fat man, Grissom, was proving to be a most unworthy adversary, well out of his depth. And as for the marshal, he was merely a lazy man who wanted much more than he had without having to work for it.

Chapter 28

The three had ridden a half mile in silence, the land rising steadily, until they were well out of earshot of the surveyor's day camp. Tucker heard nothing but the wind soughing through the tall trees.

"So, fellas, what can you tell me about those trespassers back there? It seems pretty obvious they'd been lied to by your boss, Bentley Grissom."

As if he hadn't heard a thing Tucker had said, Rummler spoke. "Just what in hell did you think was going to happen back there, boy? Telling that fine fancy man from England all them lies about us? Who do you think he's going to believe? An escaped killer such as yourself, or a couple of hardworking men looking for a way to keep the peace with a whole townful of folks with violent tendencies?" Rummler's reedy voice cackled.

Tucker glanced at Rummler, a couple of dozen feet to his left, and fixed his mind on how he might escape. Vollo appeared beside him, riding in tight. It reminded Tucker of how Emma had said the pair had crept up on her that night. He didn't think for a minute that they were going to bring him to town. But he could stall the proceedings, maybe learn something while he looked for some way to escape.

He glanced at Vollo, took in for the first time what a foul piece of work the swarthy little man was. He looked to be wearing the same clothes he'd been wearing when he shot Payton Farraday. And that had been weeks before. Now that the wind shifted down closer to ground level, Tucker found himself just downwind of the man. His eyes watered at the man's sour-sweat stink. Didn't anybody ever tell him he smelled like a gut pile, baking in the sun and drawing flies?

"Look, gents. Why don't you give me back my rifle? I'll go on my merry way—I'm busy, you know. Lots of things to do." He slowed the buckskin to a walk, hoping to slip behind, even a few steps. He might have stood a chance if he headed down the thickly treed slope that fell away for several hundred yards before leveling out at what looked to be a dried streambed.

"What do you think you're doing, boy?" Rummler dropped back and drew his pistol. "You slow us down again and I am liable to open you up with this here six-shooter like a surgeon would a man's gut. Only a surgeon has a reason to save a man's life." He smiled again. To his other side, Vollo let out with a rattling laugh that echoed down the slope.

Instead of riding ahead, the two killers matched his horse stride for stride and edged closer with each step. Soon they were sandwiching him. Their boots rubbed his, the horses bumped and nudged one another, and Jasper thrashed and fought the tight reins.

To their right, the land leveled off and the trees thinned close up. Beyond, smooth ground, the sort of terrain on which a man might give his horse its head, maybe outrun those trailing him. It also might have been too open, too easy to take a bullet.

They were as tight as they could get now, and it was difficult for Tucker to keep an eye on both killers, just the way they wanted it.

He tried the innocent approach. "It's plain we should be headed to town, but darn if you boys aren't taking me somewheres else. Now, just where might that be?"

"You never mind. I got a plan and Vollo here don't mind going along with it. It's going to be a whole lot of fun for two of us. Unfortunately for you, you ain't one of the two." He howled in loud laughter and Vollo followed suit.

As close as they were, Tucker noted that Vollo wore his pistols cross-draw fashion, and had the right-side gun gripped in his left hand. A sudden thought came to Tucker and he knew it might be his only chance. With his right hand he snatched Vollo's second pistol from the little man's left-side holster. Not tied down, it slid easily from the holster.

Tucker drove the pistol upward, catching Vollo on the chin as hard as he could. The man's tongue had been sticking out from between the black craggy nubs of his teeth, and Tucker caught quick sight of the severed pink end of the tongue as it spat outward.

The blow unseated the smelly little man in spectacular fashion, working even better than Tucker had anticipated. Vollo flopped backward out of his stirrups, somersaulting off the horse's rump. A spray of blood followed the rank man from the saddle and he offered up a sick, strangled scream.

As soon as Rummler detected Tucker's intent, the thin killer barked a string of angry oaths, and drove his right arm hard into Tucker's gut. It felt to Tucker as though he rebroke a couple of ribs that had been on the mend. The blow forced the wind from Tucker's lungs, but he kept on with his plan and reined the buckskin hard to the left, forcing Rummler's horse even closer to the slope's ragged edge.

Vollo's horse had veered off and Tucker didn't care where it was as long as it didn't carry the dangerous little killer anywhere near him for a while—he had his hands full. The thrashing back and forth between the two men frenzied their horses, and they galloped faster with each second.

Rummler appeared to finally understand just what was happening and he swung his pistol wildly, catching Tucker first on the neck, again in the throbbing ribs, landing a blow on the buckskin's shoulder, anywhere his flailing arm might find purchase. All the while he yanked hard on the reins to the right in an effort to get his horse to head away from the drop-off.

But Tucker had the advantage and finally managed to drive Rummler's horse right to the grassy edge. The horse kicked and thrashed wildly, its legs finding no purchase until it was too late. The big beast collapsed to its left side, and kept rolling. Just before he pitched over with the horse, Rummler made a desperate lunge off his saddle toward the uphill side of his faltering steed, grasping toward Tucker, hate in his eyes, spittle flecking from his leering mouth.

In those last seconds before he knew terrible things were about to happen, Tucker saw Rummler's face drive toward him, framed by a pistol gripped in one hand, the other a dirty-nailed claw grasping for anything that might help save him. From the openmouthed look on the killer's face, Tucker was sure that Rummler was screaming, but all he heard was his own heartbeat. It came as if hammer blows underwater. He tried to lean away from Rummler and the falling horse, away from the steep slope. Maybe if he had not been stunned by the man's attack, he might have reacted sooner, been able to push away.

But he didn't, and Rummler snagged Tucker's coat front in a death grip. The sideways churning motion of the killer's horse pulled Tucker right out of his saddle. He had Vollo's pistol in his hand, but the momentum of his fall prevented him from clubbing the man.

Too late Tucker realized he was headed right down the treed slope with Rummler. He vaulted over the thin outlaw, tearing loose from his grasp. Time slowed as Tucker spun outward. He saw the tops of trees below and coming up fast at him, as if they were moving and not he. He heard screams and didn't know if they were his, Rummler's, or both. He spun again and saw fear and rage and hate all warring on

Rummler's face. The gun hand had one boot caught in a stir-rup. The horse's thrashing body began its roll, its legs now upright as if beckoning Tucker, and with each passing mo-ment, Rummler's body disappeared more and more beneath the rolling barrel of the horse's body.

Before the huge animal rolled over him, Rummler squeezed off a pistol shot. It drove like a freight train straight into Tucker's shoulder. The shot slammed him backward, pinning him to the graveled drop. But only for a moment.

Then gravity took over and he pinwheeled down the slope, bouncing, it seemed to him, from boulder to boulder. His head slammed against the slope, his arms, akimbo, flailed outward, hitting trees and doing little to stop his rapid de-scent. He'd lost track of the flailing horse and Rummler, un-til he managed to slow himself enough to glance upslope.

And what he saw drove a big, hard lump up into his throat from his gut. The man and horse gained speed, whipping diagonally shoulder to rump and back again. The horse's neck looked broken and the head slammed down, then with the next surge lifted upward, only to slam down again. And Rummler's long, limp body whipped high, arms outspread and reaching as if he were in prayer to the heavens, before slamming again into the slope.

As Tucker watched, the man's body, joined by the stirrup to the horse and caroming into massive trees, seemed to be wedged for a split second, before it continued downslope. Branches, dust, clods of mossy dirt, a welter of horseflesh and legs, and the pulped rag-doll remains of Rummler all boiled down the slope straight for him.

Chapter 29

Tucker jammed his bootheels into the gravel and kept sliding, but managed to pitch himself onto his left shoulder—white-hot pain blossomed up his side from the newly cracked ribs and burst out through the bullet wound. But it wasn't far enough over to avoid the tumbling wreckage of Rummler and his horse.

The tangle of legs tripped him up and sent him rolling again. Something hard slammed into him—the horse's head—the lifeless eye of the beast told him it was dead, or nearly there. They came to an abrupt stop, a heavy weight pushing against Tucker's chest. He had no strength to move it. He tried to force his eyes open, but saw only darkness. His head wouldn't move from side to side.

He waited a few seconds, trying to figure out if he was even alive. *Maybe this is it,* he thought. Then he gagged as a cough racked through him. He was alive, pinned by the horse. A low moan rose and Tucker thought he'd made the sound, but he'd need to breathe in order to do that. A thin trickle of air leaked into him as the horse, apparently not yet dead, thrashed atop him once, twice, then spasmed, stiffening. Tucker tried to time an escape from under the horse with the animal's thrashes, but it seemed impossible. A squeak of air leaked into his lungs. He was able to twitch his left hand. He scrabbled for anything he might grab, desperate and aware that each second brought him closer to death.

There! A nub of branch, no longer than his hand and thick around as a thumb. . . . He held it tight and jammed upward once, twice, three times—and the horse, all but dead, convulsed once more. Now or never, Tucker told himself, and he rolled onto his left shoulder—the very one that had been shot. It was enough to pull in air. He also saw light for the first time and realized he was wedged not under the great belly of the horse, but under its shoulder and neck.

Atop him, the horse shuddered, then relaxed, sagged down on him. *Have to get out of here,* he told himself, wheezing and feeling as if the rest of his bones might snap any second. He lay flat on leaves and pine needles at what he guessed was the bottom of the ravine. The thickness of the matted flora allowed him to drag himself, an inch at a time, outward toward the head of the horse.

Another few wriggles and he was able to swing his arm upward and grasp the horse's harness. His fingers curled around the leather and he pulled himself toward it. For agonizing seconds nothing budged. Then it felt as if something popped. He closed his eyes and pulled, his breath coming in short grunts. Soon the pressure on his chest lessened and he collapsed back.

"What you doing down there? It's you . . . you son of a gun!"

The words rained down on him from high above. He looked upward, but between the dirt in his eyes and the sunlight dappling through the trees, Tucker couldn't see much. But he didn't need to see who it was to know who it was—Vollo. Had to be. The buzzard was alive and, from the sound of it, angry over pretty much everything and looking for revenge. So why hadn't he shot at Tucker yet? The distance, had to be it. It was too far for him.

Tucker knew the last thing he should do was sit there and

argue with himself about why the man wasn't shooting at him. He dug at the earth with his elbows and managed to drag himself out from under the dead horse.

At last his boots were freed and he glanced upward again, but saw nothing. Maybe he'd imagined what he'd heard. He didn't dare take the chance, though, and dragged himself along the decaying leaves, stirring up the musty forest floor that smelled like an old grave. *If he is above,* reasoned Tucker, *then I can at least get behind the bulk of the horse, should he figure out how to shoot at me.*

His right leg felt near useless, though not broken, but his left throbbed like a tight hatband. He was able to bend it at the knee and help push himself forward. His left arm pulsed with each slide along the ground, and he was worried what he'd find inside his coat. He felt the warm stickiness of blood, but kept crawling.

"Hey, you down there!"

Tucker paid no attention to the man. A tumble of gravel pelted down at him, and he looked up again. Had to be Vollo at the top, trying to figure out a way down the slope.

If he comes down here, I have to defend myself somehow. He realized that somewhere on the steep trip down, he'd lost his grip on the pistol he'd grabbed from Vollo. No matter, there might be a weapon strapped to Rummler's saddle. He groped for a knife, a rifle, anything, and his hand fell on something that wasn't a horse—Rummler's leg.

But it felt as though the bones had been turned to sand or jelly, and the rest of the thin killer was a dead, pulped mess. Rummler's head was partially covered by his coat, which had ridden up his bony torso until it had lodged in a circling wad up around his chin. Thankfully what Tucker assumed was the worse-looking side of Rummler's battered head proved to be the part angled away from him.

Rummler was not moving, never would be again. Tucker pushed the thought out of his mind, forced himself to recall that he had been one of the men who murdered Payton Farraday and had laughed doing it. And he'd been about to kill him too, until Tucker had forced a different course of action.

"Good grief," he said out loud, his voice a hoarse croak. "I am responsible for this mess." He looked around him, saw the horse's snapped neck and distended tongue. "Sorry, horse. You had no say in this matter."

"You're alive down there. I see you, you buzzard!"

"Wish we could trade places," said Tucker loud enough for a mouse to hear him. Not much else he could do but wait Vollo out, get his feet under him, and head along the ravine. Bound to lead to the river. He might find a landmark, and tried to recall all of the trails and river bottom features Arliss had pointed out to him on their rides of the previous weeks. As the minutes ticked by, he found himself fighting sleep, his muscles stiffening, and knew that the longer he stayed put, the worse he would feel later, might in fact not be able to get up and going again.

There must have been a reason for Vollo not to shoot him before now. He'd have to risk it. With a heaving groan, Tucker used the horse's belly to push himself up. His searches of Rummler's battered body and the man's rifle boot had turned up no weapons, not even a knife. And in a way he was relieved. Another gun would lead to even more he'd have to carry—and standing up was proving to be all he could muster strength for.

Tucker managed to shuffle forward, dragging his right leg. With the aid of a long forked stick as a makeshift crutch, he was able to take some of the weight off his pained leg. But his left shoulder was shot up, so he ended up holding the crutch in front of him, each dragging step pulling a groan from him. He went on like that for a long time, what felt to him like hours.

Finally, ragged beyond anything he'd ever felt, he collapsed to the earth, felt the jamming dull pain of a rock in his midsection, and after a few minutes of rest, found he could not get up.

Oh, hell, thought Tucker. *Here I am, facedown in the dirt, shot, bleeding, busted who knows in how many places, wanted for a murder I didn't do, guilty of driving a man and his horse off the edge of a ravine, and I'm seeing black spots. For a day with such a promising start, this sure has become one of the worst in my life. And maybe the last.* He laughed, tasted the metal tang of blood in his mouth.

Of course it's one of the worst days in your life, should be the worst, you fool. The day you die can't ever be a good thing for too many folks.

But now that he faced it, once again, he realized he didn't want to die. He suddenly had something worth living for in his life again. People who relied on him. He liked the feeling. He also realized that in the end, neither he nor anyone else had a say in the matter.

The last thing he saw before the black spots all fused together like a swarm of blackbirds drawing closer and closer all the time was a single, massive black bird leaning down at him. *Couldn't be,* he told himself, fighting to keep his eyes from closing all the way. *Can't be ol' Scratch, can it? Will I see you finally, Rita and little Sam?*

He said their names and heard the Devil's own response. "I doubt you'll die. But only if I choose to help you." Then a sigh as if someone were about to be mighty put out for their efforts. He heard saddle leather creaking and boots grinding on rock. Something grabbed Tucker by the chin, hoisted his face upward.

Tucker worked at it, fluttered his eyes open, and saw a man dressed in black with a black horse just behind him—ol' Scratch himself. *Well, hell,* thought Tucker. *That's it, then.*

Chapter 30

Something tickled his nose—a fly? Feathers? What was that? Tucker reached up to swat at it and heard a laugh, light and soft.

"Rita? Rita, is that you?"

A warm hand touched his face, a thumb stroked his cheek, a cool cloth on his forehead.

"Didn't mean to be away so long . . . the Red . . . too high, took longer than I thought. . . ."

"Shhh, hush now. Rest easy. You're safe, safe and home."

"Good . . . it's good to be home."

Something tickled him again. What was that? He forced his eyes open and saw the hazy outline of fiery blond-red hair, curly, around a pretty face, eyes close to his, looking concerned? What for?

"You are not Rita," he said, his voice sounding small and weak to him.

The person said nothing in return, but whoever it was had been touching his face, pulling at his eyes. "The doctor said to keep a watch on your eyes, make sure the centers don't go too big or too small." The voice was a woman's, lower than Rita's, but echoing, as if coming to him through a long, hollowed-out tree.

"What?" His voice sounded small.

"Samuel, you were in a fall. Your head got knocked pretty hard."

It took him a few moments to figure out just what that meant. "Fall?"

"Yes, you should sleep now."

That sounded like a very good idea to him. Maybe when he woke up, this person would stop tickling his face, tell him where Rita was.

Out in the hallway, a low voice said, "I don't know what we're going to do, girl, but I tell you one thing, and I don't give a care what all that talk in town was about, we ain't gonna let no blamed strangers take over Klinkhorn, nor the Farraday spread. I got too much pride to let that happen. And we got ourselves a stranger to take care of! I feel responsible as hell for it. Shouldn't have left him alone. Some townsfolk likely come onto him. And now he's been all shot up, took a nasty knock to the head, looks to have been dragged up one side of a mountain and down another—"

"Arliss, this isn't helping. We have to figure out how to get to a lawyer, maybe, or a judge. Somebody who knows the law who can help us."

"Lawyer? Only one in these parts is Grissom, the very man we're having trouble from. I rue the day when we fall so low we gotta call on a common vulture to stoke our fires for us."

"Do you have a better idea?"

"Yes, I'll go back to town for the marshal. See what that sloppy sack of guts can do. Leastwise I can round up a few honest men—I daresay there are a couple three left in Klinkhorn—and get them on out here, make a stand. That's the old way. You got something worth protecting, you protect it with a good gun and an even better aim."

Tucker had drifted away on a layer of something soft, moss, maybe, or leaves, the smell of pine trees all around him. The thought popped free something plugging his memories, and they flooded in unbidden, as if a crack in a weak wall had given way. And he knew everything that had happened to him. One thing after another welled, bubbled, then boiled to the surface, right on up until the man in black grabbed his face and stared at him, a large black horse looking on.

Tucker jerked himself upright, pulling in a deep breath. "Emma! Arliss!"

Chapter 31

A bitter wind had kicked up along the trail, slicing into Emma's lungs and making her wish for spring even before winter started. It would snow soon, and despite the beauty it laid on the world, within another month, they would get snow that stayed throughout the long winter months, not as much as some places to the north and west of their valley, but there would be stretches when the temperatures dropped like a stone and the snow stacked up and it seemed as if all the world held its breath waiting for spring.

Pounding the trail back to Klinkhorn on Cinda, Emma mused for the tenth time that day that nothing was going right in her world, hadn't seemed to since Tucker came into their lives. No, that wasn't fair. It hadn't started because of him, just at the same time as he showed up.

And now there was a stranger coming into the valley as if he owned it, as though he owned their land. As if they hadn't had enough to worry about with Grissom. What had her uncle Payton been thinking in taking out a loan? Had she been so much a child that he felt as if he shouldn't share their money problems with her? She felt foolish for not having been trusted and angry with him for going against what her father had intended—no outside money, no loans, and especially not from someone like Grissom, a man for whom her father felt nothing but anger. Unless what Arliss guessed was true and her uncle had been keeping her father's wishes in mind.

By the time she made it to Klinkhorn, the massing gray clouds began a slow weep, not of rain but of snow. She had to get there soon to find the marshal. She knew that Arliss would be sore with her, but there was no other way. Marshal Hart was the only person in Klinkhorn she knew for certain who might be able to help them. She had to figure out some way to get that proof that the loan had been paid off. It had to exist, and since Grissom stood to gain the most out of it, she was sure he was the one who held it.

She crested the rise that led to the town's main street, paused there to take in the normally bustling scene and let Cinda blow. The town seemed quiet, maybe because of the fresh, heavy snow scudding down and building up a thick layer. Once it warmed, there would be mud and slush, but for now it was pretty.

She continued on down the slope. As she drew closer, she saw strangers, all men, hurrying in and out of the hotel. They were dressed not as so many of the local ranch hands or miners, but in thick wool trousers, heavy mackinaws, wool caps with earflaps, and most striking of all, they were strangers to her. They were also lugging all manner of strange tools and implements. They appeared to be residing in the hotel, and from the number of them, they had probably taken it over lock, stock, and barrel. They had to be the surveying crew Tucker had come across.

From across the street, Lord Tarleton, standing inside the hotel's lobby, caught sight of movement in the street out front. He parted a lace curtain and stared into the gray light of the street, the snow dropping steadily.

He could tell by their grumbling and the brusque slamming of equipment into the wagons that his men did not want to go out into the woods today. In a way, he did not blame them, but he had a sudden and different reason: the striking young woman who had just arrived in town, who even under concealment of a man's wool jacket could not hide her curves. She wore men's denims, work boots, leather gloves, and a broad-brimmed hat that looked not to be donned for show.

This creature, he realized, was the first Western woman he had seen who looked like what he'd long hoped one of their breed might resemble—a creature of obvious beauty who might also look stunning in a dress. One who also wasn't afraid to get her hands dirty and ride a horse as it was intended to be ridden—forked, as the cowboys said.

It took Halley, the hotelier of the establishment in which they were all encamped, three gentle inquiries before Tarleton heard him. "Oh, Halley, good. I have something I need you to do for me."

"Yes, sir, but if I may, I need—"

"Your needs are not important to me right now, Halley."

"Yes, sir. How may I help you?"

That's more like it, thought Tarleton, nodding. "I would very much like it if you were to arrange for the young woman who just entered the marshal's office to meet me here at the dining room at one p.m."

"Funny you should mention her, sir. She's the one who now owns all the land you and the boys are after."

Tarleton stared for long moments between the falling snowflakes at the spot where the girl had been, and a slow smile spread across his face. This was going to be a lovely day after all.

"Gentlemen," he said to the men gathered about him in the lobby, "I thank you for your attention to the gear, but I will now ask you to go on without me. Something has come up that requires my attention here in town. I believe you should expect the best but prepare for the worst where the weather is concerned. And since it is a foul day and we are getting off to a later start because you have all been dragging your feet, you will need to count on spending the night in camp. I will see you all back here tomorrow evening. Stick with my plans. I expect that last section to be surveyed by the end of the week."

The grumbling had no effect on him, but he heard every bit of it and made a mental notation of each man who uttered a whining phrase. These were largely city men who preferred surveying streets or working for the railroad in warm weather and in flat places, unimaginative men who cared little for challenge. These would not be men who would accompany him and his crew on the first wealth-proving forays into the deeper forests far beyond the reach of town. But for a first and most fruitful reconnoitering trip, they were proving adequate.

The big marshal, as usual, was seated behind his desk, sipping a tin cup of coffee.

"Sorry to barge in like this, Marshal."

"Howdy, Emma." He slumped back in his chair, refolded his hands on his paunchy belly.

For the first time, Emma noticed the man looked more old and fat than big and strapping as he had her entire lifetime.

"You want a cup of coffee?"

It sounded to Emma like an afterthought. "No, thanks, Marshal. I do need help, though."

"What's new there?" he mumbled, leaning forward again over a stack of dodgers. He nodded toward the yellowed papers. "Been looking through these, trying to find a match to that killer I let you escape with."

"Something wrong, Marshal? I didn't mean to cause you grief."

"Well, you just keep on doing that just the same, don't you, Emma Farraday?" He stood and hiked up his trousers.

"I'll come back later, Marshal. I just remembered I have to talk with Louisa."

"Yeah, well, you just do that. I got a pile of things to attend to, you know. Don't always need to go bailing out a Farraday every time a fart's fired across your bow."

She left the office and shut the door. *Well,* she thought. *If that doesn't beat all.* That was the first time he'd ever talked to her like this, and the odd thing was, she wasn't so sure she didn't deserve it. She saw recent events through his eyes and it seemed to her she had indeed taken advantage of him and of the fact that he had at one time been close friends with her father and uncle.

Arliss had never paid him a kind word, but had been cautious about making slanting remarks about the marshal around her while she was growing up. But now that she thought on it, Uncle Payton hadn't exactly been friendly with the marshal in recent years the way he used to be back when her daddy had been alive.

She shucked a glove and dug a hand in her trouser pocket, felt a few coins. Enough for a cup of coffee, maybe a bite of breakfast at Mae's.

She worked her way out of her sodden wool mackinaw and shook a few more beads of water off her hat. By the time she had her hands curled around a cup of coffee, a shadow had fallen across her table by the window.

She looked up to see a handsome, thin man standing before her table. He wore a dandified chin beard, a curly mustache, and wavy blond hair nearly touching his shoulders. He was smiling down at her. She noticed that his clothes were of a fine quality, with colors that matched, and his overcoat looked soft and new, not like her patched wool check coat that had been her father's when he was a young man. He'd always said that a wool garment never really wore out, just got more comfortable and familiar.

The man stood smiling at her, his eyes narrowed slightly, his head tipped to the side. On him it almost looked cute. Or maybe he was trying to look that way. Then it occurred to her that he was probably the rich stranger with the surveying crew Samuel had met in the woods. The thought annoyed her, but she had to find out what he wanted. "What in the hell do you want?"

As soon as she said it, she heard Arliss in her ear, saying something about never catching a man because she was too crass, too much like a boy herself in so many ways. She bit back a sigh and kept her face stony. She was steamed about the ranch, the sour meeting with the marshal, and now with this wealthy stranger, staring like a man gone dumb, it felt annoying of a sudden.

"Pardon me, ma'am. Allow me to introduce myself." He bowed before her table, though it looked much like a curtsy and she wished he would stop it. The eatery was fairly full and most everyone in there had stopped chatting when he came in. She had a good idea who he was, and he was making a right fool of himself.

"What do you want?" Again, it sounded as if she were about to bite his head off, so she tried again. "I mean, what . . . do you want?" Still didn't sound right. Hell, she just wanted her steak and eggs and then she supposed she'd head on back home. This was turning out to be a headache of a trip. Should have just stayed at the ranch and tried to come up with a plan with Arliss and Tucker that didn't involve shooting everyone in town whom Arliss suspected of trying to get the ranch.

"My dear lady," he said. "I should like to buy you breakfast, or at least a cup of coffee."

She narrowed her eyes. "Why?" *Here it comes,* she thought. This man was looking to her as if he wanted something that maybe she didn't want to give—the Farraday land, for one thing. "What's your game?"

He ran a hand through his long hair, pulled it off his forehead. "No game, ma'am, I assure you. But if I may say so, you have captured my heart and I should like the opportunity to revel in my captivity, or at least the chance to free myself from your grasp."

As soon as he started in with his patter, Emma guessed he was a shallow dandy with something on his mind that was a whole lot different from what she had in mind, namely to have a meal and think about how she might get out from under Grissom's thumb.

The man pulled out the other chair at the little table and said, "May I?"

"Looks like you already made that decision," she said. He stood there, so she waved a hand at the chair. "Be my guest."

"Thank you, ma'am."

"Enough with the 'ma'am' business. I'm Emma Farraday." She held out her hand, aware for the first time as he shook it that his hand was soft and pink and hers was rough, callused, and her grip was firmer than his. He tried too late to match hers, all the while seeming to measure her with his eyes.

"And you are the very person I was looking for on this fine day." He gestured toward the window at the snow piling up.

There it is, she thought. *Now let's see how he thinks he has the right to traipse all over Farraday land.* She sipped her coffee and kept her mouth shut for the time being. Soon the waitress brought her food, a still-sizzling steak, two eggs, and thick-sliced potatoes with onions laid on top. She caught his glance. "You hungry, uh . . . I didn't catch your name."

"I am Tarleton, Lord Tarleton."

"Lord?" she said. "That a family name or a title?"

He laughed, a sound not unpleasant to her, and she decided as she sliced into the steak that he was not only handsome, but maybe had kind eyes too.

"It is indeed a title. I am English."

"Yep, I knew that much." She nodded, caught his fleeting look of surprise. "I can read and even walk on my own too."

"Oh, pardon me, ma'am, eh, Emma, but I was not expect-

ing so forward a personage in such a . . . pretty package. I am
in a peculiar situation, Emma." He leaned closer to her over
the table, close enough that she leaned back.

"I won't bite, Emma, I assure you. But you see, I have a
particularly large business plan in the offing and it seems that
you, dear Emma, play a large role in that plan. And with each
second that passes, I am increasingly convinced that your
role should be even more . . . shall we say, substantial?"

Emma chewed more steak, washed it down with coffee. "I
have to say, Tarleton, that I have no idea at all what you are
on about, but I will grant you that I've never heard anyone—
even Arliss—talk in circles quite like you. It's impressive."

"I appreciate your sarcasm, and it is well earned on my
part. Perhaps, after your repast, I might convince you to give
me a few minutes of your time at my office? I am set up at
the hotel, for the time being." He glanced around him and
continuing in his quiet tone said, "Without the unfortunate
number of curious ears, I will be better able to explain what
it is I have in mind."

"The hotel?" Emma stood, her chair squawking backward
on the scrubbed pine floor. "What do you take me for,
dandy?" She wasn't sure which to do first, drive knuckles
into his mustache or grab her coat. She settled for the coat
and hat.

He stood and smiled at her. "No, no, no, Miss Farraday, you
mistake me. My associates will be there as well. I have a business proposition I would like your, shall we say, advice on."

She left money on the table, gave him one more hard look,
then headed to the door, roughly brushing by him. She listened for the sound of only her boots on the sidewalk, but
heard another set behind her. The door clunked shut and she
knew without looking that all eyes in the place were on her
and the fool dandy who'd insulted her in there. She was
thankful that she had her hair down in a loose ponytail
enough that it covered her red ears. How dared he?

"Miss Farraday, please wait."

They were past the diner windows now and she turned on him, a gloved hand outstretched, a finger pointing. "No, sir, you just wait. I have about had enough of you. I was hoping to have a decent meal in quiet in there when you came in and ruined it for me. Not like I have the money to go chucking around. When I spend money on food you can be darned sure that I intend to eat it because I am hungry. It ain't for show."

"Miss Farraday, please." He tried to put a hand around her shoulder, guide her down the sidewalk beside him.

She shook out of it. "Keep your hand to yourself, mister."

"I am heartily sorry. Perhaps you will allow me to make up for it by buying your meal. After all, I believe that after I have explained what I need to talk with you about, you will want to hear more of what I have to say."

"I don't want anyone else's money and I ain't interested in what you have to say." She stomped down the sidewalk and he stayed put. *Good,* she thought, *at least I got rid of him.* Cute he might be, but he was more annoying than anyone else she'd ever met.

"Not even if I were to tell you that I own every acre of the Farraday spread?"

She stopped, her stomach knotting and coiling like a tangle of snaky rope. She'd half hoped he was just a dreamer, someone trying not to get caught doing something on someone else's land.

"And that there is a way for you to have the entire thing without ever having to resort to expensive, and ultimately doomed-to-fail, litigation."

She turned on him, too filled with confusion and fear and rage all at once, to know what else to do. He regarded her with that mix of fascination and superiority that she had seen in the diner.

She nodded and said through tight-set teeth, "I don't know

what your game is, but I guess I'd better listen to what you have to say."

"Excellent, Miss Farraday. That is all I ask, all I ask." He rubbed his hands together vigorously. "This way please. To the hotel. I will see to it that sufficient refreshment is brought in so that we might continue to dine in peace and I won't feel so guilty about spoiling your meal." He swept another low bow and preceded her to the hotel.

She was sure that the third floor of the hotel probably hadn't ever had a massive old desk up there in one room, but there it was, just the same.

"Excellent, excellent. Now, Miss Farraday, do you like tea?"

"I've had it, if that's what you're asking. But no, I'd prefer coffee. And I'll need you to get this dog-and-pony show on the road because I have to get back to my ranch before light fails us."

"Oh, Miss Farraday, I cherish your cut-to-the-chase charm. But I assure you, once you have heard what I have to offer, you will be in no hurry to go anywhere."

Emma looked around the room, anywhere but at him.

"I see you admiring the furnishings. Do you like it?" He spun slowly, his arms raised, himself admiring the furnishings as if seeing them for the first time. "I have to admit I've only been here a short time but already I have made ample improvements to this building."

"How's that?" she said, not sure what to think of the turn this day had taken.

"Why, Miss Farraday. Surely you know I bought the hotel. No? Well, it's true. And soon I expect I'll own much of, if not all of, the town of Klinkhorn. And then I'll rename it Tarleton. Or perhaps Emmaville, or something equally quaint but fitting."

"You are doing it again."

"What's that?"

"Talking in circles."

He laughed, and despite the fact that she couldn't get a straight answer from him, she liked the sound of his laughter. He seemed to be full of himself, but also handsome, rich, and not afraid to bandy words with her. But none of that mattered when she thought of what he'd said in the street. She cursed herself for letting her guard down, even momentarily. "Only thing I want from you is to know just how it is you think you own the Farraday spread."

"Oh, that's simple. I acquired the town's entire debt from Mr. Bentley Grissom. He held the lien on your place."

"I don't believe you." But her face was red as a struck thumb—she just knew it.

"Oh, my dear, finance and money are not something I take lightly, and neither should anyone else. Fortunately, other people do, and that's where people like me can come in and widen the rift, so to speak. I drive a wedge between people's assumptions and their mistakes and exploit the rift enough that a profit flourishes. It happens every time."

As he spoke he moved to his desk, unlocked a drawer, and pulled out a thick wad of papers wrapped in a leather portfolio. He thumbed through them, narrowing his eyes, making small noises that sounded like "No, no, not that, not that." And then, "Aha! Here it is, the very loan agreement signed by one Payton Farraday. I believe that was a relation of yours . . . father or uncle perhaps? Surely not a . . . husband?"

She scowled at him and rushed the desk, tried to snatch the paper from him. He pulled it back, just out of her reach, but he held the sides and allowed her to read it. It all seemed real and legitimate, and it bore her uncle's signature. "But he . . . I've since learned that he paid off that loan. It's been paid, I'm telling you."

"Oh, excellent, then. Well, not for me, naturally, because as you see I am not in the business of buying useless paper.

The world of high finance generates enough of that in a day's time. But if it is, as you say, paid off, then all we need to make this legal is the very paper issued by the bank saying that it has been paid in full, countersigned by the lending institution, in this case Mr. Grissom's fine establishment. Oh!" He held a hand to his mouth. "I mean that would be my establishment." He winked. "I bought the bank too. Can't help myself. I see something with promise and I have to have it."

She felt as if someone had punched her hard in the gut. Like the first time she'd fallen off a horse when she was just a kid. "What did you say?" She hated the smallness of her voice.

"It's true, my dear. But please, sit down, make yourself comfortable. It's not as dire as all that. My only aim is to preserve this town as it is, along with its people, who are the very lifeblood of it. I also want to encourage growth and industry."

"And what industry are you in, Mr. Tarleton?"

"Lord, I insist. And there are very few things I insist on." His face had taken on a hard look, the first time she'd seen it since meeting him earlier. "Miss Farraday, since the day is advancing, and since the daylight will fail us sooner than later, I would like to take a page from your book, unaccustomed as I am in reading such a fine manuscript, and try to cut to the chase, as it were."

She stared at him, more confused than ever. "What?"

He knelt before her, proffered a hand, and she hesitated, but finally put her hand on his, as if to shake it. He turned it sideways, and then he rested his other hand on hers.

"Miss Farraday, I was born into a world of wealth, power, prestige, and position. All in England. I became enamored with the West of America long ago, and its hold on me was such that when I came of age, I vowed to see it. I set sail for America years ago and have been here since.

"And in that time I have, because I was also blessed with

my father's business savvy, been able to parlay my ample family fortunes into a personal fortune that would stagger the United States government. But I am no charity. I have been all over the West, seen many people, places, things, events, and experienced a good many hardships too."

He paused, smiled at her. "I have seen loveliness both natural and man-made that would make the mightiest maharajah weep, but never had I seen a lovelier town than Klinkhorn, nor one so positioned on the cusp of greatness owing to its location amid a mighty deposit of such vast potential. It is far greater than the idealized frontier town of my fantasy youth as I lay in my four-poster in the old castle pile in Buckinghamshire, reading my months-old Buntline dime novels."

He nearly rose then, pulling on her hand in his frenzy. "And the lumber potential! How vast it is! It's as close to perfection as a man with such vision as I could have hoped for. And then when I saw you this morning, I became instantly aware that you, dear Emma Farraday, were the missing piece to this, the most intricate and fulfilling of life's puzzles."

Emma tried to pull her hand away, suspecting what he was leading up to and not at all sure what to do or say. But he gripped her hand tight and his smile was so sincere, she could do nothing but stare into those deep ice blue eyes and listen to him. He did have a way with words.

"If what I am leading up to isn't apparent yet, I will once again try—and no doubt fail—to cut to the chase." He smiled. "Emma, I am prepared to offer to you the world, to travel across oceans, to the Far East, throughout Europe, Russia, anywhere you desire to go. The finest in jewels, furs, the grandest of mansions, the most decadent of private rail cars, the finest of Thoroughbred horses, the best foods, caviars, the rarest of fish and fowl, anything that money can buy—and a good many things it cannot. And last but by no means least, I am prepared to give to you, by way of my sincere intention, right now and with but one string attached, the free and clear deed and title to your family's ranch, debt free forever and a day, with enough money to keep it self-sustaining in high style for lifetimes to come."

It took Emma long minutes of staring at him, at the room, at the hand that she'd finally pulled away from his, the hand she was sure one of the fingers of which would be involved with his offer, before she finally worked up enough courage to ask the question: "In exchange for what . . . Lord Tarleton?"

He smiled again, smoothed his lapels, and ran a hand through his hair. "I should think, my dear, that would be the most obvious of answers. But I will oblige you, as I know you are a woman of straightforward means. I am asking for your hand in marriage, my dearest Emma."

Considering all his talk, she had been expecting it, but it came as a shock to hear, a shock that made her entire body feel as if it were quivering. It must have been obvious because he jumped to his feet and poured her a glass of water.

"My dear, your face has positively gone white. Whiter than the snow falling outside. You should drink this. I daresay this has come as a shock, but I had hoped it would have been a pleasant one."

She sipped the water, then said, "Oh, it's a shock, Mr. . . . uh . . . Lord Tarleton. I don't quite know what to think just yet." She stood. "I have to go."

"Of course, of course, my dear. But do keep in mind that it would be in your best interests to accept my charitable proposition. I am a wealthy and important man and you would be able to significantly raise your social standing. You would also be able to keep your beloved ranch, admittedly with minor alterations. But it would be yours to do with mostly as you see fit. And your loved ones too—all well and whole and taken care of forever, living in the lap of luxury. Otherwise all will be lost to you, to them, to everyone in this town. For when I say a thing, it comes to pass. You see?"

She walked on numb legs to the door, then turned back with her hand on the knob. "You don't even know me."

He smiled again. "I don't need to, my dear. I can tell just by looking at you that you are all that I want."

"What about what I want out of life?"

He smiled, shook his head. "Oh, but you are a clever thing. I daresay we shall be most happy together."

She turned from him, closed the door behind her, and barely noticed the two men standing to either side of the door, tall men in black bristling with cross-draw guns. But she did notice them and cut wide around them. They nodded to her, touched their hat brims as she passed. She walked down the stairs and headed out through the lobby and into the snow, feeling colder than she could ever remember feeling, inside and out, in her entire life.

Chapter 32

"It's about time you showed yourself! We been worried sick here, holdin' down the fort whilst you go off gallivantin', having yourself a time in town—that is where you was at, wasn't it?" Arliss peered at Emma a long moment, leaned in close, and she could tell he was sniffing her breath, trying to determine if she'd been on one of those toots that he said all the Farradays were most apt to indulge in.

"Arliss, if you spent half the time worrying about what you were supposed to be doing and the other half ignoring the stuff you did that was just plain annoying to others, you'd be better off." She tried to make this sound festive and light, but her heart wasn't in it.

"Emma?" Arliss knew her too well. He held her shoulders and she noticed for the first time that she might be a pinch taller than him. Maybe she really was all grown-up. Maybe this was all there was to it, and that all she could hope for was to marry someone who wouldn't mistreat her. Maybe life was just a long, dark tunnel with a few brief periods of happiness separated by long times of tolerance, of acceptance of the way things had to be because the people with power and money wanted it that way.

"Girly . . ."

She hugged Arliss, then wrapped her arms tight around

his skinny neck and buried her face in his gray hair and his scruffy, whiskery face and coat collar, which smelled of old man and horses and sweat and wood smoke, and she wished things could be the way they were just two short years before when they were all there and safe from the world. She'd never known her mother, but felt somehow as if she knew her from the way her father and Uncle Payton had talked of her. Those had been good times, happy times when she thought that none of it would ever change.

Finally she stepped back from Arliss and rubbed her thumb and knuckles into her eyes. He pulled out an old soiled bandanna from his pocket and she wiped her eyes. Only around Arliss would she consider crying. She was grateful that he didn't ask her what was wrong. He knew her well enough to know that she'd come out with it eventually. And she did.

"I met that man, the stranger Samuel mentioned. The English fella."

Arliss squared off, his bony knuckles hanging at his side. "He didn't hurt you, did he?"

"No," she said, smiling slightly at his bold, selfless attitude. "He just asked me to marry him."

If the situation hadn't been so peculiar and frightening all at once to her, Emma knew she would have collapsed to the stable floor in laughter. It was too much, though, to take in, once she heard herself voice the words. And she knew she was in trouble, because saying the words out loud didn't make her feel happy; they made her tighten inside.

"He did what?"

The voice from behind her made Emma spin.

Samuel Tucker stood, swaying slightly, his head bandaged, his shoulder padded. His wounds had leaked, stained the cotton batting a reddish black, but his color was better. He wore no shirt, but his torso, still thin, had muscled and had begun filling out. His eyes stared at her, searching hers for more information. Other than Arliss's unconditional hug, it was Tucker's look of concerned anger on this cold, lonely day that made Emma feel as if she might just live through this hell that her life had become.

Chapter 33

"Just how in the hell, I ask you, Vollo, did we come to this pretty pass?" Bentley Grissom's fat head wobbled as he peered through his thick-lidded eyes like a hog in the sun on a close summer day. He looked slowly side to side. It appeared that his last remaining henchman had also deserted him. Then he heard a light snoring coming from somewhere beyond the desk.

"There that buzzard is. Sleeping and snoring his way through the day—right here in my office!"

Then the dark humor of what he'd said made him chuckle. This was no longer his office, no longer his bar, no longer his town. He slammed a pink fist to the desktop, and gritted his teeth at the pain.

From the floor in front of the desk, Vollo coughed and gagged. "Wha . . . what?"

"Get up, you sorry excuse for a Mexican. I have need of you and you are sleeping the day away."

The man sat up slowly, his hands shielding his eyes. "I don't work for you no more. We may be drinking buddies, but you and your bad plans, they always get us hurt or killed." His damaged tongue made his words sound as though they were forced through cotton batting.

"You may definitely have been part of one, but most assuredly not of the other."

"What?"

Grissom rolled his eyes, but even that simple act induced a twinge of shooting pain deep in his temple. "Never mind. Right now, if you ever want to eat again, you had better help me clean up this office."

"What's the use, boss? You ain't got no more money than I do. Plus, we don't have Rummler no more."

"It is true we don't have the services of that genetic giant known as Rummler, but we do have you. Oh, and my not so diminutive mental skills."

"I ain't so stupid that I don't know when you're poking the fun, eh? But tell me, that foreigner fella with the fancy name and all the men, he took everything from you in exchange for what, huh?"

"Vollo, I am well aware that I may have made a slightly less than prudent business decision, but it was the only avenue left open to me. I stand to gain forty percent of all the guaranteed substantial takings from the exploitation of this foul little town. And all I had to do was sign over at the outset my holdings here."

He shrugged. "It was the only way to keep this a fair fight, as they say. Otherwise, Tarleton, who has ample experience dismantling such towns, I can assure you, could have excluded me altogether. The advantage of what I have to offer him is that I was sort of an advance team, albeit unwitting, to the area. In said role, I set up the infrastructure that will, in turn, support the superstructure of his vast logging operation that will, in turn, transform this entire region of the country into the nexus of a massive logging empire."

Grissom swallowed. Why, he could swear his headache from Vollo's cheap whiskey had almost vanished. Talking through his woes always seemed to help.

"You talk too much, boss." Vollo belched and staggered to the doorway that led to the back alley, leaned there a moment before whipping open the door and urinating off the back steps into the dirt.

"Vollo! I may not at present own this establishment, but that doesn't mean I don't run the establishment for Lord Tarleton. And as the manager, I must insist that you refrain from urinating right where we have to walk."

"Huh? 'Kay, boss. But hey, what about Rummler?"

"What about him, Vollo? My gosh, man, he's dead. You said so yourself."

"He is. I went out and found him the next day, but I didn't find that other one, that killer of Farraday."

"You mean you went back to the scene?"

"Sure, I wanted to bury Rummler, thought I might piss on the body of that other one. But he was one hard fella to track down. Couldn't find hide nor hair of him."

Grissom waved away the comment. "I seriously don't think we need concern ourselves any longer with the where-abouts of the man. No doubt he crawled off to die in the leaves somewhere. Now, come here and lend a hand. I don't want last night's drunken sendoff of Rummler to be indicative to Tarleton of how I intend to run affairs here."

"Oh, don't worry about that, Mr. Grissom."

Grissom looked toward the door to see it opened wide and Lord Tarleton staring at him, arms crossed and a smile on his face.

"How long have you been there, sir?"

"Long enough to know that you are perhaps operating under a delusion. You seem to think that you will somehow be my chief of operations here in Klinkhorn, and truth be told, I have had need of someone to assist with overseeing such affairs, should the need arise. But your assumption that you will be that person leads me to question the very nature of our dealings together."

"I'm afraid I don't quite understand, Lord Tarleton. We have an agreement. A legal, binding agreement."

"Technically, Bentley Grissom, there is no 'we.' You have

nothing. I have everything, and never the twain shall meet, as they say."

"What? What is this?" Grissom swung his gaze from Tarleton to Vollo.

Grissom retreated behind the desk. "No, no!" he shouted. "I will not let you do this, Tarleton." He pulled in a deep breath. "Our agreement is null and void, sir. Consider our contract invalid."

"That suits me just fine, Mr. Grissom." Tarleton nodded to his two cohorts. "I believe we can now proceed, gentlemen. Escort this man off my premises. In fact, you'd do well to escort him and . . . that out of town limits." He nodded toward Vollo, whose grimy hands had paused in buttoning his trouser fly. He stood looking at the strange exchange with a look of confusion on his face, even as Tarleton's two black-clad cohorts advanced on him.

Grissom clawed at the loop handle of his top desk drawer and scrabbled in there for the one thing he hoped might help ease the tension in the room, back it off a bit so he could think. His pudgy hand closed around the handle of his derringer. Ever since he'd hired Vollo and Rummler, he'd gradually taken to carrying that in a trouser pocket, but always had a vision of the thing going off somehow and shooting himself in the beans. So he'd begun locking it in the drawer, except for long walks about town. And then came the day when he left it in the drawer altogether.

Had he even loaded it? Didn't matter now. He snatched up the two-shot gun and peeled back the hammer. And there sat a shell—loaded.

"Now, then, Tarleton."

"It is 'Lord' Tarleton. How many times must I tell you, Grissom? And put the gun away. Instead of having you banned from my town, I could have you jailed. How would you like that?"

"Not on your life, Tarleton. How dare you talk to me that way? I built this town. When I got here it was little more than a dry cracker with a handful of spent miners and a few ranchers looking to trade goods on the weekends. Now look at it!" He waved the derringer around his head.

"And I appreciate it, Grissom. But your time has passed here. You need to decide right now, sir, if you intend to leave quietly or stay awhile longer—as a guest in one of Marshal Hart's commodious cells."

Grissom felt that snaky vein on the side of his forehead begin to pulse and throb as he raised the derringer. From behind the smiling Lord Tarleton, an arm clad in black, its hand sheathed in a black leather glove, raised a silver long-barreled pistol, hammer cocked all the way back, and leveled it on Grissom.

Grissom traced the sight line back to a partially shadowed face, two cold eyes glinting. The same thing extended on the other side of the English dandy.

It seemed no one counted on Vollo, who they all assumed was still fumbling with his fly buttons. What he was fumbling with was his pistol. He backed to the open alley door, and as he cranked off a shot, Grissom grunted forward toward the same doorway.

Vollo's shot shattered the wooden doorframe to the right of Tarleton's head, pocking his face with spiny splinters that drew immediate bloody tears running down his face, spattering his spotless clothes with blood. The Englishman whipped sideways, screaming, and slammed into one of his hirelings, sending the man's shot scudding into the floor.

It was all the extra time Grissom needed to force his portly frame through the alley door. He and Vollo scrambled to make it out of the alley and to the livery as fast as they were able. People in the street stayed frozen in place. This was a sight to see: Bentley Grissom, red-faced and running, panting as if air were soon going to be in short supply.

"Out of my way, damn you!" He pushed at them, forcing his bulk past, elbowing and screaming between huffs and puffs.

"Boss, they ain't coming. They ain't following!" Vollo had stopped running, which itself had not been much of a chore. He barely had to lope to keep up with his boss, looking behind them for sign of a tail.

"Where did they go?"

"Getting their boss fixed, I reckon."

"I fear, Vollo, that I have somehow made an enemy of the one man I had been counting on to make me wealthy."

"Maybe you weren't never meant to be no rich man, boss."

The back of Grissom's fat hand lashed out and caught Vollo square in the mouth, splitting a barely healed lip and snapping his head back on its stem. Immediate anger flared in the Mexican's eyes like a struck match. His own claw-like hand snatched Grissom's by the wrist, bent it downward hard. "You do that again, boss, and it will be the last time—you get me?"

The fat man nodded. "Yeah, yeah, Vollo. I—"

"We best get off the street, boss." Vollo licked his lip, tasted blood. "Can you ride?"

"Been a while," said Grissom, numb from the speed of everything that had happened in the last few minutes.

As they hustled down the end of the street to the livery, Grissom said, "They'll be coming any second, I can tell. Those men in black, I never trusted them from the start. They'll come for me and shoot me, sure as day follows night."

"Nah, they don't want you, boss."

"What? Of course they do." They slipped into the side door of the dark stable.

"No, they don't neither, boss. What they want is you to be gone. You are a headache, but it don't sound like you got much to stand on. You signed away your rights to everything here. Last thing they can take is your life. Don't give it up cheap, boss."

"How did you get so smart, Vollo?"

"Never said I wasn't. That was you . . . and Rummler. Me, I just figure that if there's someone else around smart enough to make the big decisions, why should I have to scratch my thinker, you know?"

"So you're saying that I'm not smart enough to make the big decisions."

"Well, boss, you ain't been doing so good with it lately. Now, let's get out of town, think about things. Might be we can come up with a plan to take back what is yours. Course, I won't be doing this for nothing, boss. You got me?"

In the dark of the livery barn, Bentley Grissom stared into the eyes of his newest partner and did his best to not shoot the grimy man in the gut with his little derringer.

Chapter 34

Arliss and Tucker did their best to keep Emma occupied and close by them in the days following her lousy announcement, but it became apparent that she'd not let it go on that way forever. She wasn't much use to them, her mind elsewhere.

"I'm worried about her, boy. She ain't right. That English buzzard is going to pay for this." Arliss turned from the doorway of the barn and headed for the tack room.

"Where you going, Arliss?"

The old man spun on him, came at the younger man with a finger poised. "I'm going off to do what you appear to be too stupid or too scared to take care of."

"Just what's that supposed to mean?"

"Just what I said." The old man headed once more into the tack room.

Tucker followed him. "You can't just say something like that and then leave, Arliss. I'm as concerned about her as you are, maybe more. I . . ."

"There," said Arliss, smiling. "You was about to say it. Go ahead and admit it: you feel something powerful for that girl. I may be old and bent by my rheumatics, but I ain't stupid, nor blind, nor deaf neither."

"What am I supposed to say to her? She's a woman, a beautiful woman." Tucker toed the straw on the stable floor. "But I'm . . . well, you know what I am, what I have, where

I'm headed. I'm wanted by the law. Everyone thinks I killed her uncle, including you and her. Hell, I'm surprised when I wake up alive. Figure, from your point of view at least, that I've earned a bit of retribution."

Arliss slammed the harness down on the workbench and glared at Tucker. "If that don't beat all! I say, if that don't beat all! You think we'd honestly let someone we thought killed my best friend in the world and Emma's only and last living blood kin on the earth—any that mattered anyway—that we'd let him live under this here roof? You're dumber than I thought. I knew we'd be having an uphill battle with you, being a Texan and all, but I thought you might be the pick of that Texican litter, thought you might be the one sharp knife in that drawer full of spoons. But I guess I was proved wrong once again." He turned away, sputtering.

Tucker couldn't help smiling.

"Gets to be a man with a superior intellect such as myself ought not to get himself all built up, get so he believes someday somewhere someone might just prove him wrong. But no, I guess being so smart and all, I am doomed to a lifetime of disappointment."

"So you're saying that neither of you thinks I'm a killer."

"Any plainer, boy, and you'd risk it smacking you in the head. Which is what I'm about to do. And if you're fixing to talk with Emma, try to convince her to keep from making a wrong decision, for all the wrong reasons, you best get at it." Arliss turned away again, then came right back up to Tucker with that finger poised. "But you listen good. Anytime I see her crying and it ain't because she stubbed a toe, I'll be on you like flies on a cowpat. You hear me, you Texas waddy?"

Tucker nodded at Arliss, trying to keep from smiling. But it was too much for him and the old man just walked away, muttering about how foolish everyone was acting.

"Good," said Tucker. "Then I'm going to see to that busted fence in the south heifer pasture."

"But I thought you was going to go see Emma!" Arliss stared at Tucker as if he had swallowed a bee.

"All in good time, Arliss."

Outside the back door of the barn, Emma heard the whole conversation and headed back to the house. Her smile slowly faded as she recalled that the things she was thinking about could never be. There wasn't enough time, money, or people to stop the mad Englishman from taking everything he wanted—herself included. And it seemed that even Samuel Tucker, a man she'd grown fond of, didn't sound to her as if he wanted to even talk with her.

He's just playing us along, she told herself. *Healing up until he can move on.* She climbed the front steps to the house, poked the coals in the cookstove. But she knew she was kidding herself. She knew the way Tucker watched her when he thought she was busy. But it was absurd. The man was a drunk. . . . So why was she trying to lie to herself now? She slammed the top on the woodstove. What did she want?

"Emma."

She turned to see Samuel Tucker standing inside the door.

"Emma, I need to talk with you."

"I thought you were going to the south heifer pasture. . . ." She bit off the words, but too late. Now he'd know she'd been listening in on them.

He walked up to her and stood before her. A single tear slid down between her nose and cheek. She gritted her teeth, didn't dare wipe it away. She hated crying.

"So you know what I said to Arliss."

She nodded, didn't look up. He dabbed the tear, then raised her chin. They looked at each other a moment. Then he kissed her, long and slow. She put her hands on his chest and leaned against him.

They stood that way for a while in the silent kitchen, the stove's coals slowly dying out, the cold of the waning day overtaking the room. "I don't know what to do," she said finally, in a quiet voice.

"Marry me, Emma. Say you'll have me and the rest won't matter."

She pulled back, looked at him. That was not what she had expected. Two such offers in as many days. "I always assumed growing up that I'd never marry, that I'd live out my days on this ranch, the Farraday spread as everyone calls it. Managing the herds, working alongside my father and uncle and Arliss as they grew old. But all that began to change two years ago, less than a year after Grissom came to town."

"I don't want to go to Texas. You can't stay here. Arliss won't leave."

"Neither will I," she said, pushing away from him.

"What? But there's no way you can stay. We can't beat him, Emma. There's no way I can think of to best that man. He has money, power, armed men, the town's support, in part because he's getting rid of Grissom. From what you said, he probably owns Marshal Hart too."

"A couple of days ago I'd have defended the marshal, but now I'm not so sure. I think you're maybe right."

"So you agree, there's no way to beat Tarleton."

"Can't beat 'em . . ."

"Emma." He grabbed her by the shoulders and pulled her close, stared into her eyes. They were like sparks and he wanted to kiss her again, but he had to get this thing straight, settled in his mind once and for all. "Emma." He felt her breath on his face. Then she pulled away and he let her.

"You've decided, then."

She said nothing, just stood at the long scarred surface of the dry sink, the chopping board, running her callused fingers along its smooth, work-worn surface.

Tucker watched her for a few moments more, hoping there might be something he could say, but nothing came to him. He'd said it all and now felt hollow, gutted by a dull, ice-cold knife.

Chapter 35

"You have to help me, Granville."

"Grissom?" Marshal Hart rubbed a big hand through his bristly gray-black hair. "What in the hell are you doing here? You know what time it is?"

"I am well aware of the time, Marshal. I own a pocket watch."

"Probably not anymore." A voice from the dark behind Grissom snickered.

The marshal leaned out his doorframe, peered into the dark. "That Vollo, the worm?"

The little grungy man stepped forward, pushing Grissom out of the way. "Watch what you say, Mr. Law Dog. I want to know what you gonna do about that man who killed Rummler—you know, the killer you let go from your jail."

The big marshal grabbed a handful of soiled shirt, chest hair, and wooden neck beads and dragged the little man in close, their nose tips almost touching. "I'll tell you what I'm doing about it—I ain't arrested you for the murders of Rummler and Farraday yet. Count yourself lucky if that don't change in the next five seconds."

Grissom watched as the little man opened his mouth to speak, then closed it again, too frightened by the marshal's narrowed eyes and low, husky growl to say anything. Not wanting to risk annoying the marshal any further, especially not when he needed a favor, Grissom also kept his mouth shut.

The marshal let go of Vollo's shirt and shoved him backward. Vollo stumbled to the edge of the small porch and teetered there on the first step, until he grabbed a porch rail and stood still.

"Now, what's this about me having to help you, Grissom?"

"Yes, well, it occurred to me that I have done a good many people in this community a good many favors over the years, and now that I find myself in a bit of, shall we say, a squeeze, I think it's time I call in a few well-earned favors."

"Ain't the way I heard it," said the marshal, arms folded over his long-handles, his chest hair crawling out the top. "Squeeze, I mean. I heard you are in something a mite more than a squeeze, Grissom. Heard you were all but done in this town. Heard that you assaulted Lord Tarleton, forced his two bodyguards to put innocent people in this town in mortal danger by firing at you in defense of their employer. A man who, I might add, has done more for this town in driving out a snake like you and that worm there than anything you have done in your nearly three years in Klinkhorn."

"But . . . what do you mean, Granville? We have an agreement, Marshal. An understanding. You wouldn't want me to let certain people know of a certain killing or two that you were behind, now, would you?"

The big marshal laughed a low, deep sound, cold and without mirth, but it fit his mood. His mouth beneath his ample mustache was the only thing on his face to smile. His eyes were unmoving points of black light. "I ain't afraid of you. You can't touch me, can't do it." He reached back into the dark of the foyer beside him and lifted out a shotgun. "I tell you what I'll do, Grissom. I'll give you and that worm of yours to the count of five to get off my porch. I'm feeling extra generous, so I'll give you until an hour before dawn to get the hell out of town altogether. I think that's fair. Don't you?"

"But . . . how dare you? I made you what you are, gave you the ability to make good money in this town, and this is the thanks I get?" Grissom's purpling face shook with rage and his voice grew louder.

"You keep it up," said Hart, "and you won't make it to dawn." He racked in a shell and never lost his smile.

Grissom followed Vollo to the steps, and as he reached the first one, he felt a boot pushing against his ample backside and he pitched forward, hit the ground face-first, and heard that same deep, cold laugh rumbling behind him.

"Get up, Grissom. Get up and get gone from my town."

Chapter 36

Emma was pleased to find Louisa Penny home, her little house's front room cluttered as usual with all manner of dummies bedecked in a variety of dresses in various stages of construction. Patterns hung from chair backs, the floor was barely visible through layers of cloth scraps, balls of yarn, baskets brimming with other projects, and against one wall, a loom stood canted to one side. It bore a colorful project half-completed, waiting in vain for the woman who might not get back to it for weeks.

"Louisa? You in here?"

"Back here . . ."

Emma stepped with care through the clutter and made her way to the kitchen at the back of the first floor.

"Emma! So good to see you. What brings you to town today?" Louisa clunked the wooden spoon on the edge of the simmering pot and hugged her younger friend.

"I was in a few days ago too, during that snowstorm we got."

"All but melted now," said Louisa, rubbing her hands. "I hate to admit it, but I don't want winter this year. My hands aren't getting any less stiff. I can't bear to think what the cold will do to these knuckles." She held her hands out in front of her.

Emma regarded them, the red, work-hardened hands and

bumpy knuckles half as feminine as a lady of finery's hands would be.

"If I had any way of taking on less work and more time to relax doing what I enjoy doing, I'd take the chance in a heartbeat. But if needs must, or some such thing. . . . I have it better than most in Klinkhorn. I have a skill that, while it might not pay much, does keep body and soul together."

"That's what I came to talk with you about, Louisa. All this talk of money everybody seems to be having."

"I guess it's because of that Lord Tarleton and all his grand falutin' talk about making Klinkhorn into a . . . 'destination' is the word he keeps using. Claims everybody and their brother will pay to come here for what he calls a 'wilderness experience.'"

"Do you believe that, Louisa?"

"Don't you?"

Emma shook her head, then said, "If I tell you something, do you promise not to tell anyone else? Ever? Unless I say you can?"

Louisa smiled. "That depends if you're about to tell me you murdered someone."

Emma stared at Louisa, not smiling.

"Emma, tell me you haven't killed someone. I was only joking."

"No, no, nothing like that. But . . . in a way it might be killing someone's spirit."

Louisa put her arm around Emma and pulled her over to a chair at a small table in the sun. "Sit here and I'll make some tea. Then you can tell me all about it."

She set the pot and two cups down and poured the tea. "What would you like to tell me, Emma? And yes, I will keep it a secret for as long as you'd like me to."

Emma tapped the rim of the elegant little saucer under the teacup, thought about the many times she'd had tea here at Louisa's house. It was the only place she'd ever experienced the fineries that Louisa had told her so many times were a lady's privilege, even on the frontier. Most of her always thought it was a bit silly, and that Louisa was always a little too frilly sounding for her, but there was a part of her that wanted to be like that, wanted to wear the dresses. She couldn't help it. And now that such things were offered to her in spades, she wasn't sure she wanted them, wasn't sure what to do.

"Emma, what's wrong?"

"That Englishman everyone's so excited about—even you—"

"Lord Tarleton? Yes." Louisa smiled and Emma thought maybe she even blushed a bit. "He's a handsome man, to be sure. And he's—"

"He's asked me to marry him, Louisa." Emma blurted it out and then stared at the pink flowers on the tablecloth.

Her friend's continued silent shock finally drew her gaze back upward. Louisa was smiling. "You're . . . why, you're going to say yes, I assume, Emma."

"Why should I?" she said. "I mean I guess I have to, but really, why should I have to do this for everyone? Why does it have to be me?"

"Emma, what are you talking about?"

"This foul town, everybody in Klinkhorn stands to gain something if he stays, and he'll only stay if I agree to marry him."

"Did he say that?"

"Not in such words, but yes. But, Louisa, I don't love him. I don't even like him. Is this the way it's supposed to be?"

"Is there some sort of rush? Don't you have time to think about it?"

"I don't think so, no. He says he owns our place, that the loan you mentioned that Uncle Payton took out was never paid off, and now that he bought the bank, he owns all the unpaid debt, and that includes our place."

"But that can't be. Payton paid off the loan. He told me so himself, on that very day he died."

"That's the problem. No one can find the signed document saying the land was paid off. Samuel Tucker says that—"

"Wait, who? Who have you been talking with, Emma?"

The girl sighed. "You might as well know: he's the man who was suspected—wrongly, I might add—of killing Uncle Payton."

Louisa backed up, her jaw set firm. "What are you telling me? I'd heard he escaped from the jail. The marshal said he was long gone from Klinkhorn."

"Well, he's . . . Look, Louisa, you have to promise me you won't say anything to anyone. Do you understand?"

"If it's about that killer being anywhere near you or Arliss or this town, I can't make that promise, Emma. I can't do it."

"He's not a killer, Louisa. I'm telling you the truth."

"Whose truth, Emma? His?"

Emma had never seen her friend act this way before. Louisa looked as angry as anyone she'd ever seen.

"Louisa, I need to talk with you about this."

"About what, Emma? I suppose you're going to tell me that you have fallen in love with this outlaw. That he's living in your house, or some such nonsense."

Emma's eyes widened. Either Louisa was a really good bluffer or she was just taking a stab in the dark and hitting her target dead-on.

"Oh no, you're serious? Emma . . . what does Arliss say?"

"We have proof that he didn't kill Payton."

"That came from him, conveniently, right?"

"That's not fair, Louisa."

"It might not be fair, but I bet it's the truth. Now tell me you don't really love him, Emma."

"And tell you that I love the Englishman instead, right? Isn't that what you want to hear? Isn't that what the entire town wants to hear?"

Emma headed for the door, with Louisa close behind, trying to stop her, saying, "Emma, wait. We can talk this out. I didn't mean to snap at you. You just took me by surprise."

"I never should have come to town today."

She shrugged Louisa's hand off her arm and headed out the door. None of it was fair and none of it was avoidable. Short of killing a few folks herself, she couldn't think of a way to get out of this mess. But there had to be a way. She just had to believe it. The only people she could trust now were Arliss and herself. Could she trust Samuel? What if Louisa was right? Of course she'd be angry and not want to believe in Samuel Tucker—he was the man accused of killing Payton, the man Louisa had been courted by, after all.

Emma leaned against the side of the nearest building, her hands stuffed into her coat pockets, her hat pulled down low. Up until this morning, she'd assumed she had at least Louisa and Arliss to count on, but one by one everyone she thought she could trust was going away. Marshal Hart, now Louisa. Would Arliss be next?

She pushed off the side of the house and headed with purpose down the street toward the hotel. Along the way she was greeted by more people than ever before. Usually folks took little notice of her, treated her like a child or at least someone not to be taken seriously.

As if dressing like a man was cause enough to make her all that different from the rest of them. Maybe she was different? Maybe she didn't care? She never had cared before—why was now any different? Before she knew it, Emma found herself in front of the hotel.

"Okay, then," she said, reaching for the knob on the front door. And noticed most of the folks around her on the sidewalk—and a few who probably didn't need to be there—had paused and had their eyes fixed on her. Taggart had stopped sweeping the already spotless boardwalk in front of his store. Two women whom Emma knew only by sight were

stopped in the street, hands on their hats, looking at her hopefully. To her left, a pair of skinny cowpokes looked at her
from around the doorway of the Ringing Belle Saloon. And
across the street, she saw the red-and-white-checked curtains
of Mae's Diner parted, faces peering out.

She groaned and opened the door. Just inside, she paused,
took a deep breath, and went to the front desk. Halley smiled
at her, nodded as if he were agreeing to something she'd said,
even before she got to the desk.

"Hi, Mr. Halley, I need to see—"

"Lord Tarleton, yes, of course you do. He said to send you
right on up when you got here."

"But he didn't know when I'd be here."

"No, but he said you'd be in town soon and to make sure
you were escorted on up to his suite."

She looked up at the open stairway leading to the open
balcony of the second floor, the dark wood gleaming richly
in the dull glow of the lamplight and what little afternoon
light slanted in through the low front windows. The lobby
smelled, as it always had the handful of times she'd been in
it in her life, of leather and dust, as if the carpets had never
been thrashed out back on the line.

Halley appeared beside her from around the counter.
"I'd imagine it's a big day in your life, Miss Emma. I would
like to be the very first one to congratulate you on . . . that is to
say, I wish you all the happiness a fellow like me can muster."

Emma ground her teeth together until her jaw ached and
stared at him until he looked away.

His face reddened and he tried to hold her elbow and
guide her to the stairs. "This way, please, Miss Farraday."

She jerked her arm away. "I think I can find the third floor,
Mr. Halley."

"But he said to be sure I escort you upstairs."

"Well, now, you're both just going to have to live with the
disappointment, aren't you?"

She took the stairs two at a time, her boots thumping lightly on the carpeted runners. She paused only long enough in front of the door to the rooms she'd been in the other day to pull in a deep breath. That cursed Halley was right—this was an important day in her life and she didn't want to stand around dithering about it any longer than she had to.

She tugged the leather glove off her hand, catching the faint scent of Cinda, of all the days of her life she'd spent riding free and easy through the meadows and forests along the river valley and into the hills, searching for strays or telling herself that's what she was doing, but not really doing much of anything other than enjoying the countryside. All that countryside that was going to be gone from her, taken from her and everyone else around her because she was selfish enough to think with her heart and not her head?

Before she could think any more snaky, twisting thoughts, the clock in the foyer chimed one, two, three . . . three o'clock in the afternoon. Where had the day gone? She had raised her hand to rap on the big wooden slab of a door when she heard a loud voice inside. It was Tarleton's voice. She tried the knob. It turned, so she pushed it hard and it swung inward.

Across the room, turned to her, were the backs of his two men in black, blocking out the tall, slim form of Lord Tarleton. He was the one berating them. She stood in the open doorway, his voice reaching her, and what she heard made her sick to her stomach.

"Reginald and Shepler, you are perhaps the most incompetent men I have ever had the displeasure to meet. Those two men, the fat one and his filthy little cohort, we need to make sure they don't live past the end of the day. Of course, that would necessitate finding them first, and that apparently is not something you wish to indulge in, hmm?"

Tarleton must have noticed over their shoulders that the door had opened, because he stopped talking and parted through the men as if they were curtains blocking entrance to another room.

"Ah, my sweet Miss Farraday," said Tarleton, sweeping toward her. "But I told Halley to escort you up the stairs, and to knock hard before entering. Explicit instructions, you see." There was a hard glint of anger in his eye. And now she regretted making Halley feel small down in the lobby. She would apologize to him later, try to make sure that Tarleton didn't grow angry with him.

Just as quickly as it appeared, his frown faded. He motioned with his head toward the two men in black. They crossed the room and stood by the door.

"You must forgive whatever it was you think you overheard when you barged in on us like that. I am a rather theatrical man, prone to histrionics. Those in my employ, as you will come to know, choose wisely to take my comments with a grain of salt."

She looked him up and down, this man who had proposed marriage to her. He wore a suit the likes of which she'd never before seen on a man. His trousers were of a fawn color, the jacket a darker mousy hue, and it all fit him perfectly. The coat, cut short, with tails behind, the vest a gold-and-black diamond pattern over a white shirt with ruffled collar and cuffs, and a gold watch chain swinging left and right with each move he made. His chin beard and mustache were waxed and sculpted just so, and there was a curl waxed to his forehead.

"You look like you've been spending some time in front of a looking glass," she said, wondering even as she said it if she were being too forward.

"And the opposite could be said of you, my dear sweet cowgirl."

"I'm not your dear, not your sweet, and not your cowgirl."

"Ah, I apologize if I have offended you, my . . . uh, Miss Farraday. It was practically a figure of speech. Especially out here on the frontier, one begins to doubt one's speech, as colloquial ways tend to crowd out even the best schooling in a short period of time. A shame, really, that it has to be that way. But we humans are fickle creatures."

"Lord Tarleton," said Emma. "I am sorry if I've interrupted you, but I have something I need to say to you."

"Yes, my dear. I expect you do. Would you care to do this over a drink, or perhaps sitting on the divan?"

"No. What I have to say won't take long. I appreciate your kind offer, and the fact that you are richer than God and all the apostles."

The man tilted his head to the side and smiled.

"But I can't marry you. It wouldn't be right. You . . . you're not coming at this in the right way at all, Lord Tarleton. You see, when you go to castrate a calf, you don't hit it in the head with a post maul and hope it will get up and roam again one day."

His brows narrowed and his smile slumped. "I believe you are trying to make an analogy between my proposal and your . . . reaction to it? Am I correct in that assumption, Emma?"

"I guess, something like that. Look, you don't want to marry me, really. You just want to buy me like you're buying all the other things you think you want. But I'm a person. I have a life here, and friends. And we were all happy until that worthless buzzard Grissom came to town and started to poison our well, if you know what I mean. The town hasn't been the same since."

She folded her arms and sighed. "You're just the latest in a long line of things that Klinkhorn and the Farradays shouldn't have to put up with. It's not fair, but there you are—that's the truth as I see it. I promised to give it some serious thought and I have done that for two days now. And as I said, I am most appreciative, and I consider it a fine compliment, the highest I expect a person can receive, but it's not anything I'm interested in. But I would like to talk with you about making sure we find that signed receipt that shows my uncle Payton paid off that loan from Grissom."

"Oh, you are delightful! Simply delightful, my dear!" Smiling, he spread his arms wide.

"What do you mean? Don't you understand what I just said? I'm sorry, but I'm turning you down. I love someone, not you, and there's nothing that can change that."

"That's why you are the epitome of what I have been looking for. You are completely guileless in every way. And your wants don't matter a jot."

"What?" She backed toward the door, suddenly feeling as if the air in the room had changed.

Tarleton's smile became a forced thing, his eyes lost their previous mirth, and he looked past her toward the men standing by the doorway. They walked forward, grabbed her by the arms, one hand on her elbows, one hand on her shoulders.

"What are you doing?" She struggled, kicked backward, and landed a couple of good contacts with her bootheels, but if the men felt any pain, they made no sound. They just stood there holding her in place. The more she thrashed and squirmed, the tighter they squeezed her.

"I half expected the situation to come to this," said Tarleton. "That is why I have taken the precaution of arranging to sequester you here until you come around to the correct way of thinking, that is, my way of thinking. But I'm not really bothered if you never do. For we will be wed. The biggest difference is that should you have accepted my offer graciously, this town would be a very different place within a few short weeks. And while that will still happen, I can guarantee you that anyone thinking they will be able to reside here is sorely mistaken. Oh, I'll need a few locals, I imagine, for the more menial tasks, but the rest will succumb to my relocation program. That is to say, I will tell them when I want them gone, and if they don't comply, I will probably have to have them shot."

Emma's eyes widened. As if this rough treatment weren't bad enough, now he was talking about shooting her friends? This couldn't be real.

Tarleton stared at her a moment more, then broke down laughing. "I'm terribly sorry, but my little joke doesn't have the impact I expected it would. I've forever been called a man who has no sense of humor that other men might recognize."

Once again his smile slumped as he addressed the two men. "Take her to the back bedroom.

"Don't worry, my dear. You are quite safe here." He looked her up and down, as if appraising a horse for possible purchase. "I will have a bathtub sent up, hot water too. And I believe you will find the wardrobe has been filled with all manner of frocks for your enjoyment. Please clean yourself and dress appropriately. I have planned on having a fine meal here tonight, and you will not alter that plan one iota. Is that understood?"

She thrashed and bucked, but the men held firm.

"I'll take that as a yes. Especially considering you have no other choice."

He motioned toward a door set in the back wall, behind the desk. "Oh, one more thing . . ." He raised a halting hand. The two men in black kept a tight grip on her arms and shoulders, despite the continued thrashing and kicking she gave in return.

"Gentlemen, I have a little something for you to do. You two are familiar with the Farraday spread, and in particular the dwellings and outbuildings—the common, old robust structures that will be of little use to me very soon, except perhaps as a nuisance because I suspect squatters will want the place all to themselves. And this we cannot have. Am I right, gentlemen?"

They both responded, "Yes, sir."

"Good, then you know what to do." He turned back to the front window, a drink in his hand. "Burn it."

"What? What in the heck did you just say? You can't burn my home, my ranch! It was left to me and Arliss. And . . . you can't— you just can't do it!"

"My dear," said Tarleton, turning back to her, once again wearing that foul grin, as if he'd just licked clean a bowl of tasty gravy and wanted more. "You forget that I can do whatever I want. I own the entire Farraday acreage, as I own most of this town. And the rest will follow suit very soon. Oh, and I own you. Now run along and clean yourself. You smell like a stable."

Emma screamed blue murder all the way to the bedroom, and when the two men flung her on her back on the bed and turned to leave, she rushed them. They must have been expecting it, for they spun, grabbed her roughly, not really caring where they touched her, and threw her back on the bed, then slammed the door and locked it from the outside. She ran to the room's one window and clawed back the curtains. It had been boarded from the inside. She scrabbled at the edges of the lumber but couldn't get a purchase.

She bolted for the door, howling in her rage, and slammed her shoulder into it. It rattled in its frame but didn't budge. She ran at it again and again. Then finding no change in the door's temperament, she lunged at the walls. Her boots drove deep into the plaster and laths, wedging now and again, but ultimately finding success in punching through the red flower-specked wallpaper, plaster spraying wider with each driving kick.

"You buzzard! Don't you burn my home! Help! Help!"

She ran back to the boarded-up window, dragged the end of the bed closer to it, used it to brace against. Then she kicked against the boarded-up window. The planks vibrated but didn't splinter. It was long minutes before she flopped back on the bed, breathing hard and clenching and unclenching her fists. There had to be a way out of the room, had to be. She looked around—up through the ceiling? No. The floor? Doubtful. The plaster wall had given way a bit, but that might take a while. Maybe she could hit the door hard enough with something from the room.

And then the door rattled; something turned in the lock. Emma jumped up from the bed, made it halfway across the floor when the door swung open and there stood Lord Tarleton. The two men in black were nowhere to be seen, but the dandy had a nickel-plated bone-handled derringer, cocked and aimed at her.

"You, my dear, are a lovely wildcat. So lovely." And he sounded so genuine.

She lunged at him and he pulled the trigger.

Gun smoke wafting low and drifting, curling all about them, was the only thing moving in the few seconds after the unexpected blast. It seemed to take him as much by surprise as it did her.

Emma's ears rang like screaming bells, and as a second, then two passed, she wondered if she'd been shot. But she felt no pain, other than watering eyes and ringing ears. She recovered, lunged at him again, but he sidestepped, and she felt a sharp stinging pain in her side. She pulled away from him and saw something silver glinting in his hand, the hand that didn't hold the gun.

"What is that? What did you do?"

"Morphine, you perfect cowgirl. You will love me for it."

"What is that?" she said, not feeling well in the least, gripping her side and reaching out with her other hand toward the bed. He had just stabbed her with something, tried to shoot her, only to kill her with the morphine? Was that what he said it was? With a needle? She'd seen one once in the doctor's office. This couldn't be happening.

She fell to her side, forced herself to look around; then she saw him, smiling down at her. He held the pistol in one hand, gun smoke clouding low, the silver thing in the other hand. His beard, his eyes, that fancy suit . . . She felt as if she were swimming at the beach at the far corner of the Rogue where it bent sharp around the lower fields. . . .

She never made it to the bed, felt herself slump to the floor. The last thing she saw was the waxed mustache of Lord Tarleton grinning at her.

The last thing she thought of was Samuel Tucker and how she wished it had all turned out different, so very different.

Chapter 37

"You should know better than to ask that." The man speaking didn't bother looking at the man riding beside him, but he did shake his head slowly.

"Reginald, what's that supposed to mean?"

"Forget it."

"No, no, I mean it." Shepler reined up, his black horse dancing.

His partner sighed. "Okay, all right. You want to get into this? Fine. What I meant was at this point you shouldn't wonder if Tarleton says what he means, you know?"

Shepler stared at him, head tilted as if he were trying to decide whether to follow up a steak dinner with pie, coffee, or both. Finally he said, "He's not a god, you know."

"What sort of a thing is that to say?"

"Just that. He's only a man. A man with a heck of a wad of money, but he doesn't own me or you, you know."

It was the other man's turn to stare in curiosity. "You getting cold feet on this burning deal, Shep?"

"Nah, I reckon not." He booted his horse back into a walk. "Just that sometimes I like to remind myself I'm my own man. Still got a head of my own and a brain in it, you know?"

They fell into line side by side. "Yeah, I guess so. Just promise me you won't trot out that brain when we set to torching that house and barn."

"I'm fine. Let's just get it over with."

They rode on a few minutes more under the gold half-moon.

"You don't suppose anybody'll be there, do you?"

"Let me guess—that brain of yours is working hard to get you to turn around?"

"No, I'm just wonderin'."

"We'll only be setting fire to the boss's own property. But yeah, I reckon that old man will be around somewhere. And that other one too. The one you dragged on back there, remember?"

"How'd you know about that?"

"I am in the employ of a very wealthy man who pays me well to pay attention to everything going on. How could you think I'd not know?"

A few minutes more of silence passed with only the soft footfalls of the horses along the worn lane, then, "You tell Tarleton?"

The silence was uncomfortable. "Nah, what good would that do?"

"Thanks."

Ten minutes later, the farmhouse came into view. The men dismounted, tied their horses to the split-rail fence that marked the entrance to the spread's lane.

"There it is," whispered Reginald. "You with me on this?"

"Yeah, yeah."

"Then get that canvas bundle of torches over here and we'll light 'em when we get closer. Trick is to not get skylined before the light of the flames."

"I have been down this road before a time or two with you, you know."

"Way you were carrying on back there, Shep, I thought maybe I'd have to leave you on the trail, pick you up on my way back."

"You best be kidding."

"Yeah, yeah. Let's hit the house first, then the barn."

"I want to check for any animals in there."

"You're worried about animals, but not any people in the house?"

"I'm hoping there won't be anyone in the house."

Shepler made a quick pass through the barn, saw nothing in the stalls that looked like a horse, and on his way out the back door saw a paddock with two or three dark shapes, moving close to the fence, alert, maybe looking for a feed. Good, at least they weren't in the barn.

He rasped a match along the bottom side of his trousers and set it to the torch. The ragged head, soaked in lamp oil, caught with a *fwoomp!* and for a moment blinded the black-clad stranger. Then his customary single-minded purpose for his task kicked in and he dashed through the building touching dry hay, kicking piles of it close to the planks sheathing the barn's exterior. Within seconds, it seemed, the broad structure became a smoking, crackling thing, alive with darting light and dancing flame. It always amazed Shepler that way. He took it all in for a brief second, then dashed out the big door, the heat and smoke suddenly closing in on him.

He did the same around two sides of the structure before he couldn't stand to get near it any longer.

He looked far to his left and saw the once-handsome log home, a long, one-floor structure with a full front porch, take flame all around the outside.

There were no shouts from inside. He hoped no one was in there. It wasn't as if they'd been given any sort of warning. The boss was in a snit, and when he was cross, there wasn't a man or beast that the rich Englishman wouldn't hesitate to lay low. Burning out a rancher, former owner or no, wasn't something he would think twice about. Double the anger with that spitfire of a girl, and the situation had the makings of a real conflagration, a word Reginald had taught him. That was one big word, and for fires set in the name of Lord Tarleton, it seemed the perfect word to use.

It looked as if his partner had the house pretty well blazing. Cold comfort, but something nonetheless that Shepler could call to mind on those cold winter nights when he couldn't sleep. Those nights when he'd regret all the things he'd done in the name of Lord Tarleton, all the things that the law always seemed to back, no matter how they nested in his throat, choking him in the still, cold hours after midnight. All in the name of money.

At least he could tell himself that he hadn't actually been the one to set flame to the girl's house—just in case it came to pass that there had been someone in there who hadn't made it out.

Before he knew it, Reginald's partner was beside him, smiling in the glow of the flames, the sound of crackling wood being devoured by fire, brighter than anything had a right to be, it seemed.

"Let's go!" said Reginald, not bothering to whisper any longer, the sound of the fire fast overtaking them.

Shepler looked back once as they loped up the lane to their horses, the twin black beasts dancing and straining their reins. He hoped they didn't pull free. How to explain that—afoot not far from a fire, in a place he had no claim on.

He looked back again and saw that the house had become fully consumed by the flames. They curled up and over the roof edges. The chimney belched long flames straight up it; the porch had already begun to sag. He thought he heard shouts but couldn't be certain. A lot of times logs would do that very thing—make sounds like people, but it was the deep-buried pitch popping and the logs checking, twisting, cracking like gunfire.

The fire spread in runners along the ground to little outbuildings, probably the privy out back, then to something that looked like a smokehouse, the log corral that stood before the barn, empty now. He heard horses and what sounded like a mule braying.

Shepler stopped, his horse's reins in his hand. "Hey, you hear that?"

The other man, already mounted, said, "What? Get on your horse. We did what the boss wanted. The place is his. The land is his. And mostly he didn't want to give that ranch girl he's hotted up over any reason to come back here. So we just gave him what he wanted, right?"

"Yeah, yeah."

They thundered back down the lane that would lead them back to Klinkhorn proper. A quarter mile later, Reginald fished out a nearly full quart bottle of bonded whiskey from his saddlebag and let out a yip. He glugged back a few heavy swallows, then handed it to his gloomy partner. "Drink up, Shep. We did it all quick and easy. No sign of us left behind."

His partner snatched up the whiskey and pulled on it until he ran out of breath. Then he gasped for air and handed it back.

"Take it easy on that stuff. You're liable to regret it come morning." He smiled and took another pull himself.

It was a long time before Shepler couldn't see the orange glow in the sky behind them, growing and seeming to almost advance on them. It would be a much longer time before he could forget what he'd just helped to do. The knot in his gut told him it had been a bad thing. And the little bird in his brain told him that if he found out there were people in that house, it would be a very bad thing indeed.

Chapter 38

The sneeze awoke him. Tucker had never before sneezed in his sleep, though anything could have happened when he'd been drunk for two years, and he might not ever have known. But this was something else. It left a feeling of blood in his mouth, and something more . . . Smoke?

A whooshing sound above his head pulled him from sleep with the force of a gut punch. Fire? Where was he? The house, Emma's house . . . on fire? As if to answer his sleep-dazed question, he saw long snaking fingers of flame digging at the tops of the walls, clawing their way under the closed door of the room he'd been staying in—her uncle's room, the very room of the man who had died in his arms, Emma's uncle. There were other rooms—Emma, Arliss . . .

Tucker spun from the bed, fully wake, the heat stoking sudden burning sensations at him, laving him with waves that with each new assault pained him more and more. The room filled with smoke, and as he worked to tug on his boots, knowing he wouldn't stand a chance if he ran through the flaming floor in his bare feet, Tucker screamed with all the power he could muster out of his lungs for Emma and Arliss. He shouted their names and the word "Fire!" over and over, not letting himself stop. The second boot was half on and he bolted, stomping into it, as he snatched a smoldering blanket off the bed and draped it over his head. He bent low and battered his way into the log wall to the right of the door, then used the blanket to grab the steel latch and fling the door wide.

Hot snapping flames whipped at him and for a moment he backed off, considered driving himself through the small window on the back wall of the room. But he knew if he did he'd never get back into the house.

Still shouting, Tucker hugged the wool blanket tight around him and rushed into the heat. It was the most difficult thing he'd had to do since burying his wife and daughter. He called upon them now, in the maw of the raging firestorm, prayed for their help. He had to get Emma and Arliss out, had to know that they were safe.

He knew she was in her room. He hadn't heard a peep from her since she locked herself in there in the afternoon, but Arliss assured him she did that from time to time when she wanted to be alone. "Girl thoughts," he'd said, "are the deepest ones of all. Best let her be, son." And so Tucker had abided by the old man's sage wisdom, given that Arliss had known Emma her entire life, had been like a second or third father to her.

All these fragments of thoughts and more ricocheted in Tucker's brain as he staggered, crouching low, along the short hallway toward the far door. It was Emma's, and he kicked at it, tried the knob. It swung inward. But the room was a roiling mass of smoke and flame. He felt agonizing pain sneak up behind him and sink its fangs into his back and legs. It was fire devouring the blanket. He held it away from his legs as he lurched about the room, more by feel than sight. He felt the edge of the bed, hot to the touch, the wood frame raising blisters on his hands, grabbed at it, felt the buckled edges of a ticked mattress, but it had been scorched and curled now, shot through with flames.

The smoke became unbearable and he realized he was choking and coughing all at once. He tried to shout her name, lunged around the small room like a madman and couldn't feel a thing that might be the girl. He dropped to his knees and scrabbled all over the floor with his flaming, blistered hands for her body, any sign of her. He rousted the flaming mattress, wondering if she had tried to climb under the bed for safety. It didn't seem like her to give up that way, though. Emma was nothing if not a fighter. Tucker screamed her name, but his voice was drowned out by a full wall of rushing flame.

Then he felt something on his back. It hit his head, harder and harder in the same spot. He turned and dimly, beside him, he saw a shape, blackened and short, punching him, grabbing at him, screaming something.

"Arliss?"

"Come . . . on! Out! Out!"

"Emma . . . can't find Emma!"

"Die . . . we'll die!"

The next moments were to be his last. Tucker was sure of it. The stink of burning hair—maybe it was the wool blanket, he thought in passing—filled his nostrils, seemed to fill his entire head. Smoke clouded everything he might otherwise be able to see, and the sounds of whooshing walls of flame soon drowned out all the shouts of the two men huddling together. Tucker could barely move, but he knew that if he didn't they would both soon die.

But a bold image of his cherished Rita, cradling little Sam in her strong arms, their faces young and well and healthy, smiled at him. Love and warmth and light filled him deep inside, almost like a renewing, life-giving force, as if he'd been quenched and drenched in water, and that feeling of power and hopefulness, however slight, was enough to force him to bend low and scoop up the leaning little man against him, quivering and blackened and unable to stand.

Tucker struggled back through the room's door, now a wall of flame, and on through to the end of what had once been a hallway. He was equally distant from the front of the house and the side door, but he kept going for the side because it lay before him and required no further thought than to get out.

He'd never experienced such pain, and he knew he was squealing like a beast in its death throes. He had heard animals make that sound at their end, had seen a man's hands slip into a scalding pot on a pig-butchering day once a long time ago. The man, a strapping brute half again wider at the shoulder than the average man, had screamed a high-pitched sound like a baby pig being tortured. They all saw why he trembled and howled and wet himself: Layers of skin, from the elbows to the tips of his fingers, had sloughed off. As they watched in surprise, ghostly gelatinous gloves flopped free from the man's raw arms and into the bubbling, scalding cauldron.

And then Tucker and Arliss were outside into the cool air, away from the fire. Each step brought them farther from it, but Tucker couldn't walk much more. He was seizing up, and felt as if flames were dancing on him. The night was as bright as a sunny early morning. He looked down at Arliss. The old man lay huddled tight to him as if he were a baby. His long, droopy mustache was a blackened, curled thing and his hair was matted and curled tight to his head.

Tucker dropped to his knees and lowered Arliss to the cool earth. "Arliss, can you hear me?"

The old man's eyes blinked open. Tucker didn't think he saw any lashes there, but it was hard to tell, so blackened with soot was he. "Arliss, can you hear me?"

"I hear ya. By golly, boy, I'll wager you've looked prettier. You look like you've been through a house fire."

Tucker wanted to smile at the man's undefeatable resilience, but all he could think of was Emma.

"Arliss, I . . . I can't find her. I have to go back in."

Tucker made to stand, tried to slide his arms out from

under the old man, but Arliss grasped his arm with surprising strength.

"Boy, she's gone. It's okay."

"How can you say that?" Tucker heard himself shouting, trying to stand. "She's in that house, somewhere. Maybe she was in the front room. It would be better protected there, right? Maybe behind the stove, maybe she hid down behind it, where it was cooler, somehow. . . ." Tucker stood, limped a few paces toward the house.

"Samuel! Leave it be!"

Half of the house collapsed then, blasting a fresh on-slaught of heat and sparks and hunks of flaming wood at them. "Emma! Emma!" He lurched forward another step.

"She's in town, boy! I tried to tell you—she ain't in there!" Arliss's voice came out strained and weak, but loud enough for Tucker to hear. He staggered back to the old man, who'd tried to drag himself along the ground to reach Tucker.

"What? What are you saying, Arliss? Is she okay? Is Emma safe?"

The old man nodded, capable of nothing more than that, then collapsed. Tucker made his way back to him, lay down beside him. "You're telling me the truth, Arliss?"

"Yes, boy. She left a note. Said she was going to town to give her answer . . . to that damnable heathen. I knowed there was nothing to be done. I hate it, but . . . she's growed . . . and a damn Farraday. . . ."

Chapter 39

When Tucker first awoke, he touched his head, felt the damage of the fire in all its horrible intensity. What he saw, facing the wreckage of the log home, was heartbreaking. The house lay, an unrecognizable thing with the few remaining smoking timbers thrust upward at the gray early-dawn sky, clouds pregnant with heavy snow.

Beside him, Arliss stirred, groaned with a hoarse, gagging sound that grew worse, until the old man was forced to his knees and hands, heaving clear liquid, bits of soot and black nibs threading from his blistered mouth.

Every move seemed an unendurable agony, and yet Tucker knew he must. He had to figure out how this could have happened.

"Water . . . Sam . . . need water."

Tucker nodded. They had to get to the pump. It had been near the barn. Arliss began a slow, painful trek on his hands and knees toward the pump that lay beyond the remains of the house. With a mighty effort of will, Tucker pushed himself to his feet. He stood swaying for a moment, then said, "Stay here, Arliss. . . . I'll bring it to you. Wait here." He staggered forward and did his best to not look at the smoking house but could not help it. Flames were licking like hiding serpents at various spots of the ruin.

Little was left recognizable. The kitchen cookstove still

stood, its few lengths of tin pipe long gone. It looked oddly
headless, timbers leaning against it. He supposed there was
little else salvageable in the place, but there would be time
for such considerations far later. Right now he must get to the
pump and bring Arliss a drink. In what? He almost laughed
at his foolishness. He had nothing to carry water in.

He heard a noise behind him and saw the old man, now
upright on his two feet, walking in slow, measured steps beside the house. Tucker bit the inside of his mouth and felt
blisters give way. He spat viscous liquid and kept moving
toward the pump. The wooden tank remained mostly un-
burned and half-filled with water. The surface of the dark
liquid lay mottled with floating fragments of charred wood,
blackened bits of unrecognizable debris.

He reached out for the pump handle and saw his hand for
the first time, a blackened thing pocked with blisters and le-
sions. He grasped the handle and worked it until, squawking,
it gave way to motion and he was able to work up enough
gumption to coax water from the earth. Soon clear water ran
into the tub.

Tucker had no idea how desperate he was for the stuff. He
drove his face under it, gagged as the cold sensation of the
water poured on his face, choked as it filled his mouth, ran
out again, spattered in his crusted eyes. Soon Arliss joined
him and the men had an orgy of feasting on water until their
bellies distended with it. Their blistered bodies, the clothes
they had on—long-handles on each of them, in some places
seared onto their hides—were sopping wet, their burned hair
coming off in bits, loosened from their scorched scalps by
the water.

Neither man spoke for a long time. Long enough time
went by for them to both lean braced by weary arms against
the side of the wooden tank to gaze at their reflections in the
now-still surface of the water, disbelief tautening their rav-
aged features.

"The land will be here, Arliss, but if we get ourselves killed, we won't be. And if we don't get to Emma sooner than later, Emma won't be either." Tucker looked at the glowing remains of the ranch house in the dawning light. "I met the man, Arliss. He's smooth, he's smart, and he's ruthless. I could see it in his eyes. Sized me up the second I saw him, made it all seem like them being there was legal and neat and tidy. About the only thing I can give him in the way of a compliment is that he didn't seem keen on being anywhere near Grissom's two hired thugs."

"At least you done for one of them," said the old man, scowling at his grubby fingernails.

"Yeah," said Tucker. "At least there's that." He took stock of the place and there wasn't much to it. Other than Jasper, Gracie, and Julep, who had all escaped the flames by busting free of the night corral, there wasn't much else of value about the place.

They rummaged in the smoking debris, but other than a bit of warmth from the climbing sun, and the cooling, restorative effects of the water, Arliss and Tucker realized they were headed for a world of hurt.

They couldn't go to town because as impediments to Tarleton's plans, Tucker knew, they'd probably be disposed of somehow, shortly after arriving. And Bentley Grissom wasn't exactly a fan of either of them, for some of the same reasons. Plus, Vollo, his remaining lackey, was off the beam as far as Tucker was concerned. The smelly little man would probably lunge at him the first chance he got, try to sink his teeth into his face like a crazed dog. And then there was Marshal Hart, whom Tucker wasn't sure about.

"What do you think we should do, Arliss? We haven't got a pot to pee in, nor a window to toss it out of."

The old man snorted and looked up at Tucker, one eye squinted in the sun. "I ain't heard that one in a long time."

"My old gran. She was full of them. You'da liked her."

"Yep, I reckon I would have." He coughed, spat a clot of black phlegm. "I like a woman who has a way with words. She taken?"

Tucker nodded. "Long time ago. By the bite of a hydrophobic dog, of all things."

"Oh, that ain't no way to go, 'specially for a lady. I am truly sorry to hear that."

Tucker nodded. "Only worse way is for someone to marry someone they hate, and for all the wrong reasons. That's enough to make someone do something crazy." He looked at the old man. "I can't bear to think of Emma like that."

"Well, let's take stock. We got the animals and we got water. Clothes? Not much. Cold weather? Plenty. And it's fixing to snow."

"You are a font of happiness and glad tidings—you know that?"

"I have been called a lot of things in my long years, but never a fountain, or whatever you just said. But I do have an idea or two—for food and for shelter—whilst we recuperate."

"I'm all ears."

"Good, 'cause I'm all mouth." Arliss winked. "Now, that smoking mess over yonder?" He nodded toward a heap of blackened timbers set off from the house and barn. "That was the smokehouse. I reckon we could dig in there, find a few cooked slabs of venison, beef, and a ham or two, if we root hard enough."

"That sounds good to me." It was Tucker's turn to cough. He did so until he doubled over. Arliss pounded a bony fist feebly on his back. "Easy on me, Arliss. I think you just hastened along a few blisters in the healing process."

"Well, excuse me all to hell. . . ."

"Now, that's the Arliss I have come to know." Tucker straightened, dragged a soot-grimed hand across his eyes. "How about shelter?"

"Hunting camp, north of here. Beyond the river valley and

up a ways, there's a plateau. Camp's on the rim. Good hunting grounds. I ain't been up there since Emma's pappy died, oh, two years or more ago, but we used to have some wild times up there. Course, only as wild as you can have when a growing girl child is snoozing in the other room."

"Emma went with you men to hunting camp?"

"Course she did. Who's going to take care of her? Why, we three raised her. Her maw died when she wasn't nothing but a nubbin."

Tucker nodded, changed the subject. "Well, I'd guess that whoever set this blaze—and that could be any number of folks—might just come back to take a look-see at their handiwork. What say we skedaddle?"

Arliss pushed to his feet. "First, the meat." He led the way and the ragged pair hobbled to the burned-out smokehouse. Within minutes they were rewarded with two hams, a number of cuts of beef, and two venison shanks. The cuts were all burned and crispy on the outside, but they knew the inside would be just fine. And might have to serve them well for some time to come. "A stroke of luck, this stuff." Arliss smiled and patted the meat.

They unwrapped a length of old worn lariat from its task as a forgotten temporary replacement hinge on a gate. They used the old rope to bind the meats, and a few more short lengths served as makeshift reins. They climbed aboard the horses, Arliss on Gracie, who had, despite the fire, gained weight at the ranch. It seemed to Tucker she'd lost years of age. Tucker rode Jasper, and Julep the mule carried the awkward load of meats in uncomplaining silence.

As they rode north for the hunting camp, Arliss looked back. "A right shame, boy. This place was a place of love and life for many long years. Shame you didn't come along sooner. We had us some good times here. Looks like they're all but gone."

"I refuse to believe that," said Tucker. "I will work to my

dying breath to make it what it once was." He turned a steel-hard gaze on Arliss, and the old man returned it.

"Yes, sir, I do believe you believe that. And if that's good enough for you, then who am I to argue?"

Tucker meant every word he said, and what's more, it had felt good to him to say such things.

"I ever tell you I was born and reared in the Tennessee hills?" said Arliss.

"No, sir, I don't believe so."

"Well, I'm telling you now. I was. And what's more, my family was forever in cahoots and boiling up in what they called a feud with this other family, the Pendergrast clan. Nasty bunch of vipers they was." He moved his half-toothless mouth as if he were working a quid of chaw.

"I don't suppose those nasty Pendergrasts thought the same thing of the Tibbs clan, did they?"

"Oh, now you are fixing to get on my bad side. And once a body goes there, there ain't no coming back. You avoid that by keeping a civil tongue in that Texas head of your'n from here on out."

Tucker stifled a laugh. "Yes, sir."

"Point is, I got me a bellyful of backwoods, back-trail sneak-and-shoot type of living, and except during the war when it come into use, I ain't had much call to flex them old muscles, except when snipin' rabbits and squirrels and such."

Tucker adjusted the rope reins in his hands, urged the horse a quick step up a rise as they approached the river. "What are you saying, Arliss?"

"I'm saying that I think it's time we take them land boys and that buzzard who hired 'em by surprise, get rid of them any way possible until we get our Emma free."

"Our Emma," he'd said. Tucker liked the sound of that. It had been a long time since there was anyone in his life he'd called his own. "Good plan, Arliss."

"Yep, I got a few tricks I can show you. One thing, though,

I ain't interested in tying up anybody, nor keeping prisoners. I tell you that straight out front." The old man stared at him for a moment.

"I understand," said Tucker, nodding. They rode on for a while longer in silence. As they crossed the Rogue River at a low spot on a gravel bar and emerged across the other side, Tucker said, "Arliss, you recall that feeder stream you showed me a few weeks back? When we were chasing fall strays?"

"Yep. That I do. It angles over yonder." He nodded southwest. "Beyond that rise."

"That's where I was when I came upon the Englishman's surveying team. Not far from there, northward, they'd set up that camp. And it seemed to me they headed back to town most every night, but left it set up. It was a base of sorts for them—a 'day camp,' Tarleton had called it."

"Trespassers, that's all they are." Arliss spat more black gunk on the ground.

"Trespassers, yes, but trespassers with a lot of useful gear that they just leave behind every night. Might be it's under guard, but then again, might be it's not."

"You reckon they got guns?"

Tucker nodded. "I reckon."

"And clothes?"

"Maybe so. It's been cold. Anything's possible when you're in the employ of such a rich man."

"Well, what are we waiting for, Samuel Tucker? Let's get ourselves to that camp, see what we can filch from them thieves."

By the time they neared the camp, dark had begun to descend. Tucker saw the dim white bulk of the canvas wall tent in the midst of the clearing. Though they probably rode far too close to not have been heard by anyone left behind guarding the spot, Tucker made theatrical motions to Arliss to keep his mouth and those of the horses shut as he approached the tent on foot. Being weaponless wasn't his favorite feeling.

He crept forward, slower and quieter the closer he drew to the tent. He had gotten to within a dozen feet from it when something inside shifted. He paused, waited, then heard a soft, rasping snore. Whoever was the guard, he had decided to use his time wisely and snooze his way through the long, lonely hours. Hopefully the man was alone and not expecting anyone to show up. But he would probably be armed.

Tucker kept moving forward, ignoring the hot pains from his burns and blisters, from the largely unhealed bullet wound in his shoulder and the knocks to the head he had taken in his tumble with Rummler.

Tucker had almost reached the tent when the snoring inside paused. He held his breath, heard no sound for long moments, then a snorting gasp, and the soft snores continued.

From the sound of it, the man was close by his side of the tent. Just as Tucker reached the canvas to lift it and poke his head inside, he heard a horse blow softly from the east end of the camp. He paused, shocked, until it occurred to him that the camp sentry probably showed up with, or was left with, a horse—just in case he had to ride on out of there, should he be attacked by half-burned woodland savages, thought Tucker with a grim smile.

He waited a sufficient length of time and heard no further horse noises, nor footsteps of someone who had dismounted and might be lurking in the undergrowth. He had a feeling they were alone, and that he was about to come face-to-face with one startled man.

He slipped under the canvas flap easily and paused in the dark. The snoring continued with regularity. He edged closer. Once he neared the sleeping man, he rose painfully to his knees and peered closely along the length of the man, beginning at his feet.

The body seemed to be that of a fat man wearing no gun. Thank God for small favors, he thought, and with all his strength, he grabbed the snoring man by the lapels and dragged him to the ground. The man screamed as if he had been scalded.

"Vollo? Who are you? What do you want? I'm only resting here. I swear it."

The man was fat, and Tucker couldn't picture him as anyone he'd seen before, though his voice rang a bell. Where had he heard this one before? Could be he was on the street that day Emma had sprung him from jail. Yes, the more he thought about it, the more he became convinced this was . . . Bentley Grissom. The very buzzard who had caused all of this, the man who had ripped apart the town of Klinkhorn, who had invited the worm of Lord Tarleton into the apple that had been life there.

The fat man suddenly quieted and leaned his head closer to Tucker's face. "You. You? You were the prisoner in Hart's jail who broke out." He peered closer. "Good Lord, man, what happened to your face?"

"What's it to you?" said Tucker. His voice sounded like gravel grinding between river stones.

"Nothing, nothing at all."

"Then shut up. You're Grissom, aren't you?"

"Why?"

"I have a six-gun aimed at your parts, mister. You best answer the question."

"What if I am?"

"No matter, we'll get to that soon enough. Right now, though, facedown on the ground, put your hands on your head."

Tucker ignored the man's whimpering and trussed him with a coil of rope hanging off a nail on a tent pole. He kept the hemp tight, which induced more whining.

"Shut up or I'll hit you in your fat head with the butt of my gun."

Grissom lay silent while Tucker rummaged in the fat man's pockets for a gun, a knife, anything. And found both, though the knife was a paltry pocket affair more suited to cleaning fingernails and paring toenails. And the gun, a two-shot derringer, was little more than a toy, though it would be capable of killing a man—or at least annoying him—at close range. Tucker figured it would be better than nothing, which was what they currently had.

"What are you going to do with me? You . . . you're not going to kill me, are you?"

"I haven't decided yet," said Tucker, though he was secretly appalled at the prospect. "What's the story with this place, Grissom?"

"It's the camp Tarleton's men use."

"I'm aware of that. I mean why are you here and where's the guard? And why did you say Vollo's name? He here too?"

"I'm here because . . . I just thought I'd check in on my investment and then I got caught up, didn't realize the time. I figured I'd better lie low here tonight, head back into town tomorrow."

"And Vollo?"

"He . . . used to be in my employ. I don't have any idea where that bum can be."

"Something about that doesn't sound quite right, Grissom."

"And another thing, I never said my name was Grissom."

"I know it is, so stop the act."

"What do you want? I can practically guarantee anything at all that you might want. I'm good friends with the law in these parts. I'll see to it that you get a fair trial."

"For something you and your boys did? Nah, I don't think so. Now shut your mouth."

Tucker found a lamp and struck a match from the box beside it. He saw stacked crates. He used a pry bar and a ball-peen hammer from a toolbox to pry off the lids of the rough-sawn crates. Inside were various wood and brass implements such as he'd seen the men using that day in camp.

"Arliss!" he shouted. "Come on in here."

"You're friends with that broke-down old man?"

"I said shut your mouth, Grissom." Tucker kicked the fat man in the haunch and heard a grunt in reply.

He tried another crate and almost shouted for joy. It was filled with food, cooking implements, spices, flour, a pan, sacks of coffee, cornmeal, beans, a coffeepot, and more. Wait until Arliss got a look at it. He hoped it wasn't too much farther to the hunting camp.

His next crate revealed weapons of the sort he had been hoping to find: two six-guns on a single gun belt, a double-barrel scattergun, a rifle in a leather scabbard. He looked down at Grissom on the ground. The man couldn't lift his head well, but he didn't want the brute to gawk at him, to see what he was gathering.

"Well, Grissom, I can't let you go, and if I leave you here, that plays right into Tarleton's hands, something I definitely don't want to do. So I guess it's up to you. You going to come with us or am I going to shoot you now? Only problem is, unless I find bullets stashed in here somewhere, you will die of a slow-to-kill wound, because neither your knife nor your baby pistol is worth a bean." As soon as he said it, Tucker dug deeper and found shells and cartridges for each weapon in the crate.

The fat man fidgeted on the ground, tried to roll onto his side to get a look at Tucker. Tucker jammed a boot on the man's back and pushed him flat again.

"Ow! You don't have a gun of your own? You said you had."

"Lot of folks say things that aren't true. Like that I killed Payton Farraday. Not true, and yet when folks are told it enough, they begin to believe it."

Where was Arliss?

"Okay, okay. But who's this 'us'? You got a mouse in your pocket, Tucker?" Grissom laughed, and Tucker had to admire

the man's sand. He was at the center of a whirlwind of bad-
ness and he was making jokes.

"Why, Grissom, you don't think I'd be out here traveling
alone, do you? I'm tramping the woods with a full comple-
ment of soldiers, federal and state officials, and some Mexican outlaws tossed into the mix for good measure."

"Now you're funning me."

"Maybe. So, what's it going to be?" Tucker cocked the
derringer right beside Grissom's ear.

The fat man cried out as if he'd touched a hot stove,
"Don't shoot me. Leastwise not with that!"

Just then, a voice that Tucker recognized—and it was not
that of Arliss—shouted from close by.

"Hey, you in the tent! I got me an old man out here who's
starting to whimper like a little baby. You best come out, see
what he wants."

"Vollo?" said Tucker.

"Vollo," said Grissom. Then he shouted the name and
Tucker drove the butt of the tiny pistol into the side of the fat
man's head, just above the ear. Grissom grunted.

"Hey! You in the tent, you got my boss man. That's okay.
He's useless now. They run him out of town anyway. But all
I want is you. I know who you are. You should be in jail for
killing people. You killed my friend Rummler."

"I'd say I did the world a favor!" Tucker took a last quick
look at everything in the weapons crate and blew out the
lamp so Vollo couldn't draw close enough to drive a shot
right into his skylined shadow. He could tell by the sound of
the Mexican's voice that the foul man was edging closer as
they spoke.

"Okay, then, I am about to do the same to your friend.
Perhaps the world will feel the same way."

Arliss! The buzzard wanted to kill Arliss. Was he bluffing
or did he even have him prisoner?

"How do I know you have anyone there?"

Tucker heard a mumbling sound, as if Vollo was speaking low to someone. Heck, Arliss was probably arguing with Vollo. Tucker wouldn't put it past him. "It's me, Tucker. Don't give up the gold for me, damn it. I'm old—I ain't worth it!"

The sly old devil, he's trying to set up Vollo. Tucker nodded in the dark, all the while loading a six-shooter with bullets. He finished that one, strapped it on, then hefted the rifle. He had time enough to snatch up a handful of shells before he heard a rustling sound draw close, made by boots stepping slow in branches and leaves.

"Hey, gringo—I got your buddy, right? So now you toss out the gold he speaks of and maybe I won't slice him an ear-to-ear smile, eh?"

Nothing doing, thought Tucker. *Longer I play it quiet, the more seconds I can gain before Vollo calls my bluff and hurts Arliss—or worse.* Tucker dropped to one knee right beside Grissom. The fat man moaned and Tucker sneered, rapped him again on the bean, this time with the butt of the six-gun. Another grunt and the man was out again. *Too much of that and the fat fool won't have any brains left to bargain with. All I really want from him is whatever paper it is that Emma said she needed. Something about the loan being paid off. If he doesn't have it, then Tarleton does, but it might be possible that Grissom knows where it's kept.* A long shot, but the only one they had.

"Gringo. Oh, gringo? I am going to kill your friend now."

The voice sounded close by, just outside the corner of the tent to his right. How had he crept so close? And with Arliss in tow? Not likely. As if in answer to his silent question, he heard Arliss, or what he assumed was the old feisty man, making strangled half-formed sounds, as if his mouth was bound with a gag. And it sounded from far back, near where Tucker had left him with the stock.

Vollo wanted that alleged gold, figured he'd keep Arliss safe for now—just in case he needed him to make some sort of deal, maybe trade him to Tarleton to get in his good graces. Maybe he wanted Grissom too. And now the mention of gold was all it took to get Vollo lathered for a big take.

Tucker nudged the canvas in front of his face with his head, tried to keep his breathing low, even, and quiet. The tent flaps weren't tied. A plan of some sort was what he needed, but he had a half second available, and then there wasn't even time for that.

Somehow Vollo had crept closer, because Tucker saw the bottom of the tent at the corner rising in the dull glow of moonlight and sand-colored canvas. Higher and higher, like the handiwork of a letch lifting a dress, the edge of the tent fabric rose. And then he saw the hands, part of a head, a ragged white bandage hanging from it, and then an eye swiveling.

Tucker held his breath, kept his pistol aimed at the leering face, could even smell the man's sweat and breath stink. And then the roving eye fixed on him and the corner of the mouth rose in a wider leer. With finger-snap speed, a pistol barrel appeared beside it. Vollo's finger tightened on the trigger.

Tucker dropped flat to the trampled ground beneath the tent even as he pulled the trigger on his own gun a sliver of a second before Vollo fired. The world bloomed bright with the twin flashes filling the space. Smoke and the stink of gunpowder clouded the tent. Tucker held in a cough until he could be sure the man was dead.

He heard nothing for the ringing in his ears. Then he heard a squealing beside him. It was Grissom, shaking all over, thrashing his head side to side. Maybe he'd been hit. The thought didn't bother Tucker much—he knew what the man was capable of. As the smoke cleared, he saw Vollo's hand flat on the ground, the only part of him poking into the tent.

Tucker wriggled backward, not feeling as though he'd taken a bullet at all, and not daring to exit the tent in the spot—just in case the man was alive and playing possum.

He made it out under the far side of the tent and rolled to his left, pistol cocked and aimed at the spot where Vollo should be.

The man was there all right, and he lay still. Tucker got to his knees, then stood, all the while keeping the pistol aimed on the prone man. He walked up, toed him. No movement. He kicked away the pistol, flipped the man over onto his back, and as he did so he saw an injury to the man's head.

He heard the strangled guttural cries of Arliss off near the horses. He'd just have to wait. This Vollo wasn't a man he wanted to worry about in the future, so he went back into the tent and fired up the lamp again. He brought it back outside and bent over Vollo. The man's head had been severely creased. A line of bright red blood arched from the forehead over his left eye, straight back through bone and brain. Blood pumped out with a steady but slowing rhythm. Fragments of bone poked outward as if the unwashed brute had had part of a crown embedded in his head.

That man was dead, and Tucker didn't feel bad about making it happen. *Should have done it sooner,* he thought.

He heard Arliss's gurgling rants again, so he headed that way and freed the old man. "About time somebody let me go." He rubbed his arms and swung them to get the circulation back.

Tucker was breathing hard now and his pulse had quickened following the shooting. "I think that folks should thank us for ridding the earth of the last of two of the most worthless creatures ever to roam it."

"You are a peculiar man," said Arliss. "There's no doubt. Shoot a man in the head and then say a thing like that."

Tucker looked at Arliss. "You of all people tell me that? I can't believe what I'm hearing."

Arliss touched a black finger to the side of his nose and winked. "You'll do. Now, them folks leave anything in the way of foodstuffs?"

"You bet they did—and a whole lot more. Plus, I have a surprise for you."

"Oh? I like those. I hope it has to do with a hot bath, a small Chinese lady who's good at massages, and a slug or two of who-bit-sam."

"Close," said Tucker, pulling open the tent flap. He held the lamp low, and staring up at them from the ground was Bentley Grissom.

He squinted, his fat cheeks bunching. "Arliss? Arliss Tibbs, my old friend, is that you? Oh, thank goodness."

Arliss stepped into the tent and took the lamp from Tucker. He set it on the table and turned up the wick. The interior lit, he set to looking in earnest for something.

"What do you need, Arliss? Food's in that one." Tucker pointed to one of the opened crates.

"Nah. I'm looking for the place you found that there gun. I want to kill this fat tub of lard. He's caused enough grief for the Farradays in the past few years, and I aim to see he don't do the same to no one no more!" His old chicken neck stretched as he poked in the various crates, found the one with weapons, and withdrew a pistol.

"What are you going to do, Arliss? Kill him?" He moved close to the old man and spoke hurriedly into his ear. "You'll make him a martyr instead of serving any purpose in his death, and he'll be revered in these parts. The most important part of this whole thing is that we get that paper Vollo and Rummler killed Payton for on Grissom's behalf. If we kill him now, we won't be able to use him to get that paper. If it even exists anymore."

"Oh, I am quite sure it exists," said a haggard voice from the ground by their feet.

Tucker and Arliss looked down. Despite the double thumping he'd received, Grissom was smiling. Arliss hauled back and drove a grimy foot into the jowly man's face. They both shouted in pain.

"Feel better?" said Tucker.

"No," said Arliss, looking down at his burlap-and-blanket-scrap-wrapped feet. They were the only things they could find after the fire, since the old man had left his room without tugging on his boots. "I aim to get me some boots and do it up right next time."

Grissom growled something indecipherable and spat.

"You keep it up," said Tucker, "and I'll just leave the tent for a while." He turned to Arliss. "Help me rummage through the rest of this stuff. We'll take what we need, lash it to the animals. The rest we'll smash. Anything we can do here to destroy their instruments and gear will help slow them and their plans down. Not a lot, because a man like Tarleton has unlimited resources, but we'll do what we can."

"Sounds dandy to me. And lookee here," Arliss said, holding up a bundle of clothing and, under them, several pairs of boots. "Must be for anyone who gets wet while working in the woods during the day. From the looks of things, they sure was planning on a siege or a long-term campout up here. And on Farraday land too!" he crowed.

Again, Grissom laughed. "You are fools, the both of you."

Arliss hauled back to kick him again, but Tucker stopped him.

"Go ahead and kick me. I might even deserve it, sure. But this land isn't yours. Not legally, not anymore. And what's more, if a man such as myself, with my influence and power and financial wherewithal, couldn't deter Lord Tarleton, then you are fools to think you can do a thing to stop him."

"Oh, I don't plan on stopping him," said Arliss. "I aim to kill him. You too, you big sack of gristle. Just as soon as we get Emma free."

"So that's the plan, is it?" Grissom rolled to the side, grunting, trying to sit up. "Because mine is even better. And with my plan, at the end we all come out with exactly what we want."

"And what's that?" said Tucker, eyeing the fat man.

Grissom grunted again and managed to accomplish nothing, so he sagged in defeat. "I get my holdings back, you get dear little Emma back, plus your land—full title too—and we both get to see Lord Tarleton and his minions hightail it out of Klinkhorn."

Tucker was about to ask him for specifics when they heard a horse's hooves thundering away from the camp. He dove through the tent flaps and came up on his knees, pistol poised, but saw only the diminishing back end of a horse in the slivered moonlight. His breath rose in cold streams. Arliss crouched low beside him.

Vollo! He spun, his pistol pointed at the dead man . . . who wasn't there. He scrabbled around the outside of the tent. "Arliss! Get that lamp out here."

It was no use—the dead man was gone and a trail of heavy blood led to where Vollo and Grissom had tied their mounts however many hours before when they'd arrived together at the camp.

"Still alive," said Arliss, staring in wonder at the glistening splashes on the mottled earth.

"It looks like it. And headed to town to tell Tarleton what we've been yammering about in there." He pulled in a deep breath, then let it out slowly. "It seems like the element of surprise has been taken from us."

"Good."

"Good? Arliss, you know what you're saying? Even with that slim sliver of nothing, we had next to no chance of defeating Tarleton at whatever is his game, but now he'll be expecting us."

"And I say good. Because now we know where we stand. And"—he turned toward the tent—"we have a bargaining chip. Let's get some food and play us some poker."

Chapter 40

Bright morning sun slanting through the window warmed Emma's face and awakened her. Scraps of memories came to her. She'd been locked in the room by that English dandy, dragged in there by his two hired fools, and then after she'd tried to break out of the room he'd come in and . . . stabbed her with a needle!

The rush of memories awakened her further and she tried to rise but found herself held down. She lifted her head, tried to open her eyes wider, and saw she was bound by her hands and feet to the bed. And she was not wearing the clothes she'd come in with. She was now wearing a long white dress. How had she managed to change her clothes? A sudden stab of fear of what might have happened chilled her. She struggled harder against the bonds that held her strapped to the bed.

Whatever it was Tarleton had dosed her with had worn off. She felt thirsty and the light from the now-unboarded window soon became harsh and brittle. She'd had too much whiskey once in the past and she recognized the feeling as close to what it had felt like the following morning. Arliss had made sure she'd gotten up at dawn, eaten a full breakfast, and worked hard all day—while he chattered like a jay.

Arliss! The ranch, something about the ranch, those men in black. Tarleton, showing his true colors, had been about to do something bad, something wrong. . . .

"Hello, my little cowgirl. How are you feeling?"

Emma turned her head to the right, toward the voice. It seemed to echo. She forced her eyes open, and they blurred, focused.

"That's it. Take your time. You've had a hard night of it, what with all that anger and shouting you were doing. I imagine your throat is sore, poor little bird. But now look at you, all pretty and dressed for your big day."

She finally got a bead on him, and it made her heart crawl up her throat. Because at the same instant she saw Tarleton, all duded up in finery, she knew two things at once—he meant to marry her today and it came back to her with the force of a hard-driven post maul just what Tarleton had told his two men in black to do the night before. "Oh no, tell me you didn't do what I remember. . . ."

"Why, little bird? Whatever do you mean?" Tarleton rose from his chair by the wall and bent low over her. She smelled the cologne he wore, a musky odor that reminded her of a scent her father had had in a tiny glass bottle that he'd kept on his dresser. He'd never worn it when he was alive, but he had let her smell it a few times. It had been a gift to him on his wedding day from Emma's mother, and he kept it dust free, like a special little statue. Bay rum, he had called it. When they had buried him, Emma had dabbed some on his cheeks and wrists, and then she'd tucked it into his breast pocket and that had been that.

"What did you do? Did you burn my family's home? Is Arliss hurt? And Samuel?"

"I don't know what you are talking about, dearest. And I am not familiar with anyone named Arliss or Samuel, but I can assure you that the last I knew, the Farraday family ranch was as right as rain. The only thing I've done to it is bestow on it a grand gift of longevity. A lifetime free of the woes no money can bring."

"I . . . I don't believe you." This didn't seem right to

Emma, somehow. Something about his talk made her angry, uneasy. Something told her to not trust him. "Why am I tied up if everything's so rosy?"

"Emma, Emma, shortly after you came here last night to tell me you loved me—"

She shook her head no.

He continued. "That you wanted to marry me and spend your life at my side, bear my children, and teach them to be perfect little frontiersmen, how you wanted to marry immediately, that you liked the terms I had laid down before you . . . why, something happened to you. Your very demeanor changed and you acted as though you wanted to hurt yourself. You began lurching about the room."

"No, you lie. You had those two animals who work for you drag me in here. You locked me up like a prisoner, boarded up the window."

"You are mistaken, my dear." Tarleton leaned over her face, close to her, smiling down, speaking in a low, smooth voice. "You were unruly. I had to get you calmed down. I suggested you take a nap, but you kicked at the walls. The window, however, was something you did not try to jump through, thank the heavens." He leaned closer to her face, spoke softer. "And it was not boarded up, I assure you, my dear."

"Liar!" She whipped her head upward and rammed her forehead into his nose. She heard a quick snapping sound and Tarleton screamed and flipped backward, one arm milling, the other hand clutching his nose. He staggered backward, bumped into the wall, and knocked over a glass of water from the chair's arm. "You . . . you wench. You have broken my nose. Never has the nose of a Tarleton been subjected to such savagery! And on my wedding day!" Then he ran to the front of the room, banged into the door, then lurched out of the room.

Emma thrashed on the bed, then stopped, winded and frustrated. She breathed slowly, tried to calm herself. She relaxed against the bonds and found that the lengths of knotted sheet about her left wrist were loosening. One hand, that's all she needed—one hand free. She pulled her thumb into her palm and made her hand as small as possible. It was enough, and after long seconds that seemed to take hours, she was able to slip her hand free. She wasted no time—despite the dizziness that threatened her and brought dark, thudding pains in her head, she managed to sit up. She touched the spot on her forehead where she'd rammed it into Tarleton's nose. It was tender, a goose egg forming there, but it had been worth it. She felt renewed and reawakened.

It took her but the work of a few seconds to loosen and then free the three remaining bonds. Soon she was off the bed and her bare feet hit the floor and she winced in pain.

She'd stepped with her foot on something sharp that cut her—a sliver from the drinking glass that he'd knocked to the floor. She scooped up the largest pieces, stuffed a couple under the mattress by the head of the bed—just in case she'd need them later—then set one on the windowsill behind the curtain. She grasped the bottom of the glass, a round, jagged thing perfect for stuffing into that nasty royal face.

She tiptoed across the room and peered around the not quite closed door into the outer room. Tarleton wasn't there. She leaned farther into the room and saw no one. Across the way, the outer room's door leading to the third-floor landing was also ajar. Nothing ventured, she thought, and bolted for it, wishing she had her boots. She'd find them later. Right now she had to get out of there.

She guessed that he'd left the doors unlocked and open because he thought she'd remain tied to the bed. Every time she thought of him, the audacity of his actions, she gritted her teeth. *Think about it later,* she told herself. *Don't let it stop you from getting out of here.*

She reached the hallway door, fully expecting to have to dart between the two brutes dressed in black. But they weren't flanking the door at their usual posts. They weren't anywhere she could see, but she wasn't going to give them a chance to see her standing motionless. She dashed forward, the jagged remains of the drinking glass clutched in her hand, the white dress fluttering against her legs. She wished she had her boots.

Cinda. She had to get to Cinda at the livery. She had to get home. That was all she could think of doing. If she could get away from town, maybe she could figure out what to do next. Part of her wanted to believe what the liar had told her, that he hadn't actually burned her home. But the wiser, skeptical part knew that everything he said was a lie. Had to be. Nothing he'd said yet had added up. Why else would he tie her up?

She rabbited down the flights of stairs and made the lobby without seeing another soul. She paused in the lobby—same thing. Not a person in sight. It wasn't until she reached the wooden raised sidewalk that she saw other people and felt the coldness of the bright dawning day. Several people glanced her way. Most of them stopped and stared.

"Help!" she said, running toward them. They backed away from her, and when she kept advancing, they hustled away from her. One woman dropped compton shopping basket, and an apple popped free and rolled across the street.

Two horses tied outside the hotel fidgeted. The livery was at the east end of the street, and she broke into a run toward it, and looked down to see the jagged glass gripped in her hand. It had cut into her fingers, and blood ran down her fingers, spattered on the pristine white dress. She threw the glass away between two buildings and wiped her hand on the dress, held it tight to the fabric. She didn't care; all she wanted to do was get on her horse and get home. Arliss and Samuel had to be okay—they just had to be.

Off to her right, she spotted the monster himself, pounding hard down the steps of the doctor's office, his two black-clad men trailing close behind.

Tarleton saw her at the same time and shouted across the

street, "Stop her! She has become violent, deluded. She tried to kill me. I only want what is best for her!"

As he spoke, his two henchmen fanned out, intending to close in on her from each side. Emma turned, ran up the middle of the street, the cold earth painful on her feet, but the sensation doing more to revive her than the brisk air did. It felt like snow air, and this time it might well bring with it snow that stayed.

She suddenly wanted a mouthful of snow, she was so thirsty. But she had to get to the livery—and yet that was at the opposite end of the street. She could skirt the buildings along Main Street, head down the alleys, run through backyards.

But would they have thought of that already? That she might want her horse?

"Get her! Please help me save poor Emma!"

His voice trailed after her and she knew she had to do something soon. They wore boots and had guns and would soon have horses, and no one in the town, it seemed, wanted anything to do with her until she was wed to the killer.

"He set our house on fire! He burned our ranch! He stuck me with a needle, tried to kill me, put me in this stupid dress!"

"She is ranting, people. My dear sweet bride is under tremendous strain. She needs rest. I can take her away to a special place where they will care for her and nurse her back to health."

She turned, looked over her shoulder at him. He advanced, his arms out, his nose bandaged. He looked like a duck all dandied up for a day at church. His arms reached toward her from halfway down the street, his head tilted to one side. But she knew that look, knew the evil behind it. What did he want with her? Because he had taken a fancy to her and he wanted whatever he couldn't have? *Is that all I am?* she thought. She stopped in the middle of the street, looked at the faces of the people lining the sidewalks, all staring at her, shielding their eyes from the rising sun warming the length of the street.

"Is that all I am to you? To him? A head of cattle to be sold off for a song so you can all sleep easier knowing your loans won't be called in? You honestly believe what he's telling you?"

"That's about enough, Emma."

She turned to see Marshal Hart stepping down from the boardwalk in front of the jail. He had on his star, big hat, wool vest over a blue shirt. She used to think he was so fancy, such a kind man and so brave with that star and those handcuffs. Now she saw an old, sagging man prone to fatness. He walked up to her, kept his hands wedged under his belt.

"What is this, Emma?"

"Marshal, look, I know you and I have had our differences lately, but I'm here to tell you, he's trying to kill me. He burned the ranch down last night. I heard him give the order. I heard it myself!"

"Emma, this isn't like you—"

"You're right! It's not like me, so listen to me for once—"

"No, Emma. You listen to me—your uncle Payton had a big loan out on the place. He lost the ranch to Grissom when he couldn't pay it off. Then Lord Tarleton came in and bought up Grissom's bank and all its loans for a fair price. Hell, he bought a handful of businesses in town too. Claims he is going to launch a new business that is going to make every man, woman, and child in Klinkhorn rich, and the town a place on a map and not just a struggling old mine town filled with people who ain't got nowhere else to go."

"So for all that I'm supposed to marry this man? He stole my family's land, he burned my home and hell, for all I know, Arliss and . . . well, he might have been in the fire! Marshal, at least let me get to the livery so I can get my horse and ride home."

The marshal closed his eyes and sighed. "Emma, there wasn't any fire."

"How do you know?" As Emma said it, she saw the marshal's eyes flick to something over her shoulder. One of the men in black had closed in without her seeing him, and he was now just a few strides away.

Before she could get her next words out of her mouth, the big man reached out and clamped a big paw around Emma's arm. She struggled and kicked at him, but without her boots, there was little she could do. His grip tightened the more she struggled. The man in black came up and stood close enough by her side that she moved away, and bumped into the other man in black. They'd succeeded in bookending her, and right behind her she heard footsteps, turned to see Tarleton just a few feet away. The sidewalks were lined with townsfolk.

She finally slapped the marshal's meaty face. "You buzzard! You sold your soul to this . . . this puffed-up dandy." She looked beyond the close cluster of men and shouted at the gathered townies, "You all sold out to him—all for the promise of something that he'll never give you! You'll never see it, mark my words! He's killed Arliss and the other man! He's worse than Grissom."

"That's about enough, Marshal Hart. I should think we could have her arrested and locked up until she calms herself. Don't you?"

"Lord Tarleton, she's a little angry right now, but I can't just lock her up. . . ." The marshal looked at the bandaged Englishman. "On what charges?"

"I should think that would be obvious, Marshal." He pointed at his face. "The little vixen assaulted me, with intent to kill me. Do you not see that now?"

"Don't listen to him, Marshal. He drugged me, locked me up! Hell, he even changed my clothes—I didn't put this dress on myself!" She struggled more, but the marshal wasn't about to let her go. He had both of her wrists gripped tight in his meaty paws. She twisted her arms and struggled, but to no avail.

Emma saw the searching look the marshal gave Tarleton. And the Englishman gritted his teeth, shook his head. Something unspoken transpired and Emma knew she was sunk. She suddenly felt horrible. She was barefoot, Arliss and Samuel might well be dead, and no one would believe her—or if they did, they were too afraid of losing whatever it was they'd been promised by this man.

She was tired, cold, thirsty, and her head hurt. None of this was fair. She stopped struggling, looked around at the faces of the people she'd known her whole life, people she thought she knew. And among them stood Louisa Penny, her old friend. Emma felt her heart beat a little harder when she saw Louisa, but then the older woman turned away, couldn't hold Emma's gaze. *So that's how it's going to be,* she thought.

"Marshal, if you're going to be spineless and not let me go, then you can at least let me go to the jail and get warm before you lock me up in a cell."

He mumbled something but, like Louisa, couldn't meet her gaze.

Behind her, Lord Tarleton said, in a voice loud enough for the entire street to hear: "Don't forget to lock it tight, Marshal Hart. We know how . . . porous your cell block can be. I'll be by later to personally check in on dear Emma, make sure she has been given proper accommodation, and perhaps by then she will have come around to reason. Perhaps she will stop being so selfish and realize that denying the keys to the golden city is unwise not only for her own future life, health, and happiness, but also for those very things for all her dear friends in this perfect little frontier town!"

Lord Tarleton ended his brief speech with his arms upraised, as if advising everyone to look to the heavens to see the glorious vision of the way their lives would be, should Emma only marry the man. All she could think of was how satisfying it had been to drive her forehead into his perfect nose and hear it snap.

Come what may, she thought, *for the rest of his days, at least he'll remember me every time he looks in a mirror.*

Chapter 41

"Okay, fat man." Arliss gave himself a rubdown with canteen water, then donned new boots—a couple of sizes too big—and clothes—even bigger. Tucker suppressed a smile, especially when he considered that he too wasn't much heavier than Arliss and he had to pull on similar clothes. But clothes of any sort were a warm and welcome relief.

"You say you have a plan, Grissom. Let's hear it. And don't try to negotiate with us. It won't take much for me to leave you alone with him. And don't mistake that calm demeanor for someone who wouldn't harm a fly—Arliss is as savage as they come."

Both the other men looked at Tucker as if he had two heads. He shrugged, his attempt at levity lost on them.

"You have a piece of that ham you might share with me?" Grissom looked hopefully at Arliss, who was noisily gumming a thick hunk of gristle-rimmed meat.

"Why, sure, Bentley. Soon as you fill us in on your master plan—and it had better include all the doings that English rascal has planned for Klinkhorn."

The fat man licked his lips. "I can't . . ."

Tucker reached for the ham and carved a thick slab for himself. Aside from trying to get Grissom to talk, he was just plain hungry. He had wanted to head on out away from that camp right after Vollo had left, but Arliss had insisted they stay awhile, that Vollo, even if he managed to stay alive, would take forever to get to town. If that was the man's destination, and if he lived that long.

"Okay, okay, but I have to have food, I tell you. I can't hardly think without food."

"That's a shame, Bentley, because I ain't inclined to give you a thing until you give over with what we need to know. And that's my final word on the matter."

Tucker was impressed with Arliss's negotiating skills. And even more so when Grissom relented and began blurting out his thoughts, eyeing the meat all the while, sniffing and licking his lips as he spoke. "A long time ago I recognized that there were plenty of other ways in the world to make more money than just by digging for gold. This entire region is prime for logging—"

Arliss threw his hands up. "Oh, here we go again. I tell you, them trees are best left alone, right where they are. You and your kind all want to log it off, leave us a stump field, and vamoose with the pickings. Why—"

"Arliss, let the man speak. It's a little late for opinions, don't you think?"

The old man looked offended, and set to work on his ham with renewed vigor. Tucker nodded to Grissom to continue.

"So anyway, I heard about this English fella, some sort of big moneyman, who was buying up all manner of prime forest land along big rivers. He's been setting up logging operations all over the West."

"I'll just bet he has." Arliss glared at them both.

"So I contacted him, told him about Klinkhorn, told him how I might know some folks who could use some cash for the timber on their land." He looked at Arliss. *Bold of him,* thought Tucker. "Might just be a way to save their property."

"Let me guess," said Tucker. "And then just when Lord Tarleton is due to arrive, lured to Klinkhorn on the promise of your vividly painted descriptions of riches beyond his belief, of logging off forests belonging largely to the Farradays, you get paid a visit by one of those pesky Farradays—namely, Payton."

Tucker looked at Arliss, who had slowed his chewing and alternated his concerned gaze between Tucker and Grissom.

Tucker continued. "And it just so happened that Payton paid off the loan he had to take out—much to his regret—to keep his ranch floating until he could get paid for the next season's stock. Which he did. But that wasn't enough for you, was it, Grissom? You had to have that paper you'd been forced to sign, the one you never thought you'd have to sign because when you gave Payton Farraday that loan, you did your best to make sure he'd not be able to pay it off. You secretly made life tougher for the Farradays while that loan was out."

"No, I—"

Tucker turned to Arliss. "You have lots of unusual losses of head of cattle? High numbers of aborted calves? Start to thinking maybe rustlers had come into your range? Strange sicknesses in the herd?"

"Hey, yeah! That's the way it was. But we just knuckled down harder and worked like devils, all of us, me and Payton and Emma. Poor girl worked like two grown men just to keep hold of the place. Never asked for a reason, just assumed it was what we all had to do to make it through till next season."

Arliss turned to Grissom. "I knew some of what was going on. Payton told me about the loan, asked me to keep it under my hat where Emma was concerned. Mostly because he'd made his brother a promise that he'd not ever bargain with the likes of you. But there comes a time for some folks when you're left with no other option but to make the best of it. Swallow your pride and beg for forgiveness from the dead for going against a deathbed promise."

He rasped a hand across his burned face. "By golly, how

that ate at Payton. He worked like a madman to make sure we'd pay off that loan. If me and Emma worked double hard, Payton drove himself ragged. But it worked. We got that loan paid off. We was going to have a little celebration that night. He was also going to start courting Louisa Penny more regular now that the debt had been cleared up."

"But he never got the chance."

"No, sir, never did."

Arliss wasn't a large man by any stretch, but he seemed to Tucker to loom and glower in a seething rage over the fat form of Grissom, who had propped himself up against the side of the bunk on which he'd been napping.

Grissom tried to cover his face with his bound hands. "It's true that Vollo and Rummler were in my employ, but I never told them to kill him. I just wanted that slip of paper. You have no idea the pressure I was under. I couldn't let down Lord Tarleton. I knew he'd show up soon. My whole future rested on this deal—the future of Klinkhorn. You don't understand."

"I understand plenty." Tucker wanted to hit the man in the head again with a pistol butt, maybe keep on hitting him until the pig never awoke. But that would not help Emma, and would make him no better than Vollo and Rummler. He turned away from the man. "Arliss, how long will it take us if we left now, headed straight north, to get to the cabin?"

Arliss rubbed his chin. "Hard ridin'? Couple hours. Why, what are you thinking, boy?"

"I'm torn. We're not in good shape, but I'll bet anything Emma's in trouble. I have to get to town. And if she's been hurt at all, it won't matter."

"How's that?" said Arliss.

"Because I'll kill every last one of the men who hurt her—or stood by and watched."

"And then they'll string you up." Grissom shook his head, a disapproving smirk on his face.

"Yep," said Tucker.

"I suppose we got to drag his carcass around with us." Arliss nodded at Grissom. "Don't worry, tubby. It's a figure of speech. We need you alive, at least for a while. Might be you'll be useful in knowing where Tarleton keeps his important papers, or in getting us closer to that dandy than we might get on our own. You better hope so anyway. Elsewise you don't stand a snowball's chance. Then we throw you to the wolves."

"Wolves?" said the fat man.

"Yeah," said Tucker. "The townsfolk. You know, the ones you've been shafting for the past three years."

"I thought we had come to an agreement!"

"I didn't agree to anything. Except that I'd give you a piece of ham if you yammered long enough. I reckon you lived up to your end." Tucker picked up a piece of gristly meat. "Open your mouth." Grissom did, and Tucker stuffed the meat in.

"We'll have to skirt Tarleton's men. They'll be headed here. I figure if we ride north, then angle east to town, we'll have a shot at sneaking in come dark."

Arliss rummaged in the weapons box, loading up his pockets and cradling a shotgun. "Ain't much of a plan."

"Nope," said Tucker. "But then again, we ain't much to look at."

Arliss cackled. "Don't count this old Tennessee hill boy out of the game just yet, whippersnapper." He winked. "Now let's ride." Arliss kicked Grissom on the haunch. "You too, fat boy."

Chapter 42

Marshal Hart barred Tarleton and his two cronies from entering the jail with him and Emma.

"You don't need to be in here," he said. "Anything you needed to say has most likely been said out there in the street. We'll get her in here, let her cool down. And you all can go about your business."

Tarleton leaned against one side of the open doorway and talked low to Hart as if Emma hadn't been standing just inside the door, wanting to edge closer to the warmth of the stove.

"Marshal Hart," he said in a low tone, "you seem to forget your place. I intend to marry that girl, and in so doing, make this town one hell of a special and rich place. I will not be denied anything. Do you understand me?"

The marshal's response surprised Emma.

"Lord Tarleton, you seem to forget that I am wearing a badge pinned on me by someone who has more legal right to tell me what to do than any ten rich Englishmen."

But Emma saw the sweat collect on Hart's chin, saw the muscles of his left eye jounce and jump. And she was sure Tarleton saw much the same.

After a few long seconds, he said, "Keep her here until the poor little dove regains her senses. I will be in my hotel. Send for me." Tarleton turned away, then paused and looked back inside, but this time he stared straight at Emma. "And don't make me wait too long, Marshal. I do not like being denied. I will not be denied." He stared at Emma, touched his hat brim, and flanked by his two black-clad hirelings, Tarleton strode off the porch, down the steps, and crossed the street.

The marshal stood at the open door for a minute more. Emma gave brief thought to braining him in the back of the head with a length of firewood.

"Fixing to snow, I reckon." He breathed in deeply once more, then turned to face the room, closing the door behind himself. Emma had retreated to the feeble warmth the woodstove offered.

"Marshal, let me—"

"I can't, Emma. I can't do it, so don't ask me to let you go. I'm . . ." He turned from her, hugged his arms, his back to her. "I'm in this too deep. Been in it for a long time. Longer than that fool Tarleton knows."

"What do you mean? In what too deep?"

He rummaged in a cupboard beside the desk, came up with a pair of wool pants, a stack of mismatched socks, and a knitted wool sweater. "Here," he said, stacking them up beside her. "And now for the important stuff, coffee." He tried a weak smile and poured them each a cup.

She pulled on the trousers underneath the dress, and the marshal looked way. Then she put on the socks and bunched the dress up under the sweater. The dress wasn't anything she wanted to wear, but it did add a few layers of warmth. She dipped the ladle in the water bucket a half dozen times and drank her fill. She turned her attention to the coffee and the greasy biscuits the marshal had set out on a tin plate on the tabletop before her. Emma guessed he'd been saving them for his noonday meal. She didn't care; she ate them all.

"What did you mean, Marshal, when you said you were in too deep?"

"Got to get you in that cell, Emma. I'm sorry about it.

Here's a pair of boots. They're a mite worn and no doubt too big for you, but they'll help keep the warmth in and the cold out. And there are plenty of wool blankets, no worries."

"Why lock me up? I've done nothing wrong. Let me go! I have to check on Arliss and Samuel. You know there's something wrong here. What aren't you telling me?"

"I have to lock you up, not because you're dangerous but because they're the dangerous ones. I think the only place you'll be safe for the time being is in here. I can hold them off for a while yet."

"Hold them off? What are you expecting to happen, Marshal Hart?" Emma paused in chewing the last biscuit, sipped coffee to wash it down.

"I don't expect much to happen until they get tired of waiting and come after you." He looked at her then for the first time since they'd come into the office. "And when I don't let them in, there'll be hell to pay."

That made her feel a little better about him, but far from impressed. "What if they hurt you? Then I'm stuck in a cell, a sitting duck? That hardly seems fair. At least let me go, let me get a head start on out of this powder keg."

"No. I can't do that. It's too dangerous for you out there. There are people out there who have things they think they have to do to other people, and I'm thinking that one of them will find you and use you as an excuse to get to other people."

"You're talking in circles, Marshal. Let me go."

"No!" He spun on her. "Let's go, Emma. Back to the cell. Please don't fight me on this. I'll explain it all later. Trust me."

Emma began to protest, then looked in his eyes. Something there told her to not push this. That somehow maybe the marshal knew something she didn't. But she sat unmoving until he sighed and pulled out his pistol. "Emma, now."

He got her in the cell, clanged it shut, and turned the key in the lock. She grabbed the bars and pressed her face close to them. "Marshal, what did you mean? What is going on here?"

He walked a few steps away, then said, "I . . . I have to make it right, Emma. I can't do this anymore."

He half turned to face her. She saw the light from the back door's window slant in, shadows forming lines on his tired face.

"Emma . . . I killed your father."

Chapter 43

"I think he's gone round the bend on this one." The speaker, a short, densely built man with a thick brushlike black mustache that hung over his top lip like a sleeping creature, sat in the seat of the narrow work wagon, the lines looped loose in his hand while he waited for the mule to drink its fill.

His partner on the seat stretched, yawned, and adjusted his dusty bowler hat. "I hear you. We've been working for Tarleton, what, three years now? Every town he finds a new filly to set his cap to, right? But there ain't never been one to tell him no like this one, not ever. And that's what's got him all bunched up."

"How so?"

"Ain't you ever noticed how he hates it when there's something that he can't have? Always makes a new way around the tree."

"Yeah, and he always ends up with what he wants. I reckon that's what makes him so successful in business."

"I guess so, but betwixt you and me, I don't like what he's doing to this girl. Hell, I'm not so sure this town deserves what he's planning to do to it."

"Well, forcing the girl to marry him is one thing. Mostly out of spite for the fact that she's told him to go whistle on his own. Right or not, that's just one person. But setting all of Klinkhorn out on its ear? I don't know how right that is. And most of the boys feel the same way too."

"Good thing none of us is getting paid to think too hard."

"Yeah, but I tell you what, that can only go on for so long before I get my fill."

"I hear that. Getting out of town while he marries that wildcat is about the smartest thing we done all week. I expect the camp is just fine, but you never can tell if a critter has gotten into things. And telling him that if our equipment is fouled up it will slow us down, now, that was genius thinkin'."

The driver slapped the lines on the mule's back. "Hup there, mule! I do have my strokes of genius."

"They're just few and far between."

"Since you never had one, how would you recognize one?"

As the two bickering men rumbled along in their loaded and tarped work wagon, Tucker peered out from behind the streamside boulder where he'd been crouched. He and Arliss and a bound-and-gagged Grissom had crossed the stream earlier and had paralleled the track Tarleton's work crews had made through the woods in getting to their day camp.

By the time he made it back to Arliss and Grissom, snow had begun to fall at a steady rate, large, thick flakes that clumped on tree limbs and hat brims. Tucker wiped the gathered snow from his sparse beard and decided he would have to ride on ahead. The town could sell its soul for a dime—he didn't care—but there was no way he was going to risk letting Tarleton marry Emma.

He pulled Arliss aside and explained what he'd heard. And to his surprise, Arliss suggested the very same course of action.

"You going to be able to keep tabs on Grissom? And without killing him?" Tucker almost smiled as he watched shock and desire war on Arliss's face.

"Don't you worry. I'll bring him in, one fat piece and alive. Once I get him to town, though, I can't predict what will happen to him."

"Fair enough. Grissom said Tarleton is most likely holed up in the hotel, so I'll head there first, try to get Emma out of there without too much fuss. Maybe we can meet up at the livery?"

Arliss nodded. "I'll tie up outside town, creep on in. You really think it's gonna be this easy?"

"Hell yes." Tucker smiled. "Don't you?"

Arliss shook his head and mounted up. "Good luck, boy, though I reckon you're so full of beans and vinegar you don't need luck." He held up a hand. "This snow, can't decide if it'll be a help or a hindrance to us."

Tucker gave the old man a last look. "It'll be what it'll be. Nothing we can do to change that." He nodded toward Grissom. "Watch him," he said, looking at Arliss. "I don't trust him as far as I can throw him."

"Unless you got more muscle than what you're showing, I'd say tossing him is out of the question."

Tucker gave a final wave and rode on, booting Jasper into a swift run. His best guess was that he'd make it to the town close to dark. A wedding ceremony was one thing, he thought. But from what the surveyors in the wagon were saying, Tarleton was a user who didn't love her, didn't seem to love anything but money, and since she'd refused him, he wanted her more than ever. Just because he couldn't have her. What lengths would such a man go to just to get what he thought he wanted?

The only possible answer made Samuel Tucker boot the big buckskin hard and head for Klinkhorn.

Chapter 44

As the afternoon wore down and the storm clouds bunched tight enough to become one cloud, daylight lost its struggle and a raw wind kicked up, blowing the new snow straight down Main Street, Klinkhorn, from the east, forcing it between buildings, through gappy windowsills, under eaves, and down chimneys. Wood smoke drafted back into sitting rooms and kitchens one minute, pulled hard out of chimneys the next with a rush that burned firewood fast. It allowed little precious heat to fill the rooms where residents sat close, gloved hands outstretched toward the roaring stoves, layers of clothes all but covering their faces.

Huddled in her stone cell, wrapped in six wool blankets, Emma Farraday sat dumbly, oblivious of the cold. Every so often a shiver jerked through her body.

As soon as the marshal had said he was the one who had killed her father, she froze inside. None of it had made any sense. And then as she sat on the bunk in the dark, wrapped in the blankets, the more she let her mind work back, she began to unravel the knotted threads that made up the hellish two years since her daddy had been taken from her, shot by some unknown person. They'd all suspected Grissom, but no one could prove it. And he had of course denied it repeatedly. Now it looked as though he might have been telling the truth.

But why did Marshal Hart kill her father? He had been

with the Farraday brothers during the war, and then they'd all come west together to try their hand at finding gold. Young men with muscles and dreams and bellies full of killing. So what had happened?

Emma had an overwhelming urge to shout to him, to ask him to explain himself, but every time she wanted to demand that he unlock the cell, a creeping futility seemed to sap her strength and leave her more tired than before.

So that was the real reason why he locked her up before he told her. She didn't blame him. She promised herself she'd kill him the second she got the chance.

Chapter 45

The storm was blowing in hard from the east, and the snow grew thicker by the second. Tucker was thankful that Payton's horse was a stout beast that showed little sign of flagging, but even with that advantage, the situation was grim.

He hoped Arliss was able to make it through and trusted that the old man knew the terrain. Tucker played over in his mind what he remembered of the town and found he recalled very little. That first night, he'd ridden into Klinkhorn intent on getting food and drink, and by the time he'd been dragged to jail, he was both battered by the marshal and feeling the effects of the whiskey. Then when he left town, it had been under a tarp in the back of Emma's wagon. But she'd saved him then, and now it was his turn to repay the favor.

For a man who had come to town with next to nothing, a man intent on dying any way he could, and the sooner the better, he had ended up with the few things no man could ever pay for—renewed health, new friends, and the promise of love. And he'd be darned if he was going to give up on any of them now.

Scarcely two minutes more found him rimming a little ridge to the north above town. Far below, to his right, he saw intermittent flickers of warm light from the windows of the houses of Klinkhorn and reined Jasper toward the far end of them, close by where he knew the livery sat.

"I'm coming, Emma," he said aloud, the words whipped away by the bitter wind.

By the time he reached the livery, it was full dark, no moon or stars. As Tucker dismounted, he looked up the main street and saw little other than already drifting snow, and a few weak clouds of light barely strong enough to cut through the storm.

The hotel sat to his right, a third of the way up the street, and was one of the few buildings to offer more than a single light from its many windows. But it was the third floor, where Grissom had said Tarleton had set up shop, that Tucker was most interested in. Could she be up there? As likely a place as any. And so, a perfect place to begin his search. He lashed the horse to the rail out of the wind behind an angled section of chute used for funneling stock from one corral to another. His pockets were filled with ammo for the six-gun holstered and strapped on his waist over the wool mackinaw, and he cradled the rifle across one arm. His burns throbbed, as did his wounded shoulder, but the blowing snow provided a welcome relief to his seared features and uncovered head and hands.

He knew what he looked like because he'd seen his reflection in the stream earlier in the day, before Tarleton's men had come along with their wagon. He was not a pretty sight, and neither was Arliss. They'd both be scarred for the rest of their days, though how many of those days were left to them, neither of them knew. Come the morning, if they were alive, they might better be able to hazard a guess. Rescuing Emma was his only goal right now.

Tucker cat-footed around the backsides of the stark structures lining the right side of the street, past the back door of the saloon he'd visited when he'd first come to town. He paused, jerked back into the deeper shadows against the building. He swore he heard a cough. Too soon for Arliss to have made it to town. Someone else out on such a night? Or was he being watched?

The thought made his gut tighten, turn cold. "In for a penny," he whispered, and double-timed it to the hotel. A quick glance upward toward the well-lit third floor verified his guess, and he groped against the dark wall of the building for a door. It took him longer than he had expected, and only when he tripped over the snow-buried bottom step of the back stairs did he find what he was looking for. He paused on the top step, his hand on the doorknob, turned it slowly, and it gave under his hand. The door swung inward, a long, drawn-out squeak accompanying it. He stood outside, peered in down the long corridor that he knew must lead to the lobby.

As he stepped inside and closed the door behind him, he heard the voices of many men, talking, laughing, socializing, possibly from the front parlor. He'd been in enough town hotels to know the basic layout of the place. They would be Tarleton's men, gathered on such a night in the warm downstairs room, the one with a stove or a fireplace. They would be drinking, and perhaps less inclined as the night wore on to want to fight for their boss. Or perhaps they would because their money source would be worth protecting. If that was to be the case, he hoped they'd be drunk, less accurate with their hurried shots.

He passed several closed doors. Behind one he heard what sounded like pots or pans being clanked together. The kitchen staff was busy with supper preparation or cleanup. All those men to feed would make for a big mealtime and lots of work. The place smelled of polished wood and something more, maybe mold and cooking smells that wafted through the hallway.

There might well be a back staircase to the top floor, but he hadn't seen sign of one on the outside and he didn't know the interior well enough to venture a guess and end up stuck in a closet. So up the central staircase he'd go. He didn't dare go slow any longer—every second he stood without someone stumbling on him was a second wasted. He took the stairs two at a time, made it to the landing of the second floor with no interruption. And by the time he reached the third, he guessed he'd been given some minor gift by whatever god was up there watching over him.

And that's when he saw the two men in black.

Chapter 46

Arliss dismounted as he led his string of beasts and one prisoner to the livery gate, slipped in the snow, and came up slowly, scrabbling for the shotgun that he'd dropped when he fell. "Damn it all to hell anyway. . . ."

The horse he rode, old Gracie, like the others, hunkered low, bent against the east wind and the driving snow. He turned back to the mule and Grissom, ready to yank the fat man down. But as he turned, he walked right into him. "Grissom—what are you doing off the—"

"Howdy do, Arliss." Grissom stood before him, no rope binding his wrists and a gleaming little derringer in his hand, aimed right at Arliss. "This had been misappropriated from me earlier, and I took the opportunity of filching it back. Hope you don't mind."

Arliss knew he'd have no time to jerk the shotgun up, cock it, and pull a trigger. And that was all he had time to think about, because in the next instant, Grissom shot him.

"Damn you to hell, Bentley Grissom!" Arliss gripped his side, felt the hot wetness of his blood spilling into his cupped hand. He pressed his knotted fist tight against the ragged seeping wound in the too-big wool coat.

"I got a two-shot gun here, Tibbs, and another bullet rattling around in a pocket somewhere, but no time to fish for it. So you can just bleed out instead of me ending it quick for you. You and that clan that you work for have been a pain in my backside ever since I met you, and you've only gotten more painful as time wore on."

"And you talk too much," said Arliss, doing his best to stay upright as a sick feeling rode up him like a racking shiver.

"Coming from you, that's rich."

Arliss's teeth began chattering, but even through his near-instant fever he felt the powerful regret he'd not killed Grissom earlier, when he'd had plenty of chance.

Grissom crossed behind the stable, grunted his way up onto the sidewalk, and marveled at the lack of activity in town. "Just a snowstorm, for Pete's sake," he mumbled as he hustled along the boardwalk.

Time to get a better weapon and get in that hotel. He'd deal with those two fools in black, and then that should leave Tarleton defenseless—for negotiation. And whenever he came across him, he'd be sure to kill that cursed Samuel Tucker. Though he had to admit that Tarleton's men had done a pretty good job of trying to do that.

"But once again," he said, "Bentley Grissom is left holding the bag, cleaning up other people's messes." He sighed theatrically, peering up and down the street. He edged closer to the dim light cast from a second-story lamp two buildings up from the hotel. Still no one. He saw the marshal's office across the street, guessed that Hart was in there, keeping warm, his feet up on his desk, his door locked and windows shuttered. If he knew anything about Marshal Hart, it would take a whole lot of odd noise, such as gunfire, to bring him out on a night like this.

He hurried on, passing slowly through the dull ring of light from two windows of Taggart's store.

Across the street, Marshal Granville Hart squinted out between the thumb-width gap in one of his storm shutters and couldn't believe what he saw—almost didn't trust his eyes. It looked like Bentley Grissom across the street, skulking on up the sidewalk. No, he would be long gone by now. Nowhere for him to stay; nobody would have him. Then the large shape moved farther up the sidewalk and paused again. And that's when Hart was sure that he wasn't seeing a phantom shape, something conjured of shadow and swirling snow and scant light. It really was Bentley Grissom. And in that instant, the marshal's rock-solid plans for the evening changed.

He hadn't been expecting to see the one man he wished he had killed, the one man who had ruined everything for him. The one man whose presence in Klinkhorn had been bad enough, but whose departure left ripples that some folks had to deal with, and he had been one of them. Since Grissom had disappeared from town, at Hart's insistence, Hart had experienced nothing but one bad turn after another with Tarleton.

Now Hart was sure that all of Tarleton's fancy talk about dragging Klinkhorn up by its bootstraps had been nothing more than lies to gain his toehold in the town long enough to shuck it clean of lumber, then leave it a husk, high and dry and lonesome. But it had been Grissom who'd started the ball rolling.

Hart snatched up the cell keys, pulled on his wool mackinaw and gloves, and headed back to the cells.

"Emma Farraday," he said, in a bigger voice than he'd intended. She was sitting as she'd been when he last checked on her, wrapped in blankets and unmoving. "I have had a change of heart and a change of plans. I'm unlocking the cell." He paused, watching her. "And I know what that means." After a few moments, she moved her head, and though it was dark back there, he guessed she was looking in his direction.

"I'll be back shortly and I'm sure you will have things to

say to me. I have some to tell you. And then . . . well, we'll see what we'll see." He cranked the big key, the others on the ring jangling in the cold, dark cell, his breath rushing from him. "But right now I have something I have to do."

He cracked the cell door, left the keys hanging in the lock, and walked out the dark corridor to the front of the jailhouse and left that door open behind him too. He retrieved another box of shells from a top desk drawer and stuffed them in his pocket, unbolted the door, and stepped outside into the stiff wind. He clinked the door shut behind him and flipped up his collar. Then hurried across the street.

Chapter 47

"It's all because of you, Grissom."

At the mouth of the alley between the hotel and the store beside it, Grissom spun toward the street. "Hart!"

"It all started to go wrong when you come to town," said the marshal. "I'll never forgive you for that."

"It is fortuitous that we meet like this. But I don't want your forgiveness, you oaf! I want your neck, I want your star, I want your money, I want your life, you pathetic wretch. And I got it all too. Well, all but that last." Bentley Grissom palmed his derringer and thumbed back the hammer. "But soon I'll have that too." A leering smile split his fat cheeks, pocked with paltry stubble—the fact that he could never grow a decent mustache or beard had bothered him his entire life.

"You made me kill him. You made me kill one of my oldest friends."

Grissom cocked his head to one side. "Who in the heck are you talking about?"

"Mitchell Farraday!"

"That is old news, you idiot. You shot your friend, not me. I gave you money, all the money you needed to cover your gambling debts. You bet everything but your own mother's bones—maybe those too, come to think on it. Never has a man been born more incapable of knowing when to fold than you. And yet you kept on piling up the debt. I asked for one simple favor, one simple thing, and you keep bringing it up, month after month, year after year. Deal with Farraday, I said. How you interpreted that was none of my concern. Thankfully, you chose to deal with him in a most permanent and expeditious manner. And thanks to that, my interests grew increasingly—and I grew most appreciative."

He aimed the pocket pistol at the marshal's head. The big man closed his eyes, his nostrils flexing faster, a nerve at his eye corner jumping out of control. Grissom pulled the trigger. Nothing happened. He growled and thumbed back the hammer again. Pulled the trigger, and a close whip crack of a sound came out of it, smoke curling up from the snub barrel as if it were the glowing end of a cheroot.

Marshal Hart stood before Grissom, a frown pulling down the ends of his big mustache. His eyes were no longer closed. They brimmed wet, and then a runnel of red tears slipped down alongside the man's nose, seeped into his big bristling mustache, around his mouth, then off his chin. The marshal dropped to his knees, said, "I'll be damned," then fell prone on the wooden sidewalk.

"Yes, you will. Me too, I'm sure. But not just yet." Grissom giggled and swung the hotel door wide.

Chapter 48

The two men hadn't yet seen Tucker. He pulled in a long, silent breath, raised his rifle. From his distance of twenty feet, they were close enough that he covered them both easily. Getting the two gun slicks to comply would be another thing entirely. Tucker stayed in the shadows. He peeled back the hammer as he spoke. "You two men best not do what you're thinking of doing, which is shucking those pistols. Leave 'em where they're at."

But as he guessed they would, they both rabbited, clawed at their guns, and let fly with a shot each, even as they rolled out of the way. He felt a stinging just above his knee on his left leg, and a buzzing by his right ear. The second they reacted to his voice, Tucker had dropped and cranked off two shots. One splintered woodwork; the other gave up the dull thudding sound of a bullet digging deep into flesh. A teeth-gritted bark verified he'd hit one of the gunmen.

The door they'd been flanking opened and one of the shooters scrambled inside the room and slammed it behind him before Tucker could shoot.

He was trapped at the top of the stairs, not a good place to be, he knew, because from below he heard the approach of low voices and cautious steps on the first floor. Judging from the lack of further shots, he guessed the remaining gunman was either too badly wounded to shoot or he couldn't see where Tucker lay hidden. His leg throbbed like a bag of bees, but he didn't dare move. He kept his rifle trained on the spot where he knew the remaining gunman to be.

"Hey," said a weak voice. "You aren't dead? Are you the man I pulled out of that horse wreck?"

The man's words hit Tucker like a slap to the face. "That was you?"

The man tried to say, "Yeah," but it turned into a wet cough.

When he'd finished and grown quiet again, Tucker said, "Thank you for helping me."

The door behind the man opened a crack a couple of inches wide. Low light from inside leaked out. "Shut up," hissed a voice from inside.

Tucker squinted at the crack, tried to make out a face. "I've come for Emma Farraday. She in there?"

The man out front coughed again, then said, "No . . . she isn't here—"

A blast from the doorway stuttered the coughing man into permanent silence. Tucker bit down on his lip. Whoever was in there was heartless. Had the man been telling the truth? What profit would there be for him in lying? Especially given that Tucker's bullet had obviously struck something vital. Either way, the gunman was past all caring now.

The voices from downstairs were slowly drawing closer. They would be Tarleton's men, confused maybe, but concerned for their employer? Given what the two men in the wagon had said earlier, Tucker wasn't so sure that when gunfire erupted, these men were prepared to risk their lives for the man, no matter how good their pay might be. They were surveyors and lumber specialists, merely the advance team that would spell out just what, where, and how the loggers would operate.

Their voices drew closer—probably near the second floor by now. Tucker knew he had to move, get away from the top of the stairwell. But what if someone were watching from the doorway? The voices became more defined, closer. He'd have to risk it.

Tucker pulled himself to his feet, keeping his rifle trained at the doorway, the more immediate threat. Hot slices of pain knifed up and down his wounded leg. It nearly gave out, but he stiffened it and swung it wide as he walked forward. One stride, two, three . . . The door cracked open. Tucker was quicker, and sent a round crashing into it, cranked another one in there and dove to his left, rolled over on his wounded leg, and groaned in pain.

From inside, he heard a mingled scream of rage and agony. A second later, the door kicked shut.

Good, thought Tucker. *I hope it was Tarleton I hit.*

Tucker grabbed the top of the dark wood wainscoting lining the hallway and lurched down past the doorway he'd just shot into. No one else poked their head out.

He looked down the hall behind him. There didn't seem to be any way off this floor except for the staircase he'd come up—the one filling with Tarleton's men. He retreated farther down the hall. Might as well see this thing through. If he somehow got out of here now without checking that Emma was here, only to find later that he'd been so close to her, he'd never forgive himself.

Maybe one of those other doors connected with Tarleton's room. He backed up, deeper into the shadows. The next door down was locked. *Now what do I do?* He was just about to venture back up the hall, to risk kicking in the door, when he heard a familiar voice from the stairwell. Grissom? It couldn't be. He was with Arliss. Unless . . . That might mean Arliss had been hurt, or worse.

The voice drew closer, along with the *clump, clump, clump* of heavy feet on the stairs, accompanied by equally heavy breathing. Definitely Grissom. A few voices sounded, asking him just who he thought he was. Then Tucker heard a pistol's hammer cocking back and Grissom saying, "I am your biggest headache, boy, if you don't back down against the far rail and keep on walking down those stairs."

Though he heard his steady, slow approach, Tucker was surprised to see the fat man's head, then shoulders appear at the top of the stairs. He gained the landing and didn't seem to much care about keeping quiet, or surprising whoever might be up here. Tucker was tempted to draw on the fat man's chest and let him have it.

The door opened again. Tucker braced himself for the flash from a gun barrel, then to see the fat man tumble backward down the stairs, flop, flop, flop all the way down. But neither happened.

"That you, Lord Tarleton?" said Grissom.

"What do you want?" That was definitely an English accent. Tucker's lip rose in a sneer. *I will dive sideways and send a bullet into that fiend if need be.*

"Lord Tarleton," said the fat man. "I come in peace. I have a solution to your current problems."

Tucker heard a distinct snort of laugher. "What problems might they be, then?"

It was Grissom's turn to laugh. "I think you know all too well what I'm talking about. And the simple solution I'm talking about is a little thing called mutual back scratching."

"That, Mr. Grissom, is a most unsavory vision. But I will consider what you have to say. Come ahead."

Tucker watched the fat man as he lumbered with purpose, six-gun poised—no fool was Grissom—along the corridor, hugging the shadows perhaps a bit more than one might normally. Just before he reached the cracked door, Tucker thought, *In for a penny,* and lurched ahead, half dragging his wounded leg, hopping with the other, his rifle trained on the fat man.

The sound of his struggling maneuvers stopped Grissom.

He peered into the dark, his pistol pulled up tight to his chest. "Who's there? I'm going to shoot."

Tucker was a half second faster than the fat man. "No, you're not." He slammed the rifle stock into Grissom's face, followed it up with a downward chop with the gun butt. The fat man folded like a bad hand of cards, slumping to his knees and wheezing in a sloppy pile. Tucker kicked away the pistol and just managed to jam the rifle barrel into the door's opening as it slammed shut.

"Now, I can lever the door open, Tarleton, and just start shooting, or you can open the door and let me in. Your choice. But I'd advise you to make it . . . right now."

At Samuel Tucker's feet lay a groaning, blubbering man. "Get up, Grissom. And stop rooting in your pocket. Jerk your hands clear of your clothes or I will shoot you in some fatty part. Might take a few rounds, but I daresay I'll invade your vitals before too long. Your call."

Chapter 49

Yellowed light from the oil lamp spilled down the hallway to the cells. It was a long time before Emma swung her legs down from the bunk. She sat for a moment more, listening to the wind whistle in through the gaps around the back door, rattling the shuttered window.

When Marshal Hart got back, she'd find out everything she needed to, and then she'd kill him. It was a simple plan, and somehow she'd bet he knew it had to be that way. If he didn't yet, he would soon. She'd go find a gun, a stick of firewood; she didn't care what she'd use. The idea warmed her. After all, she had nothing to lose.

She clumped down the hallway to the office. Maybe he had coffee on the stove. Coffee while she waited—that sounded good. She swung through the door into the office, headed straight for that stove. It was plenty warm. She added two sticks of wood, then hefted the coffeepot.

"Hello, girlie."

Emma spun, the pot in her hand. Vollo stood in a dark corner by the marshal's desk. He stepped out of the dark and she gasped. His head looked as if it had been cleaved by an ax.

"I don't look so good, huh?" He laughed, a low, dry sound like paper rustling in a breeze.

He didn't sound so good either. His words sounded as if they had been dragged through mud.

"What do you want?" Emma shrugged off the wad of wool blankets she'd held clasped about her neck and stepped backward.

"I want you to put down that coffeepot and keep your hands where they won't do no harm, eh?"

She moved another step closer to the door.

"Do it now!" He walked forward, closer to her and into the weak ring of light from the oil lamp sconce on the wall.

What had been Vollo's face was now a crusted, blood-streaked mess of dirt, bristled beard, broken nose, split lip, and one eye purpled and swollen shut. Shards of bone jutted outward from his head wound like shattered porcelain. Whatever had done it—a bullet, she guessed—had plowed up his skull bone and left his bloodied scalp a raw, glistening thing. "Painful" would be far too weak a word to describe how it looked, let alone how it must have felt. No wonder he sounded odd and winced with each breath.

"You are going to take me to your lover man."

"Tarleton is not my man and certainly not my lover."

Vollo laughed. "No, no, no. I don't care about him. I am talking about that man who killed your uncle. The man who killed my friend, Rummler. You know the one. That starving drifter."

He didn't know his name, but Emma knew whom he was talking about. "Samuel? Samuel Tucker?"

"*Sí*, yes, yes. That is the man."

Emma shook her head. "You're wasting your time. I . . . He's dead."

Vollo laughed again, long and loud. "Not unless he died in the last couple of minutes."

"What do you mean?"

"I know he was coming to town. I heard him and that skinny old dog talking, the one who does not stop yapping. I should have shot him when I had the chance. Or better yet, gutted him."

"Arliss?"

"Yes, that's the one. Nasty old thing, he is. Neither of them looked too good. They should have burned in that fire, I think, eh?"

Emma felt a glow of hope. They had lived through it—so it had to be true. She begged with all her heart for it to be true.

Vollo stepped closer. Emma moved away. He drew his pistol, turned his good eye on her, and cocked the hammer. "You should sit down in that chair there, away from the stove. I heard shots across the street, and your sweetie was pretty lathered up to see you. So if he lives through that big party over there at the hotel, then I bet he'll come here looking for you."

"Why do you care? What's he done to you?"

Vollo's good eye widened and he gestured broadly with his hands. "To me?" He wagged the pistol at the gaping wound in his head. "He did this to me—for no reason! And to my friend, Rummler, he killed him too. Yes, that man is a killer man. He is a no-good seed. My mama said that about me, but this one, he is much worse. He is *el Diablo*, for sure."

Vollo leaned closer to Emma, and she smelled his breath—blood and cigarettes and old food. In a low voice he said, "And Vollo don't forget that you did this to him neither." He pointed toward his broken nose and the crusty sore of his split lip. "He don't forget." Vollo winked at her and limped away to look out the gap in the shutters.

Emma didn't much care what he did or didn't forget. She was allowing herself to enjoy the real thought that perhaps Arliss and Samuel were alive. She had to get out of here and find them. Before they came to the jail looking for her. It might only be a matter of time before they found out she was here. But what if Vollo was right and they were mixing it up with Tarleton and his two hired guns right now? Samuel Tucker and Arliss were no match for those expert killers, even if they hadn't been through a fire. And Vollo had said they didn't look too good.

She got up, but her big boots scuffed and clunked on the floor. Vollo adjusted his gaze with his usable eye, and waved his pistol from side to side. "I tell you to keep yourself sitting, and what do you do? You stand up. Just like a woman. Tell her one thing and you end up getting blamed for another."

"I was going to make coffee. I need a cup of coffee."

He didn't move, but the gun lowered a few inches.

She reached slowly for the near-empty coffepot steaming on the woodstove.

He just watched her.

"I'm going to fill the pot and put it on to boil, so we can have coffee, okay?"

"Yeah, yeah, okay, I'll have some. But make it fast. I don't have all night to wait, eh?" He wagged the pistol barrel at his head again.

It was disturbing when he did that, and even worse that he just assumed he would soon die from the head wound. That meant he knew he had nothing to lose. Somehow she had to let Arliss and Samuel know Vollo was here, waiting for them.

Chapter 50

The door in front of Tucker opened wider and there stood Lord Tarleton, directly in front of Tucker's rifle barrel. The belly of the man's vest was spattered with fresh blood. Tucker looked at the man's hands, but they were held behind him as if folded there, a pose he seemed quite comfortable with. His ornate chin hair and waxed mustache looked haggard, droopy. Above the mustache was a bloodied bandage, edges plastered to the man's face. Someone had gotten in a good lick and broken the dandy's sniffer. His nostrils twitched and his eyelids flickered as if he'd been too long without sleep.

"Where's the man I just shot?"

The smug smile on the dandy's face drooped. "Is that any way to greet your host?"

"You are no host of mine, mister."

"I assure you, I am no mister. I am a lord. Lord Tarleton, as you well know. And you are still the much-sought Samuel Tucker."

"Yep. Now, where's the man I shot?"

Tarleton reached with a boot toe and nudged the door open wider. Tucker tensed, followed the move closely with his rifle barrel.

"Rest easy, cowboy. I am merely going to show you what you wish to see."

On the floor behind the dandy, a man dressed in black lay sprawled on his back on the carpet. His right hand outflung, a mangled claw from Tucker's close-range bullet. But that's not what had finished him. He lay wreathed in a two-foot-wide puddle of red-black blood sopping into the carpet, his throat a deep-sliced gash separating stark white lips of flesh and muscle.

"Somebody cut that man a new smile."

"Yes," said Tarleton, glancing down at the man. "It does rather look that way." He looked back up at Tucker. "Oh, that was me, by the way. It seems the frontier is a persuasive place of such violent inducements." He looked back down to the dead man. "I did him a favor, really. His partner was dead and this one wasn't half the shot the other was. Plus, he's no use to me now, a mangled hand and all. I would guess you are to blame, really."

"How do you figure that?" Tucker kept his hands tensed. He heard Grissom's measured breathing from the floor behind him.

"If you hadn't shot my men, I would not have had to take such drastic action as . . . this." He pulled his arms out from behind his back, gestured at the dead man. The sleeves of Tarleton's fancy frock coat were soaked in blood, his hands slick with it, and a straight razor was gripped open in one, blood stringing off the end of the square-ended blade.

"Where is Emma Farraday?"

The man cocked his head and squinted at Tucker. "Why? What is that uncouth hussy to you?"

"Where is she?"

Tarleton looked puzzled. Then his eyebrows rose. "Ah, it's love, isn't it? Good Lord, what on earth could she love about you? You are a savage cowboy who looks as if he's been dragged through a keyhole in both directions. Whereas I"—he folded his arms across his chest—"I am an English lord."

"Yeah, yeah, so you keep sayin'. And I for one don't give a rat's ass. I—" As he saw the sudden rage spread on the dandy's face, Tucker heard a grunting, wheezing sound from behind him. He dodged low, slipped to his left into the room just as Tarleton lunged for him, razor thrusting. Something grabbed at Tucker's dragging bum leg and he pitched forward, trying to spin as he did. He cracked off a rifle shot, but it went high into the room.

In the doorway, he saw the skinny English dandy on his knees, slashing at the squealing Grissom, who had risen on one knee and slapped at the crazed Englishman with a meaty paw while rummaging in his pocket with his other hand.

Tarleton's razor found purchase, first in the fat man's suit coat. The next swipe slit the shirt and welled red. Grissom shrieked like a baby and pushed at the Englishman, but Tarleton had the advantage of height and a handy weapon. His slashing attack continued in a flurry. His weaponless hand clutched at Grissom's face, grasped a mat of sweaty hair, and he brought the razor in to deliver a vicious killing stroke to Grissom's throat.

As the razor touched the thick-jowled flesh of Bentley Grissom's neck, Samuel Tucker considered not pulling the trigger of his rifle. But the split-second thought passed and he sent one, two bullets into the kill-poised body of Lord Tarleton.

The Englishman's entire body spasmed, his head whipped backward, his eyes snapped impossibly wide, and bright red blood gurgled upward. It fountained out of his gaping mouth, staining forever his fancy waxed mustache and chin hairs. Lord Tarleton pitched backward and lay still, the straight razor gripped in his bloody hand, his legs bent beneath him.

When the smoke broke apart, Tucker saw Grissom, bloodied from a dozen slashes and slices, on one knee, wheezing.

The fat man looked over at Tucker. "Took you long enough."

Tucker struggled to his feet, using the wall for support, then stepped over to the big desk and poked inside the top drawer. He pulled out a small leather folder and untied the rawhide thongs holding it closed. After a few moments, a weary smile spread across his face. He tucked the paper into his shirt pocket and set the folder on the desk.

The entire time, Grissom watched him, wheezing, sweating, and bleeding.

Tucker pushed by him and headed slowly into the hallway.

"Where are you going?" said Grissom.

Tucker stopped, looked down at the fat face. "I am going to round up some townsfolk. I believe they'll be interested to know you are back in town . . . and open for business."

"Oh, don't do that. They . . . they hate me here. I did my best for them. It's true, but . . . Tarleton, it's really his fault. He ruined it for everybody. He was greedy—that's the truth of it. Greedy."

Tucker shook his head and made his slow way down the hall.

"I can pay you, damn it."

"No," said Tucker. "No, you can't." He didn't hear another word from the fat man.

Chapter 51

Tucker paused, looking at the scene beneath him in the hotel lobby. People filled the room. Among them a half dozen townsmen with guns were herding the last of Tarleton's surveying crew back into the sitting room off the lobby. Tucker's gaze landed on one figure. "Arliss!"

He bounded down the last flight of stairs, stumbling and righting himself on the banister. He made his way over to the long leather divan where the old man lay, gray-faced but awake. He held a wad of bloodied cloth to his side.

"Arliss, you're hurt."

"Course I'm hurt. That buzzard Grissom shot me. You'd be hurt too if'n you took a bullet." He looked at the awkward way Tucker stood. "Oh, I guess you did. Well, then, you know how much agony I'm in, don't you? Instead of simpering over me, why don't somebody fetch me some whiskey, dull the pain till that useless doctor gets here? Why in the hell do pregnant women always pick stormy nights to whelp anyways?"

"Speaking of," said a short, bald man. "Where did Grissom get to?"

Tucker looked over his shoulder, back upstairs. "He's up there. Waiting for you all. I expect he's ready to take his medicine."

Just then they heard a single gunshot from far upstairs.

"Hart's gun," whispered Tucker. "I should have remembered it."

The hotelier, Halley, who'd been rummaging behind the check-in desk, emerged with a half bottle of bonded whiskey. He avoided his wife's stern glare and brought it to Arliss, who promptly uncorked it, then offered it to Tucker.

Tucker shook his head. "I have to find Emma." He turned to the others in the room. "Where's Emma Farraday? And don't you dare tell me you don't know—I'll tear every board loose from this town to find her!"

He drag-walked from face to face, man, woman, it didn't matter. He stared each one into submission. Finally Taggart, the storekeep he'd remembered who bought Payton Farraday's gun from him, said, his bottom lip trembling, "She . . . she's at the jail. Marshal Hart took her there."

Tucker narrowed his gaze and headed for the door. From behind him, he heard Taggart say, "But Hart's dead, just outside the hotel door. We think Grissom did it."

Tucker didn't turn around. He opened the frosted-glass door and headed into the storm as the townsfolk swarmed the stairs.

Chapter 52

Tucker leaned into the wind, headed diagonally across the street. He'd just nearly stepped on the snow-blown form of Marshal Hart, and knew he was dead. Tucker had suspected as much since Grissom had shown up in the hotel with the marshal's cherished gun—a man like Hart wouldn't give up his sidearm without a fight, or an ambush. Tucker made straight across the street for the jail, hoping against hope Emma was safe.

A sudden gunshot barked and a gout of flame flared from the jail. Tucker lurched back deeper into shadows. After a moment, he shouted, "Emma! It's me, Samuel Tucker!"

Nothing, then: "Hey, you! Killer man!"

Tucker squinted into the whipping snow. There, something moved behind wooden shutters in the jail. "Who's that?"

"It's Vollo and I got me some little ripe banana in here, eh? You gonna try to take her from me or am I going to have to just shoot her now, and then you after? It's up to you which order we do this, killer man."

So close now, thought Tucker. He hoped that meant he'd not hurt Emma. He risked a hobble-run across the street, and flattened himself against the shop front next to the jail.

"Why are you calling me that when you and Rummler are the ones who killed Payton Farraday? Answer that, murderer!" As Tucker spoke he moved out away from the front of the building and back into the street, the drifting snow slowing his wounded leg's efforts. He half crouched behind a frozen water trough.

His comment didn't have the effect on Vollo that Tucker had hoped for.

The bloodied killer just laughed. "You trying to get me all worked up, eh? Admit to something? You'd like that."

"Vollo, why go to the grave with that on your conscience?" *Not that he has one,* thought Tucker. "For that head wound of yours will surely be the death of you, anytime now."

"Yeah, yeah, I know all about it. And the only thing I want to do before I die is to see you die. You killed Rummler and now you killed me. The least I can do is to kill you too, see?"

As Tucker watched, the jailhouse door cracked open, and a face peered along the edge. Too dark, and barely lit from behind—Tucker didn't dare risk a shot in that direction until he was sure Emma was out of the way.

Then the door swung wider, no one in the doorway. As it opened all the way, a face peered around it again and shouted, "Where are you, killer man? I ain't got all night, you know. You seen to that!"

Tucker didn't respond, just waited him out. In very short order, he suspected he'd know soon what the man intended to do. Tucker just had to be one step ahead of him. With a bum leg.

Then Vollo moved farther into the light, jerking his head to one side as if he were trying hard to hear or see. He held the pistol before him, kept angling his head and then his torso farther into the open. "You hear me, killer man?"

As Tucker watched, Emma appeared behind Vollo and swung her arm up hard and fast. She held something dark in her hand. It arched up high above Vollo's head and for the merest sliver of a second, Tucker thought he saw stunned surprise on Vollo's face as he realized the girl was behind him.

Then Tucker saw a steaming coffeepot slam down on Vollo's head, smacking hard, the tin top pinging off and scalding-hot water pouring out of it and down the man's already wound-raw head. She jerked her hand free of the coffeepot and it rattled to the floor.

Vollo screamed, a high, howling sound, flailed his arms, and jerked the trigger of his pistol. Tucker dashed forward, felt the bullet whistle past his head. By the time he got to the man, Vollo was down on his knees, weaving, the pistol gripped in his fingers. The skin on his head had bubbled immediately and the earlier furrowed bullet wound gushed anew. He tried to raise the pistol, but it seemed too difficult a task for him. Tucker pulled the pistol from Vollo's grip. The man made a grunting noise and flopped to his side, dead, his tongue distended, blood from his head pooling on the gritty wooden floor of the dead lawman's office.

After a few quiet moments, Emma hugged her hand close to her chest, only then realizing she'd burned it by grabbing the scalding metal handle of the coffeepot. Tucker stepped over Vollo's body and took her hand, kissed it softly, then led her out the door and across the street to the hotel's lobby.

Chapter 53

Emma Farraday and Samuel Tucker pushed through the door, edging apart a handful of townsfolk. Louisa Penny shouted, "Emma!" and rushed to her. She hugged the bedraggled girl, but Emma didn't respond in kind. Louisa pulled back, looked closely at the younger woman. "Emma, are you hurt?"

Emma looked at her for a few seconds. "Yeah, I am." She took a deep breath. "I can't talk to you right now, Louisa. Later, maybe. But not right now."

Louisa looked down, nodded. "I understand," she said, and left through the front door. The few remaining people, red-faced, drifted off to the parlor.

"What are you wearing, Emma?" Tucker looked her up and down, taking in the rumpled, oversized jailhouse cast-offs, all pulled on over the bunched-up and bloodied wedding dress.

"It's a dress, sort of. A wedding dress."

"I reckon you look better in ranch-hand duds."

"Good, because it seems every time I wear a dress, bad things happen."

"Then on our wedding day, you can wear whatever you want."

Emma stood back, regarded him a moment. "That's mighty bold of you, Samuel Tucker. But what makes you think I'd want to marry you?"

He pulled her close. "Who else would have you?" He kissed her before she could reply.

From his corner on the long leather divan, Arliss took a pull on the whiskey bottle and chuckled softly. "He'll do. Oh, I reckon he'll do, all right."

Read on for an excerpt from
another Ralph Compton Western
by Spur Award–winning author Matthew P. Mayo

The Hunted

Available now in paperback and e-book.

"That's what you got for me? That?" The dealer nodded toward the cards laid before him. His words came out too loud, and as if he'd been waiting long minutes to say them. The thin man with oiled mustaches, black visor, and arm garters shook his head and winked at the gawkers gathered about his table.

Across from him, his customer sighed and closed his eyes for a moment. He was a mammoth man with a broad back turned to the rest of the room.

The dealer and the others clustered by the table flicked eyes at each other, then settled back on him. The player's rough-spun coat, the dark color of axle grease, strained across the shoulders as he brought a hand up to scratch the stubble on his face. "I'm out," he said quietly, nodding toward the table.

"You about were anyway." The dealer shifted his cigarillo to the other side of his slit mouth and winked at the watchers. Their soft laughs chafed Charlie, but he'd earned them. Coming in here half lit and feeling as if he knew more about playing blackjack and bucking the tiger than any man alive. Heck, three hours and he'd spent more time running from it than wrangling the tiger, and what did he have to show for it? A whole lot of empty in his pockets.

He had his emergency five-dollar piece in his vest and that, plus his mule, Mabel-Mae, and his meager kit, was about all he had in the world now. Three hours earlier he'd been halfway to owning a sizable chunk of land in a pretty mountain valley. Now he'd set himself back by two years—that was how long it had taken him to earn that two thousand dollars. Those two years had all but killed him, he'd worked so hard. And now? Now he was two years older, and as his father used to say of his family's lot in life, he was poorer than an outhouse rat.

"Hey, how about letting someone else take up space in that chair?" The dealer squinted one eye against the slow curl of silver smoke rising up the side of his face from the cat-turd cigarillo. Charlie wanted to smear the smugness off his face, but he'd avoided jail for too long now to cozy up to the idea of being near broke and tossed in the calaboose in Monkton, Idaho Territory.

He pushed away from the table, the chair squawking back on the boot-worn boards. He kept his eyes on the dealer's the entire time he stood, taking longer than he needed to. It wasn't much, but showing off his height was about all he had. It worked. The dealer's grin sagged at the corners and his cigarillo drooped as his eyes followed the big man's progress upward.

He'd not been there when Charlie sat down at the table, so he didn't know how big the fellow he'd been mocking was. And what he saw was a giant of a man, closer to seven feet than six. Charlie was wide enough at the shoulder that by now, at thirty-eight years of age, he naturally angled one shoulder first through doorways and ducked his head a mite. It didn't guarantee he'd not rap his bean on the doorframe—there weren't too many weeks of the year when he didn't have a goose egg of sorts throbbing under his tall-crowned hat.

Charlie's stubbled jaw—he'd not taken time to clean up before hitting the saloon for the first time in many months since he'd sold off his latest claim—was a wide affair beneath a broad head topped with brown curls, tending to silver, forever trapped beneath his big hat. It added nearly another foot to his height, but he didn't mind. It suited him somehow. His hands too were wide, callused mitts with thick tree-branch fingers more suited to dragging and pounding and stacking than tapping out cards. He should have known better than to think he could best the house.

The dealer eyed Charlie's hands covering the entire top of the now-wobbly wooden chair he'd been seated in. He swallowed once, began to speak, gulped again as the big man took his time straightening his coat, squaring that mammoth hat. The big man still didn't look away from the dealer's face.

The dealer finally managed to whisper, "Thank . . . thank you for your patronage, sir."

Charlie nodded once, turned, and heard the dealer let out a stuttering breath of relief. Despite his new financial situation, Charlie half smiled. At least he had his size. It wasn't worth much, but this big body could, by gum, still earn him a day's honest wage most anywhere labor was needed.

The big man strode the length of the narrow room, making the long walk toward the front of the saloon, the floor squeaking and popping under his weight. Everyone he passed gave him the hard stare. He felt certain they all knew he'd lost all but his shirt.

Midway to the door he passed a cluster of men at the end of the bar. He felt relief that they were chattering among themselves and not concerned with him. Then he heard a voice that about stopped him in his tracks.

"Shotgun? Why, by God, it is! As I live and breathe, it's my old friend, Shotgun Charlie Chilton!"

Though it had been many long years since he'd been called that, Charlie's step hitched, as if out of dusty reflex. He paused right there in the middle of the room and closed his eyes. He knew a couple, three things: He should have kept on walking, he'd never had many friends and most of them had died away in the war, and the man who all but silenced the room with his drunken shouting was no friend.

Anybody who called Charlie by that old name was no one he wanted to know anymore—and should by all rights be dead by now anyway.

Charlie knew he should have kept right on going out that door, headed to the livery where he'd intended to bed down for the night in the stall beside Mabel-Mae, his old mule. And then come tomorrow he'd lick his wounds out on the trail, put some distance between himself and the town of Monkton. And once he did, he'd cipher out a way to earn money again, make up for the last couple of years' wages he'd blown at the faro table.

Though Charlie knew all these things and thought all these things, he still opened his eyes and slowly turned to face his past. And that's when what had begun as one of the best days of his life, which had gotten pretty bad, got a whole lot worse.

For who he saw annoyed him to no end. Jacob "Dutchy" Erskine. They had called him Dutchy because he looked as though he might be a Dutchman, though he wasn't any more Dutch than Charlie was the king of China. But the fool was grinning at Charlie, and judging from his rheumy eyes and leering mouth, his boilers looked to be half-stoked with liquor too.

Charlie turned back to the door. He hadn't gone another step before the voice stopped him again. All eyes were on them both now. Even the lousy banjo player in the corner had stopped.

"Shotgun Charlie, as I live and breathe!" Dutchy slid away from the elbow-smooth bar top and stumbled the few steps toward Charlie.

The drunk man was still a good couple of strides away when Charlie held up a hand. "I . . . I don't know who you are, nor what you're after, but you've mistook me for someone else."

The man halted, weaving in place, his smile drooping. "What? Charlie . . . aw, you're funnin' me."

Charlie pinned a broad forced smile on his wide, wind-burned face. He looked left and right, nodding and smiling at the staring faces. Seemed as though there were a whole lot more people in here than when he'd come in. He felt his cheeks redden even more. Curse Dutchy for a fool.

"I'm telling you . . . fella," he said in a lowered voice. "I ain't never seen you before. Now do us both a favor and back off."

"No, no, I ain't neither. Come on over here, meet my new chums. You can buy us all a drink with your faro winnin's." Dutchy's smile turned pinched; his wet eyes narrowed. "Unless you'd rather reminisce all about the old days right here in the middle of the bar." He raised his arms wide to the room.

Charlie saw the two missing fingertips on Dutchy's left hand. They had healed poorly after they'd been shot off long before Charlie ever knew him. The hard pink scar nubs looked like pebbles or warts, and Charlie had always wanted to pare them off with a knife. If they had been on his fingers, he'd not have been able to live with the look, nor, he suspected, the feel of them.

Dutchy giggled, looked around at the silent, expectant faces. "Maybe you'd like to tell 'em all about the last time we seen each other. Wichita, wasn't it? Something about a lousy Basque, wasn't it? All them sheep running all over the place, and Charlie here, he . . ." Dutchy stopped and leaned forward. "What's the matter, Charlie? You look like you seen a ghost. Maybe one of a little girl? One who's been all trampled by a . . . horse?"

It had been a long, long time since Charlie had dreamed of the little girl. But it hadn't been any longer than that afternoon that he'd thought of her. He'd been walking on into town leading Mabel-Mae when he'd seen the children playing before a white-painted schoolhouse a few streets away from Monkton's main street. He thought of her every day, in fact, and this man, this damnable Dutchy, was fixing to rip it all wide open again.

Big Charlie Chilton had tried hard since that accident to make sure he was slow to start a thing. But once he set to a task, he dedicated himself to it and rarely gave it less than his all. But when his great ham-sized right fist drove like a rock hammer square at Dutchy's grinning face, Charlie hadn't known it would happen. Like the old days he'd worked so hard to put behind him. No warning, just action. He hated the fact that it felt good when his tight knuckles jammed hard against Dutchy's leering face.

The strike happened so fast that the entire room was still silent, listening with rapt attention to the drunk's account. The next thing they all heard was a muffled snap and Dutchy's head whipped to one side as if he were gawking at a passing bullet. His body followed suit and spun in a dervish dance before slamming into the bar leaners behind him. They parted fast and let Dutchy drop, his head clunking the mud-scraped brass rail.

The early gasps had given way to scraping chairs and now yammering as standing people leaned, trying to get a look at the collapsed victim.

"He dead?" someone asked.

As if in response, Dutchy groaned and rolled his head to and fro, the left side of his face already swelling and purpling.

An old man with a cob pipe leaned close over Dutchy. "Naw. It was his jaw that cracked." He plucked the pipe from its customary spot in his mouth, the groove worn by it in his teeth. "He ain't dead, but he ain't gonna be right by a long shot for a long time to come, mark my words. . . ."

That was the last thing Charlie heard as he bulled his way through the double front doors, the glass panes rattling as he pawed them shut behind him. His big granger boots punched squelching holes in the slushed mud of the early October street as he stepped off the sidewalk. The livery. That's where he had to get to. Had to get on out of here before someone set the law on him.

Charlie didn't hear the doors open and close again behind him, fast footsteps hammering the boardwalk in the opposite direction, toward Marshal Watt's office.